BLESSED
WATER

ALSO BY MARGOT DOUAIHY

SISTER HOLIDAY MYSTERIES

Scorched Grace

POETRY

Bandit/Queen: The Runaway Story of Belle Starr

Scranton Lace

Girls Like You

I Would Ruby If I Could

BLESSED WATER

A SISTER HOLIDAY MYSTERY

MARGOT DOUAIHY

GILLIAN FLYNN BOOKS
A zando IMPRINT

NEW YORK

zando

Gillian Flynn Books is an imprint of Zando.
zandoprojects.com

First Edition: March 2024

Text design by Pauline Neuwirth, Neuwirth & Associates, Inc.
Cover design and illustration by Will Staehle

The publisher does not have control over and is not responsible for author or other third-party websites (or their content).

Library of Congress Control Number: 2023944374

978-1-63893-026-6 (Hardcover)
978-1-63893-027-3 (ebook)

10 9 8 7 6 5 4 3 2 1
Manufactured in the United States of America

BLESSED
WATER

WHETHER IT'S GOD, science, or magic doesn't matter—you can swallow a glass rosary bead and survive. I know because I swallowed one that awful weekend and didn't die or double over.

Cheating death on Easter. Classic.

After my prayers for clarity, for forgiveness, for a cigarette, for a way out of this fucking mess, deep inside the wet cave of my body was an unmistakable tickle. I could even hear the rosary bead sloshing in the chem-dark bathtub of my guts.

Contractions of a tiny, secret heart. Still beating. It breathed liquid, as we all did. One body inside another body—we prepare for life fitting perfectly. In the womb, fluid night. Before things become beautiful or terrible, there's no separation. No good or bad. Until we're pushed into the light.

The bead fought my stomach acid for hours, leaching its blessing or poison or unmet wish. Anything hidden always finds a way to escape, no matter its careful sealing.

A glass bead, divinely translucent, stubborn as a bullet. A solid Glory Be. A cold prayer trapped in my warmest place. Like wanting to eat a moment to keep it. Closing your eyes and say-ing, *I will never forget this.*

So, yeah, I swallowed it.

Too ridiculous to be true, but a true story, nonetheless.

If you're asking how a grown-ass woman could ingest a piece of glass on purpose, don't. That's a dumb question. You open your mouth and down it goes.

What you should be asking is *why*? Why is it tied to the Polaroids, the flood, the bodies, and the bloodshed?

The *why* is what matters.

The *why* dredges everything to the surface.

GOOD
FRIDAY

7:00 A.M.

SISTER HOLIDAY IS WHAT I prefer to be called. Not Holiday, not Sister, and definitely not Sis. But I let it slide when Riveaux called me Sister Goldsmobile as she tapped her left canine, as if I'd ever forget that I had a gold tooth. Without mirrors in the convent, maybe I could've.

Besides being a nun, I was a music teacher at Saint Sebastian's, a part-time private eye, and a full-time pain in the ass for PI Magnolia Riveaux, the hellcat who ran Redemption Detective Agency, one who could out-sleuth Sherlock and out-nose the swankiest perfumier in Paris. Riveaux smelled rain clouds a state away when the wind was right. She could have been my blood sister with the ways we protected and irritated and appreciated and disappointed each other. Riveaux was the brains; I was the bear trap. Metal teeth and all. Once I latched on, you'd have to gnaw off your own leg to get rid of me. But we understood each other. Not that we were always sunshine and unicorns. More like hailstorms and cobras.

Riveaux agreed to train me for a hundred hours on the sly, so I could take my PI exam and do good things with the bad cards

I was dealt. Or at least shuffle the deck to stay out of trouble. Like trouble wasn't my true calling.

Our agency office was a scalding slice of unrenovated warehouse in Carrollton, near Riveaux's family home. Part PI headquarters, part perfumery. Her two passion projects in one spot. It was so balmy in there, spring rainy season in full drip, that walking from one corner to the other felt like being the victim of a felony. The air was thick with her pungent concoctions: jasmine, peppercorn, leather, and spices I couldn't name if you paid me. The combination made my eyes water. The ceiling was high, the wall was mostly windows, and the space was outfitted with supremely scuffed up furniture.

Riveaux reached over her desk, scarred with a dozen coffee rings and cluttered with perfume bottles, beakers, and an overflowing ashtray, to hand me a PI apprentice certificate.

"Better not lose it," she said with her trademark wry flourish. "I'm never filling out all that paperwork again."

"I thought stepping through red tape was one of your specialties," I said.

"More like stepping into shit."

"Speaking of, what's on today's shit list?"

She smiled and closed her eyes, her eyelashes clumped behind her glasses. "Go to Pier 11 and meet the client. She's expecting us at eight sharp. I'm headed home for the extra camera battery, then I'll meet you there." She placed a tower of coins in my gloved palm for streetcar fare.

Belligerent wind rattled the windows. I looked out and saw a bald spot on a palm tree where the storm had peeled off its bark.

Riveaux re-Velcroed her back brace, then wrapped her left elbow with athletic tape.

"Hope those contraptions keep you from falling apart," I said.

"Watch it. Even with my busted body I could make you say 'uncle.'"

"Don't you mean 'Hail Mary'?"

She grabbed her cane. "Don't make me regret forgiving your ass."

"*We* forgave each other's asses," I corrected.

"More than I can say for most friends."

"Or nuns."

In the line of duty, Riveaux had blown more discs than I knew existed in the bendy straw of the human spine. She used a cane now, but was off pills of any kind. Even Advil. Extreme, sure, but better to go all in than halfway. Cigarettes were her last vice. Mine too. At least that's what I told myself. Riveaux looked rested. Younger. Her divorce from that jackass Rockwell in the works. Stinging with the ferocious focus of a new chapter. A double-act comeback. We both deserved do-overs. Even the bare agency lightbulbs glowed a godly yellow, like the nodding heads of goldenrod.

We had our first official case as PIs.

We were on the edge of glory. Toes hanging over the deep end, ready to dive in. Fire didn't burn us. Painkillers didn't kill us. Healing was miraculous, but it fucking hurt like hell.

7:17 A.M.

RIVEAUX SHOUTED FROM her swivel desk chair, "Snap out of it and stick to the damn plan!"

The handover of my certificate—applause of thunder, the only fanfare—marked the official start of my PI apprenticeship. I wasn't sure what I'd hit first, my permanent vows with the Diocese, a hundred hours of sleuthing, or the end of my rope.

I left to meet the client, Mrs. Jasmine Norwood, at the Mississippi River, Pier 11. The streetcar took me to the southern end of the line, then I hoofed it in the rain to the water's edge.

We forgave, but Riveaux didn't fully trust me. And vice versa. It was for the greater good, but we had double-crossed each other.

Trust is earned, and I was all cashed out.

My trust in God felt different, too, after losing Jack, Sister T, Voodoo, Sister Augustine. But my mother and the Holy Ghost, willowy angels, whispered their vapor voices into my ears and guided me back to the righteous path. My faith was running up credit even though I'd already paid. Would keep paying. With interest.

And Moose, my brother, I owed him most of all.

Would my younger brother always feel like a son I had lost? A hurt, scared kid I sent down a rough-rapid river? Did all siblings play tug-of-war between grief and joy, anger and adoration, or was it just us, the queer Walsh kids?

All I knew was this: Ruin can be sweet, too. No one's a pure saint or sinner. Miracles lived everywhere. In black coffee. In rubble. The shattered pieces that fit back together enough to catch the light.

Rain blasted me as I walked to the pier to meet Jasmine Norwood. Its stop-start-stop rhythm like the most proficient torturer. I clung to my umbrella but still got drenched. Soaked through my socks. My eyes burned with wet. Why was I surprised when the levee fractured?

Finally, I saw PIER 11 printed on a green sign in the watery haze.

Right on time to meet our first client.

Part of God's plan. Like the storm that hallowed weekend. Test after test to baptize me and see if I could swim. Because water cleanses and ravages. Because water replenishes life as quickly as it ends it.

Rain slammed the sign, PIER 11, terrorized it, but the words remained.

8:00 A.M.

MRS. NORWOOD HAD EMAILED Redemption the day prior, writing, "I want y'all to dig up dirt on Mr. Clay Norwood, my sorry excuse for a husband!"

It was exhilarating, seeing her message come through on Riveaux's fancy computer. Our soon-to-be client needed hard evidence that their nuptial vows had been breached—a tale as familiar and predictable as pounding your body during a cannonball dive. You wouldn't think water would hurt so much, but it's all about the angle, the way you enter a new world. Like marriage. It only works when the delusion is shared, when you know the rules of the game you're about to play.

One gay nun's opinion—take it for what it's worth. Or don't and suffer.

Riveaux and I had to learn the Norwoods' daily schedules, the husband's travel routes. We needed proof—evidence of motel stays, Mr. Norwood's GPS data or a car tracker, receipts for mistress gifts. We'd trail him, catch that dirtbag in the act using Riveaux's million-megapixel camera.

In Mrs. Norwood's email, she specified that she wanted to talk it all through with us "in person" before we started. IRL, as my students said.

But I waited at Pier 11, and Mrs. Jasmine Norwood never showed.

Riveaux was taking forever to get the battery. For twenty minutes I prayed for the Sorrowful Mysteries and cursed in the annihilating wind and rain, my umbrella useless, my gloves, scarf, and pants dripping wet. My sensible nun shoes were sopping messes.

So much of my life in New Orleans felt preordained, even the events that unfolded over those three hellish days—starting with the gentle placement of that PI apprentice certificate into my gloved palm.

I scoffed at the anchored *Creole Queen*, a riverboat jazz cruise monstrosity designed to lure tourists in with its milquetoast, whitewashed version of New Orleans. As I studied its stupid exterior, something caught my eye.

In the water, there was a bag. No, an animal. No. Bobbing against the red paddle of the riverboat was a body.

Rain powered down in glass hammers. I ran from the pier and yelled for help, though I couldn't see anyone or anything.

Into the backwash of the river, I jumped. Tried to pull that manatee of a person up to the embankment, but it was impossible, like dragging ten of myself. The head was swollen. The comb-over, thin wisps. The dead hands, tied behind the back, at the wrist, palm to palm—reverse prayer position.

I cried again for help, dog-paddling, choking on the rain and thick river water.

"Why the fuck you swimming?" Riveaux hollered from the dock, her hands arched into a bridge to shield her eyes.

"Call 911!" I threw my head back to scream. "There's a god-damn body in here!"

"Get it out! Pull it in!" In her floppy red rain hat and strangely adorable oversized rain slicker, yelling with her whole body and pounding her cane, Riveaux looked like a pissed-off Paddington Bear. Was it only anger I saw in Riveaux that Friday morning? Rage was a trendy cover for disappointment. For sadness. For something unnameable, maybe even unknowable.

I propped myself up and sat on the flat ledge of the ship's red paddle, half in, half out of the gritty water, one hand on the body to keep the Mississippi from taking it.

The swollen head marbled like rotting meat. The face submerged. Trying to stay afloat with a body that big was a repetitive exercise in failure.

Failure, my brand. At least God kept things consistent.

Minutes later, a cop lifted the corpse high enough for EMTs to grab the body and pull it out of the water. I was breathless, coughing up water. Needed a cigarette.

I reached up to a beefy medic who pulled me onto the concrete lip of the embankment. Strong and weak at the same time, I was electrified by the discovery but hated needing help, hated needing people at all. The medic's strength was bold, confident, a bodily conviction. To be so alive in the flesh, less caged in the gerbil wheel of a mind. Was that what my brother, Moose, felt as he patched up soldiers on the battlefield? He sure as hell didn't learn his bravery from me.

The pounding rain blurred the details, no edges, couldn't even see my own tattoos. A terrible smearing. The water held me, and, in a sick way, it was spellbinding.

The corpse from the river was clad in all black, like me. I leaned closer and saw that both its eyes were gouged out.

Eyebrows gone. Large crosses branded deep into bloated cheeks.

Someone tried to erase his face.

But despite the butchery, I knew the dead man. I knew his faceless face.

Father Reese.

8:48 A.M.

I BLESSED MYSELF, dropped to my wet knees.

"Father Reese."

"You know this guy?" A fist of wind knocked Riveaux's hat off. She jumped for it but missed, and the hat disappeared into the lacerating air.

"My priest," I said. "Father Reese has been at Saint Sebastian's for forty years."

His skin looked boiled. My own, freed from my gloves and scarf, felt stewed.

I pulled the mushy pulp of my PI certificate out of my pocket. Shocked that it took a whole hour before I destroyed it.

The police, as they arrived, worked to lock down the area and tape off the scene. The yellow hazard tape fluttered in the merciless wind.

Riveaux and I looked pathetic. Drenched rats. The EMTs and police moved in quick but fluid steps. The rain powered down like it wanted to devour us. Acts of God, like anything we cannot control, equalize us.

Eyeless Father Reese. Not so much a human, but a relic scooped out from a forgotten pit. I still knew it was him.

Dear Lord, hear my prayer. Maybe share some bullet points of your divine plan? For fuck's sake.

I caught my breath on the filthy embankment of the filthy river in the jewel-toned city I loved. It was raining so hard a palm tree broke its own neck. Like the memory of the best sex you've ever had, New Orleans taunts as it redeems. It's the sweat that never leaves you. A siren song. What enchants also ensnares, then you're fucked.

Coughing up water, every limb felt heavy, sandbagged to the muddy ground. With Father Reese bound like an Easter ham on Good Friday, tell me God doesn't have a wack sense of humor.

You don't have to believe in God or a higher power. Megachurch leaders are insane, the "religious right" is neither religious nor right, and most radio preachers are about as legit as the belief that you can fly after huffing glue. But trust when I say that pulling Father Reese out of the water was a form of birth. A new reason to wake up, a new door to redemption.

I should know. At thirty-four years old, I was the youngest servant with the Sisters of the Sublime Blood by forty years, although there were only two of us now. Six months away from my permanent vow ceremony. I had settled into my routine, my simple room in our modest New Orleans convent. No car, no phone, no TV, no nonsense. No money of my own. Anyone who wanted to get ahold of me wrote a letter or rolled up in person. People who felt suspicious or sorry for me didn't get it. My life made more sense and had more grace in it now than most modern existences brimming with fuckery and hypocrisy. Rules were clear, and I stayed in line.

Most of the time.

I looked at Father Reese's body again. Someone had ended his life, left his flesh to the hungers of the water. The divine took his spirit, crane-gamed his soul to a different plane. There was still an expression on his mutilated face, a yearning. Even in death, when you're long gone, the you of you reaches back, reaches for home.

9:11 A.M.

SIRENS BLARED. Crude and jagged. Like the pulse of the devil. Through the downpour, forensics managed the moment with quiet intensity. After hundreds of crime scenes, such orchestration became second nature.

In the freshly erected medical tent, I saw a familiar face.

"You?" It was Mickey, the EMT with the chin dimple as deep as a well. "Fucking hell, Sister Holiday. When am I going to stop seeing you?"

"When I stop saving the day." I made the sign of the cross.

"This guy's day is looking unsavable at present," said Riveaux, who leaned on her cane.

Riveaux cradled what I presumed to be her camera under her big rain slicker. Mickey draped a towel around my shoulders and eased me into the mesh chair he had unfolded.

Father Reese was a sap, frequently on the road for conventions and lectures, boring us to tears with lukewarm homilies on the Sundays he happened to be in town.

Our second priest picked up the slack. Father Nathan arrived from Ascension Parish three months earlier—a plucky, young priest, newly minted after seminary. Reese was supposed to show him the ropes, but it was Nathan who had the deeper, more meaningful relationship with God. I could tell by the way he preached and prayed. In the silences he allowed. Father Nathan was special. He cared. An ally, like Sister T. Me and Nathan were friends in a hard place. Comrades because we shared the one thing you cannot fake: true faith.

And, yeah, Reese didn't even know my first name, but he didn't deserve such a brutal end.

I'd get to the bottom of this, like I did last time.

Crows darted over the riverbank like black flames. Detective Reginald Grogan stalked into view looking like a good ol' boy Captain Ahab, cocky and tall but tight as a fist ready to break somebody's nose. Mine most likely. Obsession had carved age into his face.

Sergeant Ruby Decker walked a step behind Grogan, but they were exactly in sync. Two limbs of one authorial body.

"Sister Holiday," Decker said with no attempt to conceal her disdain, "you have a gift for being in the wrong place at the wrong time." Rain shot down on the tent with brute force.

"I have many God-given gifts," I said. The towel felt soft and warm on my body, but I could feel my eyes reddening with each cough.

Grogan brought his mouth close and parted his lips near my face but said nothing. His breath smelled like two-week-old tobacco juice and the kind of coffee that scraped your throat on the way down, then sent you sprinting to the john.

He stood and eyed Riveaux up and down. "Why you here, junkie?"

Riveaux brushed it off, but I saw her glitch. "A client named Mrs. Jasmine Norwood hired us."

"Hired a joke-of-a-nun and a druggie?" Grogan laughed. "For what? A pill-popping gay prayer circle?"

I piped up though the rain dulled my voice. "We're working a case."

Riveaux nodded. "Redemption Detective Agency, ID number 6—"

"666?" Grogan wasn't funny but acted like he invented comedy. Did all cops think they were gods? Or just the ones in my life?

"Isn't your boat in the marina nearby?" Riveaux probed Decker. "The one Rock and I joined you and Sue on last Fourth of July?"

What card was Riveaux playing? Showing off her investigative chops and memory? Or reminding her that they were once colleagues? Pals?

"Yes, it is," Decker said through clenched teeth.

Grogan cast down his gaze on Father Reese's corpse. "All kidding aside, congrats Maggie, on that PI thing. But y'all need to clear outta here now. Scoot." He swept us aside with his big hands.

Grogan was a hard-ass. Who knew what that man had seen, all the pain he'd soaked in. All the cases that went cold. Detective work was in his family, like mine. Grogan's old man was NOPD Chief Albert Grogan, long dead. My father, who was still alive but dead to me, was NYPD Chief Frank Walsh. Policing was scary, sure. But it didn't give them a license to bully, to kill, to harass with impunity. I watched Grogan take control of the scene.

"He's in a foul mood," I said.

"I heard Grogan and his wife are having problems again," Riveaux said. "I can sympathize."

Riveaux and I were finding our way back to trusting each other, but it was stunningly clear that Decker and Grogan weren't going to kiss and make up with her any time soon. My dad told me that once you leave law enforcement, you're out. For good.

Determined not to cause more trouble for Riveaux, but unable to help it, I said to the Homicide Squad, "So you can only do your jobs when no one's watching? Performance anxiety?"

Decker was incensed. "What did you—"

"What Sister Holiday meant to say," Riveaux interrupted, squaring her shoulders, "is that we are here to tail a cheating husband, so our client can get a better settlement in her divorce. She was going to pay our retainer here, in person, this morning." Riveaux was being earnest. She held up her PI card. Mist clouded the lenses of her glasses. "Transparency."

Grogan huffed as the rain hastened its tempo. "Don't see any client around, do you?" He spit brown tobacco juice into the wet wind.

"She emailed the agency yesterday."

I cleared my throat and clutched my towel. Decker stared at my inked knuckles, at the grime under my fingernails.

"At least I found Father Reese before he washed away," I said.

"We'd have found him sooner or later," Grogan said.

"You're jealous I got the action, again."

The change in Grogan's face, the corkscrew of his lips, made it clear I was under his skin. Exactly where I wanted to be. He hated that I could get to him.

"When did you first see him in the water?" He refocused.

"Twenty after eight, over there." I pointed to the red paddle of the riverboat tourist trap.

The Homicide Squad left my soggy self behind and did their thinking aloud as the forensics swarm clicked photos and bagged evidence, wearing protective white suits, gloves, and hoods. One white woman crouched low, gently brushing away wet grass to reveal something unseeable from my perch. Another expert a few feet away worked the ground with tweezers.

"What if Mrs. Jasmine Norwood was a ruse?" Riveaux pushed her glasses up her nose.

I laughed at *ruse*. Don't know why. Like biting your lip when you're parking or trying to remember a name. No reason. Not sure if it was my faith stopping or starting again, but I felt an engine rev deep in the meat of my heart muscle.

The energy of a new case was holy. It routed all my mania onto one target. One goal. We'd crack the case together, me and Riveaux.

Obscene rain drummed the tent. Father Reese was a molted casing, a sad reminder of human cruelty. The ultimate riddle of God.

Somebody might have set us up. It would have been the logical cue for any sane person to get the fuck out of dodge, trash the Redemption PI Agency before we even began, and save ourselves from all the torment the discovery of the body unleashed.

But the fastest way out is through the dead center. It's also the most dangerous path. Like Moses through the tidy split in the Red Sea.

9:46 A.M.

RIVEAUX DROVE ME BACK to Saint Sebastian's—my campus, my new home—before the second period bell rang. It was a miracle I didn't start teaching until ten on Fridays, and, since it was Good Friday, we had an early dismissal.

I had to talk to Father Nathan, to learn everything he knew.

The two priests lived together in the Saint Sebastian's rectory. Like roommates. Or inmates. Or lovers. When you share a dwelling, alliances and rivalries form. Hard to tell them apart. Nathan was different from any other male-presenting cleric I had ever met in New York or New Orleans. He didn't fall for the pseudo-reverent congregants. He wasn't duped by the wealthy folks looking to ensure a fast track through the pearly gates with their church donations. Hypocrites.

A quick rosary brought me back to myself. In the convent, I took a one-minute ice-cold shower, towel-dried my hair, and changed into a clean black uniform. As I buttoned my blouse, I read the ink that was tattooed from my jawline to my toes. A biblical plague of tatts. Words, faces, names, and vignettes that melted into my nervous system, colors that felt different day-to-day. Lines Nina used to trace, to kiss. But now my ink was concealed by the black gloves and scarf I still wore every day, even though Sister Honor didn't require it. Old habits were hard to break. Any nun would agree. I enshrined it as my own rule. My nun-sleuth uniform.

No one could decipher me, and I liked it that way. To strangers, I imagined I looked like a clean slate.

In the convent kitchen, I slugged back a cup of atrocious coffee before I dashed out. The sludge was so caustic it burned my throat. Like her request for forgiveness after our latest dustup, Sister Honor—sanctimonious starlet of God, the only other Sister left in our Order—bungled the coffee-making. Pride got in the way. Sister Honor could not or would not ask for help, then she played the victim. Her favorite role.

No surprise.

In my music room, catching my breath, the bell rang as the rain outside gathered strength. The cataclysmic downpour droned in my inner ears. I had river crud, shower water, and who knows what else jammed in there. I tilted my head, bounced up and down, and let my ears cry.

Ryan Brown (the noodge), Fleur, Aisha, and Rebecca all answered "present" as I took attendance, but they didn't look up. I still recited "Prince Dempsey," though I knew I'd hear no smart-ass jab in response. Misfit Prince had skipped so much school recently it would take a holy decree for him to be handed a diploma. Not sure the kids realized Prince had been so frequently absent, though. Their attention was welded to the open palms where their phones lived. Where stigmata circled Jesus's sacrifice. I could have been ramrodded by extraterrestrials, suspended in a spaceship tractor beam, and my students would not have noticed. The here and now were neither. No one was anywhere anymore.

Advanced Guitar Ensemble was an exercise in group trust. We learned and tried and failed together. But for all intents and purposes, I was alone.

"Morning," was all I could offer the class.

A loud burp from Ryan Brown was the only reply.

"Phones away," I said, "and let's begin."

A chorus of grumbles and groans erupted. At least they were in unison.

Lord, forgive my low threshold for dweebs, for rich and entitled teenagers with dynastic wealth.

After synchronized swimming with Father Reese's carcass in the river, I resented having to teach. I was ready to go, to pop off and fight. There were clues to find. A killer to smoke out. I needed to talk to Father Nathan. The crime scene had to be revisited. Still wasn't sure if I could trust Riveaux, and absolutely knew I couldn't trust the cops. Another dead body in my sight line. Another lost soul on that Friday of biblical rains. No Mrs. Jasmine Norwood. Was she a distraction, a perp, or a second victim?

All the while, it stormed, slick and awful, like fangs biting down.

My zillion hours of PI apprenticing had begun, and I needed to sleuth. I had picked up a trick or two from Riveaux already—she always zoomed out for the big picture.

I had a bad track record taking instructions from others. A pasty frat boy at the Bay Ridge Y tried to teach me and my kid brother how to swim. I was seven and a half and Moose was nearly six. Moose took it slow. One stroke at a time. I dove into the deep end and prayed for a miracle.

Still in the deep end decades later.

"Nice of you to join us, Sister Holiday." I didn't need to turn to face the doorway. Knew it was science genius Rosemary Flynn by the superiority in her voice and the percussive *t* in *Sister*. We'd been sharing a classroom since the east wing fire last semester. That morning her anxiety pricked the air. Maybe a real heart was clicking somewhere in the porcelain jail of her polished body. Couldn't tell. And yet, when I did turn, Rosemary Flynn looked so goddamn pretty, as always. Strawberry-blond hair in a tight bun. Ruby-red lipstick. A quicksilver flash of something alive—mischief?—in her gray eyes. She stood upright, her whole body strong and erect with the brutalized conviction of a ballerina's big toe. She sneered at me. With us, it was either hate or lust. Maybe both. But never disinterest. "You missed the morning meeting," Rosemary said, her arms symmetrically crossed, red fingernails rapping.

"Would love to chitchat but . . ." I pointed to my students, who were flinging guitar picks at one another's heads. Of course, I needed to talk with Rosemary, Father Nathan, and everyone else about Father Reese's death, including the students. One-on-one. But I would have to wait until class ended. Our students had been through so much. Drag them and complain about them, sure, but they were my charges. And if they were hiding something, it was up to me to figure it out. The police couldn't find a needle in a goddamn pile of needles.

Rosemary motioned to me with her aggressively manicured hand, and I stepped away from my student circle. Her eyebrows lifted as her voice lowered. "Was Father Nathan with you? We can't find him."

"What?" I whispered. My stomach turned.

She sighed. "His history class is waiting for him, and Sister Honor has been looking for him all morning. I thought since you were both gone, and you are friendly, maybe you were together."

I walked into the hallway and signaled for Rosemary to follow me out.

"Father Reese is *dead*," I said. Thunder rippled the roof. The rickety hallway lights flickered.

"Oh no." She blinked with genuine shock. "Did he pass away in his sleep?"

My face was so close to hers I could smell her rose cologne. The scent was so velvety, I wanted to cry. "I found him in the river this morning. Murdered. Bound up and slashed."

Rosemary inhaled, grabbed her mouth, held it tight with her hand as if her lips might leap off her face. "No."

I shifted my weight from my left foot to my right and tried to not to stare, but the intensity of the moment and the potential of her unraveling held my gaze.

"Where the hell is Nathan?" For a split second, my heart stopped. Father Nathan was uncharacteristically absent. On the morning I found Reese dead.

Rosemary shrugged. "I truly don't know. I haven't seen either of them since yesterday. Bernard searched the rectory and said he didn't see anyone."

Bernard Pham, my comrade, the janitor at Saint Sebastian's, cleaned up everyone's messes. And God's chaos. He was also an experimental noise musician, which some found baffling but endeared him to me even more. He was solid. If Bernard said the sky was falling, which it essentially was, I believed him.

Father Nathan had no cell phone, so we couldn't call or track him.

"Have you noticed anything else unusual recently?" I asked Rosemary. "Anything off?"

She said, "A pair of rubber gloves were taken from my science lab. I noticed during my weekly count. Some test equipment, too. I figured I should tell you."

"You do a weekly count?" I was slightly impressed.

I made the sign of the cross, let it sink in for real.

Father Harold Reese was dead. The old priest I had known for nearly two years.

Father Nathan Troy was MIA. The young priest I had admired for three months.

I hoped Nathan was late. Or lost. Anywhere but floating in the river, God forbid. Or connected to the murder. Nothing was impossible; even good people were capable of barbarity. The thought made me sick.

I stuck my head inside our classroom and saw pencils pro-truding from the foamy ceiling like errant rockets piercing an innocent moon.

Back in the hall, I held Rosemary's eyes, wouldn't let her look away from me.

"I need to find Father Nathan," I said.

She cocked her head. "What if he doesn't want to be found?"

Despite her know-it-all air, she rarely helped or had anything to offer. No tidbits. No clues. And yet, I couldn't help feeling like Rosemary Flynn held a piece of the puzzle. A puzzle that shape-shifted every time I looked at it.

10:50 A.M.

AT THE SIGHT OF SISTER HONOR marching down the hallway, Rosemary Flynn left me at the classroom door and swiftly caught up with her. Chin up, Rosemary dutifully followed our default Mother Superior.

Good holy and true Lord in heaven, why does the human species dote? Why do we cling to the people and creatures and places that don't need us and can't keep us?

As Rosemary panted after Sister Honor, I raged against the pathetic memories of my own weakness. My awful patterns. How I continually chased, then ran from Nina. How I failed Moose again and again. How I could only show up for him in the wake of a crisis. Moose was always trying to get my attention, holding up a mirror. Fuck that. I knew too well what shame looked like. Didn't need his constant reminder.

"Hey, Sister!" Bernard Pham had appeared from around the corner with a mop and bucket.

"Have you found Father Nathan?" I asked.

"Not yet. Duty keeps calling." He pointed to the mop and bucket. "The roof can't handle this storm. Like a waterfall up there."

"Seriously?"

"Yup. I'm literally bailing us out every time it rains. The whole shebang's gonna give."

"Not exactly the ambiance we want for optimal learning."

"We need a better solution. I have to bend Sister Honor's ear."

He trotted to track down Sister Honor, who was long gone by that point.

I resumed teaching, or my best imitation of it.

Only a few more minutes before the bell, before I could sleuth again, before I could look for Father Nathan. For any clues to his coordinates. He never missed class. This was bad. But how bad and what brand of bad, I wasn't sure. My body felt it first. The way my chest seized, like an invisible force choke-chaining my heart, said danger. Something was very, very wrong. Flesh knows what the mind cannot rationalize, tries to deny.

Father Nathan came to Saint Sebastian's from Ascension, a parish located an hour northwest of New Orleans, to share leadership duties with Father Reese and teach history. I couldn't help but think he also came to help us heal, to comfort us after Sister Augustine's grisly end. A fresh start. Our Moses in a baby-sized basket.

Clearly, I'd solve yet another case at Saint Sebastian's, but I'd have to do it faster than last time. Cracking a case isn't about reenacting the moves and countermoves of a psychological chess match; it's about finding gaps. Missing pieces. Following the heat, feeling for wind in the tunnel, charting a way through the dark.

Class concluded with the squawk of the half-dead school bell. Students shuffled away. Their emo malaise was spiked with the excitement that accompanies a holiday schedule and early dismissal.

My music room door slammed shut as I slipped out and walked swiftly downstairs to Father Nathan's history classroom. I had to be there, alone, to dig through Nathan's desk. And if he came back while I was searching? He'd understand. Perhaps I could find something, anything, pointing to his whereabouts. A receipt. A ticket. The corner of a sticky note torn in haste. Or on purpose. Ghosts of split-second decisions. Cosmology of bad choices.

What was Father Nathan up to? Ordering extra blessings for the holy water at the Guild downtown, or was he drunk on Communion wine, or dead, on the train to the heavenly plane? Could he have been the victim of a hate crime? Bigots despise progress. And those bastards would be especially offended by Father Nathan, a leader, a Black man rising through the ranks, maybe steering an old ship in a new direction. I was getting ahead of myself. A workplace hazard as a PI apprentice nun.

He didn't seem upset yesterday. But everyone was masking something—what was his secret?

Did our new priest murder the old priest, then flee? It was as far-fetched as any grainy mystery on PBS, but it's a stunning miracle we can trust anyone. We don't tell ourselves core truths, let alone one another. People we are closest to will tell the biggest lies. Trust is the greatest suspension of disbelief. I should know.

Father Nathan's desk was freakishly organized, not like my overflowing shitpile, with PI manuals and logic puzzles hidden under music theory books, zines, and the Bible. I rummaged through every corner, every drawer of Father Nathan's station. Other than a single key sitting right on top of a book about WWII, I found zilch. The key was a sleek enigma. A metal cipher. Smaller than a car key, bigger than a post-office box key. I tried it in every lock I could find in Nathan's classroom, but nothing opened.

Did he have a bike? I couldn't recall. I did remember when Nathan first arrived on campus. He was twiddling his thumbs, waiting around for crotchety Reese, so Sister Honor asked me to welcome him and give him a tour.

"Father Nathan, as in Nathan's Famous Hot Dogs?" I asked. "New York tradition."

He rolled his eyes. "Never heard that one before."

"My humor is fresh and exciting."

"Clearly. And yes, I'm Father Nathan. *Famous* was my nick-name in high school, probably because I had no friends."

A loner, like me. Instant point.

I showed him the rectory kitchen, which Reese should have done himself. But priests didn't bother with such pedestrian admin tasks when us nuns—lowly women—could do their work. Typical. On our tour, Father Nathan opened the kitchen cabi-net, grabbed a jar of peanut butter, dunked a fork inside, and licked it clean. The extreme randomness of the fork won me over. Later, he showed me his deck of cards with crosses printed on them, like he was marrying faith and vice, then gifted me a matchbook for no reason. Deck of cards. Peanut butter fork. Just-because matches. Father Nathan was my kind of guy.

Later that week, during Nathan's first sermon, I sulked in the corner of the church, waiting for the service to begin, jealous I couldn't be up there, riffing on the Word. My black gloves, scarf, and dyed hair clashed with other parishioners' conservative attire. I didn't care. I was there to pray, to feel the light, like everyone else. Then Nathan walked up to the pulpit, his collar royally askew and his shoelaces untied. When he started to speak, I didn't tune out. He wove musical motifs and an exquisite tirade against white privilege into his sermon. Divine. The unexpected references made it feel like Nathan was speaking directly to me. Such an odd sensation—inspiration—after I had grown so used to the painfully boring blah blah sessions from Father Reese, the human Ambien.

After the service, I approached him.

"That was not a waste of time," I said. "You know how to 'rock' the pulpit."

"Heaven help us," he said with an emphasis on *us*. "I play music, too."

"What instrument?" I asked, expecting to be disappointed by something intellectual like harpsichord or accordion.

"Bass."

We started trading favorite guitar licks, and I was delighted to learn that Father Nathan was a punk fan. I forgave him for preferring the Clash over Siouxsie and the Banshees; nobody's perfect. Except God. As we talked, I realized that Nathan and I were both insider-outsiders, drawn to the Catholic Church, to music, to big changes and outrageous choices. We mocked Christian rock—gag—and debated which Nina Simone record was the best of all time. Deal sealed on week one.

Everywhere I turned in Nathan's history room, I felt his large but calm presence. Even in absence, bonds have quiet efficiency, like a fisherman setting a hook.

Rain lashed the windows. If the storm didn't let up soon, New Orleans would be in big trouble. Water rises and rises until the pressure is too much. Something always has to give. I hated that my new city was constantly under threat.

The history room was empty, but Nathan's void flooded the space.

Father Nathan was the one priest who offered me kindness—me, the impostor. Seemed like he wanted to know the real me. Two survivors on the sinking ship of a religious institution. We were the newbies, the underdogs sparking energy into a shrinking congregation. Maybe I had it wrong. Maybe we were going down with the ship, too.

Since my desk search didn't reveal much, I left to call Riveaux on the phone in the teacher's lounge.

"Redemption Detective Agency," Riveaux recited after one ring. I could tell she was smiling, could hear the shape of her face in her voice.

"Father Nathan, our new priest, is missing. I have a bad feeling."

"Dang." She cleared her throat, said, "Let me call Homicide, see if they have any info," and hung up.

I used the bathroom and was startled by how heavy everything felt. The door. The faucet knob. My own body.

Less than five minutes later, Riveaux called back. I jumped, not used to the ring.

"No news from them on Father Nathan. But they've changed their tune." Riveaux's voice was buoyant on the other end of the line. "Grogan wants us on the case. They offered a détente. NOPD is going to subcontract Redemption to find Father Nathan and—"

"We're not working for the cops," I interrupted. "No way in hell."

"Hold up, Goldsmobile." I swore I could hear her tapping her left canine as she schooled me. She was usually late to the party but always first to dispense humor. "Grogan's annoying as fuck, but he stays connected. He and Decker can get us access to all the scenes. We'd be working for *ourselves*, our agency, not them. Where do you think Nathan is? How long has he been missing?"

"Don't know. Nobody's seen him since yesterday, as far as I can tell. I already searched his classroom desk. Only found a key."

"What does it open?"

"Not sure. I tried it on a dozen locks but nothing opened."

"I would have found out by now," Riveaux said. "Step it up, Goldsmobile."

"What's it like all the way up there?"

"The fuck you talking about?"

"On that pedestal," I said.

"You begged to be my apprentice, remember? Could the key have been planted, question mark?"

"Impossible to tell."

The rain slammed harder, started to seep through the window jam in the teacher's lounge. New Orleans was unrelenting, never dry yet still thirsty, never satisfied. When I closed my eyes, I saw Reese's meaty head in the water.

Riveaux got serious. "Did the two priests get along, question mark?"

"As far as I could tell. Wasn't around them together too much outside of Sunday Mass."

"Was Father Nathan the old guy's enemy or a Reese mini-me? Junior Reese in training? One of Reese's pieces?"

"Father Reese was a flatliner, usually out on the road on one of his book tours. Father Nathan was a good guy. My friend. He cared."

"Be objective. Remember the three *F*s of PI work?"

"Forget Friendship or you're Fucked. Trust no one, look at everyone."

"Correct. Do you think Nathan had anything to do with Reese's murder? Stay focused."

"I'm telling you. What you see is what you get with Nathan. If that's ever the case. But, of course, he *could* be involved. Anything is possible."

"Don't I know it."

"I can't imagine Nathan killing Reese, but . . ." I couldn't finish the sentence. Hated letting my mind kick up suspicion about Father Nathan, a decent guy, one of the few people my age who got it. And by *it*, I meant God. I hated questioning him the same way I hated questioning Sister Augustine. Look where that got me.

Burned.

"So, Goldsmobile," Riveaux said, trying—and failing—to keep her tone even. I could feel her patience wearing thin as a needle.

"What?"

"Nathan's gone. Stay objective."

I rubbed my temples too hard. "Yes, he's currently missing, but I just can't see him being involved in murder."

She scoffed. "When you can't see the forest for the trees, you gotta start chopping."

"Someone's already done plenty of chopping on Reese," I replied, eliciting a groan from Riveaux. "Can you pick me up at one thirty?"

"Yep."

"I'll be done with my last class then. We can head back to the riverbank and see what we can find." I had to get back to the crime scene, put my hands in the river again.

Ask, and it shall be given to ye; Seek, and ye shall find. Matthew 7:7.

We're born liquid—drooling, pooling, supple cheeks, juicy knees. Humans are mostly water, but we can still drown. If only the water could answer all the prayers, all the questions we scream into it as we sink.

11:28 A.M.

I HAD A FEW more hours before I could break free and work the case with Riveaux.

The rain continued its crazed dance.

My anxiety must have been contagious because my students shed what minor manners they possessed. A shadow wobbled as Ethan Ellsworth, another polo-shirted bullshit artist, reached for a phone eleven seconds after I'd last said, "No phones in class."

"It's not a phone," Ethan said as I glared.

"Oh?"

"It's my emotional support device." He smirked.

Hail Mary, full of grace. Grant me the saintly serenity to refrain from unleashing a holy throttling.

Yes, I prayed for grace, for guardrails. I needed patience to endure my hapless class. My gears were turning. But I'll confess: Tension can be irresistible.

Addictive even.

Everyone talks about the miseries and winged terrors unleashed by Pandora, but keep in mind that in the minutes before she cracked that box open, Pandora existed in the most delicious state of life, pure anticipation.

"Put it away. Now." If I couldn't smack the damn phone out of the kid's hand my tone had to do it.

"Fine," he replied, his supply of smarm depleted.

The bell rang and students left. Lunchtime. The Good Friday schedule had things moving at a rapid clip. We were nearing the finish line.

Rosemary Flynn returned, entering our shared classroom with chalk dust on her hands and the shoulder of her pink silk blouse. She took a long drink from her fine pink teacup. I was about to ask if she had heard any news about Father Nathan, but I buckled, too distracted to speak as I watched her swallow the tea. The rain slapped the glass like the hard knuckles of a backhand. "Where on earth is Father Nathan?" she inquired, reading my mind.

"Dunno," was my pointless reply. "Where do priests go when not teaching or in service? The Guild? The top-secret priest clubhouse? No nuns allowed."

I walked backward to my desk, eyes on Rosemary, as I pawed for my notebook. When I found it, I scribbled:

1. Good Friday

2. Mrs. Jasmine Norwood=a ruse?

3. Father Reese=dead in the water. Hands tied and face slashed. Body with coroner.

4. Father Nathan=missing but why. Where? Hail Mary. WTF.

5. Key.

"What are you writing?" asked Rosemary as she plucked a thumbtack from the corner of her Newton's Laws poster. Her red nails were long and sharp and the color of pain. Like they could draw blood with the lightest touch.

"Listing the clues so far," I responded. I didn't tell Rosemary that Riveaux's requirement for me joining the PI agency was that I start therapy. Bespectacled Dr. Connie wasn't helping, but she wasn't not helping. Listing and counting became stress-management tools. Though listing and counting stressed me out, too. I noted Rosemary's posture, her expression, the earringless ears, the plumpness of each lobe. I wanted to touch them, to bite them.

"What clues?" She was asking a lot of questions.

"That's for me to worry about."

"Do you think Father Nathan is okay?"

"Are any of us okay?"

"Depends on your definition." She glanced out the window, then at me. I tried to slow down my heart rate. I hated when she looked at me like that, because I wasn't sure what to do about it. "When do you think this storm will stop?"

"Rainy season is both necessary and inconvenient, don't you think?"

"Never thought about it," Rosemary said as she wrote the word *pressure* on the chalkboard.

"'Forty days and forty nights, and I will wipe from the face of the earth every living creature I have made.' Genesis 7:1. Did you know Noah was six hundred years old when the flood began?"

"I honestly feel six hundred years old." Rosemary blinked at her hands and brushed the chalk dust from her fingers, delicate as blown glass.

"Well, you don't look a day over five hundred and fifty-five."

The severity of Noah's story seized me. In every day and every way, God reminds us of our fragility and power. Two sides of one mysterious coin. Water feeds the world, then uncreates the world.

"That passage is so melodramatic." Rosemary theatrically swept her hand to her forehead. "How can you read that nonsense, let alone believe it? It is so ridiculous, so artificial, written by men about men for men. You of all people . . ."

She said no more. Didn't need to.

I cracked my neck. "Genesis is the root beer of biblical books, sassy and unexpected."

"Gives me indigestion." Of course, Rosemary Flynn was the type to say *indigestion* instead of *heartburn*. She leaned against the wall and tapped her foot nervously. With a remarkably flat voice, she said, "You look very tense."

"I pulled a dead body out of the river this morning, so I guess you could say I'm a little tightly wound."

"Tension seeks release," she said. "It's a scientific principle."

She moved closer and brought her face to mine. A shiver passed through me like a slow dagger.

"I guess I could use some release," I said, standing taller, matching her dead delivery.

"What do you have in mind?" she asked.

"What do *you* have in mind?"

"You're the tense one."

She pointed to my scarf and gloves, took my cross between her fingers and gave the gold chain a tug so imperceptible I might have imagined it. But the necklace cut into the back of my neck with delicious urgency as she pulled harder. I readjusted my scarf and squinted, trying to suss out what the hell was going on with Rosemary. Every nerve in my body was a live wire severed by lightning, frying me, toying with the raw need.

Was Rosemary coming in hot for the sake of the heat, a cat-and-mouse chase? Or was she messing with my head in a telltale attempt at misdirection? On the morning of my tragic discovery, it felt off. Like she was trying to derail me from Father Nathan's trail. Dear God, in my old life, I loved rassling with sexy, inscrutable, ice-queen doms like Rosemary Flynn. So curated on the outside, you knew they'd be total freaks in bed. All that top energy could only nosedive. Like coke benders, those wild nights left me hollowed out the day after. Because what I would never admit, not even to myself, was that for all my lesbian Lothario stagecraft, I wanted only Nina, my high school sweetheart. I wanted to marry her, indulge all the traditional BS that I used to rail against. I wanted to shack up somewhere we wouldn't be kicked out of for playing music late at night. Rescue an elder cat or three. Raise some kids we loved fiercely, then whined about when they started thinking for themselves. We'd live and complain and make messes together. Me and Nina. I was convinced we'd still be crushed out on each other in our nineties.

Rosemary and I were close and far, staring then looking away, unsure of the next move but enjoying the awkwardness, like slow-dancing to Aerosmith at prom. She smoothed her pencil skirt. When I hesitated and said nothing, her face changed.

"Forget it," she said under her breath. "I have to prepare for my next class."

What the everloving fuck?

I left Rosemary Flynn alone in our classroom. Had to keep searching without distractions. But wherever I went, trouble was waiting. Like the sick grip of an undertow. Hands in the darkness, pulling me down.

11:40 A.M.

MY NEXT DESTINATION WAS the school library. Third floor of the west wing. Our school's east wing was a singed ghost, still out of commission after the fire. No money to raze it. I hated looking at it. A graveyard with no tombstones.

Our new English teacher, Alex Moore, walked into my view, carried by the spooky gait of a leggy spider. He had been called up from a Catholic school in Thibodaux after Sister Honor became Saint Sebastian's principal. Real chummy with the Diocese, Alex Moore. He ran the library but wasn't a librarian. And judging by the state of it, Alex was running our little library into the ground. Books collapsed in sloppy towers. Nothing was alphabetized or categorized. He cleared his throat. Alex must have been six foot three. Or four. Scalp practically touching the scuffed ceiling.

"Hello, Sister!" he said with an intense warmth that made me flinch. "What brings you—"

"Show me how to work the computers."

"All we have is the *one* computer," Alex said. "Brought it myself. I saw y'all didn't have one and thought, oh, shoot!"

Father Nathan employed a similar habit of substituting curse words with wholesome ones, but when Alex Moore did it, I cringed. "I had an extra, and even though y'all need at least ten to run a proper lab up here, I'm truly honored to share it."

Instead of thanking him, as I suspected he was expecting, I said, "One is all I need."

Alex Moore, like most people, banked on being liked. He was the kind of "charming guy" that gives "good meeting," pounds you with clever perspectives and weak humor. A persona, a set piece. Look closely, though, and the illusion is eerily clear. It takes time to see the real human hiding inside carefully constructed walls. But I would break through. Or break it all down.

Alex walked me to the computer in the corner of the library. An old tank of a machine in a dark, musty room, but it was worth a roll of the dice.

"Let me turn this on for you, Sister Holiday." He reached his long Gumby arm across me and tapped a key.

I had to stop myself from slapping his hand away. "I got it."

"You sure? I can show you how to—"

"I can manage." I turned my back to him and faced the screen. "I'm a quick learner."

"Sure thing, Sister!"

Alex Moore didn't hate me. Not outwardly, at least. Was he trying to be the hero? Or did I entertain him? Tempt him? He couldn't have been barking up a queerer tree. I loved being queer—my greatest asset, on par with my sleuthing abilities— though provisional vows with the Sisters of the Sublime Blood meant dating was off the menu. And Alex would never have been on my dance card in a billion years. It's not like I was leading him on. I didn't smile much, to hide my gold tooth, the result of a bar fight and a parting gift from New York.

I punched some clacky-ass keys on the antiquarian keyboard and wondered in which decade the machine had last been used. The desktop betrayed no personalization, with only default applications against the abstract wallpaper. I searched and clicked through dozens of documents—gradebooks, the tragic employee manual from the Diocese, post-hurricane damage reports—the only point of interest was a folder labeled OREGON TRAIL. No doubt it was Alex's addition, some repository of dumb lesson plans. I clicked on it to see what was inside, but it was protected by a six-character password. I tried all zeros, all ones, all sevens, Jesus's birthday. Nothing worked, and since hacking wasn't my forte, I moved on to the web browser. After slamming my fist on the mouse.

Licensed PIs have special access to a statewide investigator database. Riveaux gave me our login credentials. She even laminated a card for me, which I glued inside my notebook. The database had the pastel colors and clip art of a 1995 chat room and was hard to navigate. I couldn't find anything on Father Nathan or Father Reese. Couldn't find them at all.

I kept wondering where the hell Nathan was, kept seeing Reese's dead body bobbing in the water, his skin torn and swollen like infected gums.

No doubt, all men of the cloth had secrets, and I'd find Reese's and Nathan's. Would they be like Sister Augustine's? Or was there a secret even deeper, older?

A life-giving element like water will corrode and collapse plumbing from the inside out over time. Not if but when.

IN THE TEACHER'S LOUNGE, lunch was painful and quick.

My heart was so heavy, but I couldn't tell if it was anguish or anger. Or both. Parfait of dread. I was so sick inside, had to force myself to eat, to put bread into my mouth, chew, swallow. Repeat the steps. Not like the stacks of Oreos I used to demolish on Saturday afternoons with Moose, watching cartoons in a sugary frenzy, twisting cookies, scraping off cream filling with my teeth until we kicked back a whole sleeve.

That day I didn't want to eat or deal with other faculty. All I wanted in my mouth was expensive tobacco and cheap whiskey. And maybe a fast-talking woman. How I missed kissing. Making out. A simple, steamy make-out session with a hot lady.

"Father Reese is dead," I told the group. Judging by the lack of reactions, they already knew.

"I informed everyone on staff already," said Sister Honor, without a trace of sadness or alarm in her voice. Either the police or Rosemary had told her. "Now, who would like to begin with grace and a prayer of remembrance, an Our Father for our Father Reese?" Sister Honor spit as she talked, and the warmth of her saliva spray landing on my cheek snuffed out what little remained of my appetite. Her habit was fixed confidently to her head.

Our priest had been murdered, a man she'd known for decades, but Sister Honor didn't seem undone. Didn't even seem upset.

She asked again with vigor, "Who shall start the prayer?"

I raised my hand high, gloves pulled down to cover my tattooed wrists.

Sister Honor stared directly at me, at my raised, animated hand, following the length of my arm, and said, "No one? *Nobody?* Okay, I shall begin. Let us pray for Father Reese. Our Father, who art in heaven . . ."

My right cheek cramped from grinding my teeth for the duration of Sister Honor's prayer. Unlike most assholes who worry about social norms, I never fake-smiled during meetings or any other time. But I ground my molars and plunged my tongue into my gold tooth every time Sister Honor said something absurd. Pain—a familiar companion. Reminded me I existed. It soothed the preverbal, primordial me.

Rain oozed through a crack in the ceiling; a fat drop landed on Alex Moore's nose, which, in profile, looked like a bony butt squatting.

Behind the armory of Sister Honor's skull was the giant poster for our next Big Read: *Exodus 14: The Red Sea Crossing.* Our school-wide book club would read about Moses crossing the Red Sea. That guy led people through a crisis. A folk hero—a dude Judith. Brave. Started off as vulnerable as you could possibly be, a baby in a freaking basket sailing down a river. What faith, sending your kid away, trusting God to keep him alive.

What faith it took to have a kid in the first place. To bring a new life into this strange world. An act of tremendous selflessness and major selfishness.

"In the beginning . . ."

In my usual seat at our round table, I tried to make myself small. Rosemary Flynn, who shot curious looks in my direction, sat to my left. And to her left, lanky Alex Moore, in John Vander Kit's old spot. Poor John. According to Bernard, John had dried out, too, like Riveaux. And me, for the most part. Sure, I stole cigarettes from whomever in the student body was foolish enough to bring them to campus. Luckily, alcohol was harder to find in my new life. We all needed to quiet the noise, dull the edges of anguish. So much loss that year. The body count cranking up. I had become the Patron Saint of Losing People. Sister Holiday, God's mercenary in the earthly realm who kept taking hits.

Though I wasn't hungry, I ate. Needed strength. It was also a small comfort to break bread and eat in community. I thought of Father Nathan preparing for transubstantiation: *Take and eat; this is my body . . . This cup is the new covenant in my blood, which is poured out for you.* Luke 22:19–20. On my palm Nathan placed the holy wafer, letting me bring it to my own tongue. The luminous disc of new life, white as bone.

Rosemary had made everyone sandwiches with Sister Honor's bread. Cheddar cheese, Creole tomato, and mustard. Our new principal's baking was exceptional, no question. She channeled her fury into tender crusts and aerated dough. Hatebaking. We shared sticky figs and satsumas from our convent garden. I made an urn of strong chicory coffee and said a silent prayer for Nathan, fallen Sister T—my friends—as I sipped the lifeblood.

Sister Honor poured a perverse amount of half-and-half into her coffee and sipped. I watched in dismay as she poured in even more cream. I always took my coffee black. No sugar, no milk. Didn't want anything to get in the way of the caffeine.

Questions, like the rain, kept intensifying. Some maniac killed Father Reese and threw him in the water. Nathan had missed his morning classes. I quietly panicked for his safety. And worried about his involvement. But I prayed and ate with everyone anyway. People carry on. It's what we do because it's what we must do. Selective amnesia is a curse or a cure, depending on which side of it you're on.

The group needed to be questioned, their alibis logged in my steno. I started by asking the usual questions: who, what, where, when.

The why—that came later.

I sipped my coffee and spun the mug. "Where was everyone this morning?"

Sister Honor was offended by the question. "Had you been at the morning meeting you would have known that everyone was there. Everyone except for *you*."

"I mean before the meeting," I said. First line of inquiry and I'd already poked the bear.

"Like, our alibis?" Alex Moore asked.

"Yes."

He paused, looking out the wet window, the only one in the lounge. "Boring story for me. I watched the morning news—"

"Which channel?" I asked, even though I had no idea what channels were what. I hadn't watched TV in years.

"Channel eight, *Live with Eileen!* Their Doppler radar is never wrong. Never."

"Thrilling. Then what?"

"Rode my bike to school."

"In this crazy rain? Even though you watched the weather forecast?" The guy was dumber than he looked, which was saying something. I didn't recall if Alex was wet when I first saw him. I removed my glove and tapped his shoulder. He felt dry, but it had been hours.

Alex nodded. "The climate catastrophe is no joke. It's all drought and wildfires or hurricanes and floods. We all have to join the movement. Every one of us."

"The Sisters of the Sublime Blood have been advocating for environmental protections since long before you were born, Mr. Moore," Sister Honor jeered.

I scribbled *ALEX SUCKS*, then I turned my attention to Rosemary. "And you?"

"Me?" She tapped her chest with her long, red nails. I was worried she'd stab herself.

"Yes, you."

"Home, naturally. I woke at six, made breakfast, and drove to school."

I studied everyone's faces as they chewed and talked nothing-talk. Sister Honor was riled up, maybe because she was actually sad and needed to mask it. Glances with intentions too microscopic to decode were being traded between Rosemary and Alex. I watched in repellent detail as he shimmied his chair a nanometer closer to Rosemary's ironed skirt. I imagined her freckled, pale thigh underneath it, how the fabric hugged her skin like hot water.

"Oh, and I found the missing gloves I mentioned," added Rosemary, "from my supply."

"Where'd you find them?"

"A student stole a pair, inflated them, and stuffed them into his sweatshirt sleeves in the cafeteria."

"You need to set some rodent traps, Bernard." Alex Moore was disturbingly calm. Took himself ever so seriously. "Sounds like Mickey Mouse is on the loose."

Bernard snorted as he walked into the lounge carrying a Snickers bar, a can of Coke beaded with sweat, and something wrapped in foil that smelled heavenly. His hair was coiled into a knot on the crown of his head, and his long eyelashes cast shadows on his cheeks.

"Hey, Bernard," I said, happy to see my ally.

"'Sup?"

"What's in there?" Alex Moore pointed to the foil.

"Bánh mì xíu mại," said Bernard. "Want some? My auntie gives me hell for not being married, but damn can she cook. Here, try some." Bernard grabbed a knife from the utensil drawer and sliced off a sumptuous chunk for Alex, whose eyes rolled back into his head as he chewed. "Right? Super good."

For an artsy guy, Bernard had a sensational lack of pretension. He was urgently himself and didn't give a fuck. I loved that about him.

Rosemary cautiously sipped what appeared to be her twenty-sixth tea of the day. Bernard drank his Coke in one gulp, then said, "TGIGF."

Looking at Bernard's kind face, with the stinging memory of Father Reese's mutilated body, I started to cry. The fragility of life. How quickly the precious can turn painful. Love to hate. Like a thundercrack severing the silent sky.

The tears felt sublime and leaden as they fell, a heavy release.

"It's healthy to cry!" exclaimed Alex Moore. He leapt out of his chair and knocked a glass of water all over his lemon Hubig's pie and Sister Honor's plate, drowning her symmetrical sandwich. His bumbling made me reflexively jerk back, and I fell with a thud. "Don't be afraid of vulnerability, Sister Holiday!"

"Stop talking!" I said from the floor, hot, salty tears dripping into my eardrums, down my neck. "Leave me alone." I hated crying and wanted to show Alex Moore what vulnerability really was. By punching him until his own father wouldn't recognize him. By standing on his throat until lights out.

But the truth was that crying was sacred. Mysterious. Every tear a revelation. The inside world pushing through, escaping. Crying is our first language. The mother tongue.

Bernard helped me up. My eyes were burning, hollow in the center where the black ponds dilated. When water drips from eyes, it's the body and mind begging the pain to stop, the planet to stop shaking.

"I'm sorry," I said to the group with a tinge of embarrassment. I splayed my fingers in my gloves, flexed my thumbs. Why was I so undone?

Rosemary Flynn looked at me with concern and intrigue, halfway between running away and leaning closer.

"Sister Holiday, always the center of attention! Every single tragedy must revolve around her." Sister Honor's favorite hobby was dressing me down. Her second favorite was talking like I was not in the room. "Dear, dear, dear." She sucked her teeth. "Look at this wasted food!"

Bernard said, "Oh, please. Chill. Main man Reese is *dead*, Padre Nate is nowhere, Sister Holiday's hitting the skids, and we're all supposed to what . . . do business as usual?"

"Who saw Father Nathan last?" I asked. My hair was wet with tears.

"I saw him around eight last night," said Bernard, "walking to the rectory with a box."

"What kind of box? Big or small?

"Medium-ish." Bernard held up his hands like he was showing us the size of a catfish he'd caught. "I shouted to Nathan, but he was in a hurry, and it was raining."

"He didn't turn around or say anything?"

Bernard shook his head. "Maybe he didn't hear me."

I jotted details in my steno, frantic scribbles I prayed I'd be able to translate later. My brain moved too fast for my body. "Anyone else see Nathan last night?"

Besides Sister Honor muttering to herself as she made the sign of the cross, no one made a sound.

Alex tapped his stubbly chin. He looked at Sister Honor and said in a low voice, "I am so, so sorry about Father Reese." He turned to me. His forehead was the largest I had ever seen. "He was your priest, your *Father*. You obviously miss him, Sister Holiday."

Sister. The word still surprised me.

Contrary to most people's assumptions, being a nun is the easier path—patriarchy and all—for someone like me: addictive personality, race car of a mind, genuine love for the Lord, a desire to know more. The Order strips away clutter and space junk. Being a Sister of the Sublime Blood helped me find balance. But that didn't mean I liked the hierarchy.

I never loved it, but you don't have to love something to need it.

12:40 P.M.

"SISTER HOLIDAY, please come to the main office."

Our receptionist, Shelly, was so consistently peppy I was convinced she was either a phony or spiking her coffee with Baileys. I was almost to my classroom, my last class of that truncated day had just begun, when I heard the announcement. Hoped it was news about Father Nathan but assumed Sister Honor wanted to put me in the stocks for some infraction. Showing too much emotion? Despite our trauma bond from surviving the fires Sister Augustine had sparked, Sister Honor wouldn't let me come too close.

I walked into the main office and saw him.

"Moose? MOOSE!"

"Goose." He blinked.

The image of my brother was blindingly bright, strong yet delicate, the way Jesus must have looked when he walked on water. Glowing. Unreal.

"Moose!" I screamed again. I could not believe what I was seeing.

My brother found me, arrived in my new city—in my new life—at the worst possible time.

As if there were a good day or good way to repair a rift, to say hard words.

Without thinking I leaned in, and we completed our double high five—the Walsh family rule—which Moose turned into a huge hug after he grabbed my arm.

Moose's haircut was shorter than I had ever seen. Army chic. Rain dripped from his dark brown beard, which was shot through with cindery threads of cardinal red. His eyebrows were auburn, too. In a surreal second, he was a living portrait of the whole Walsh family—a son, mother, father, sister, and brother, all in one.

He was soaked, from the rain or tears, I couldn't tell. Like when I saw him in the hospital, after his attack in high school, wet with tears and blood. When I couldn't protect my baby bro. When my prayers and revenge could not fix him. Couldn't fix us. I was wet, too, from holding him.

"Moose."

We hugged again and he wrapped his tree-trunk arms around me. I heard clanking in Moose's backpack. He eyed my black gloves, then my scarf, which was tight as a fitted sheet on my neck.

"In disguise?" he asked.

"For once, no."

Things never happen as you predict or rehearse in your mind. They are more marvelous. And more scary. That's how it felt to hug Moose in my school's office. He was sopping wet, and his frame was unrecognizable. Biceps so big and hyper defined they were almost comical. Like he was wearing a kid's Halloween costume with plush muscles.

But why was he there and where the fuck was Nathan? Where in the angelic realm did he vanish?

Moose and I stood in silence for a moment, my worry so loud it stirred in trapped air, the ferment of decomposition. How would our lives have been different if I hadn't fucked up so royally, so often?

"What are you doing here?" I asked, studying his face and hands. I must have looked like a freak, eyes wide, making sure he was real. His fingernails were clean, filed, evenly shaped. Cuticles trimmed down to the quick. His cheeks were nicked, from fistfights or rushed shaving jobs, I couldn't tell. Bruises wrapped around his thick arms.

"Moose, your arms. What happened?"

"That? Nothing. Still your clumsy brother. That hasn't changed."

Just a few minutes together and he was already lying to me. Couldn't push him too hard too soon. My little brother was so much bigger but more fragile. Two opposites can be true simultaneously.

"I'm moving here, to N'awlins," he said, trying on the local pronunciation.

His words stunned me. "Did the army give you a sabbatical or vacation?"

"No. I'm all finished."

"With your second tour? Or first?" I had no idea how the military worked or how long medics were in service.

"No, discharged."

"What? Why?" I asked.

"C'mon, show me around your school," he said. "I want to see where you live."

"I'm . . ." I said, my voice charged with shame. "I can't do this right now."

"It's okay, Goose, I don't blame you for anything. Not anymore." He chewed his thumbnail. "I'm here now. That's what matters."

"This is the worst time for you to visit."

"I'm here just the same." He smiled, and I let myself feel his warmth. "We can celebrate my birthday together."

Oh, God. Moose's birthday was Sunday. Easter Sunday.

The timing was never right with us. When he needed me most, I was too late. Always too late. Too busy drowning in my own shit. He needed so much, too much, far more than I had to give. Can two lost kids find a path out of the forest, or are they always destined for some witch's oven? But I made a vow, a fucking oath, to do God's work, good work, to never lose the people I loved again. No matter what life threw at Moose, I wanted to help him kick its ass. He was my blood. I didn't want him to suffer alone anymore.

But I was the avalanche. I was the flood. The explosion. What my giant little brother truly needed protection from was *me*.

"You have to go, Moose."

The rain was impatient, like it wanted to knock down the door.

"We haven't seen each other in like *two years!*" He poked me in the ribs. "I'm here! It's me."

"You can't stay."

"I don't have anywhere to go." He chewed his thumbnail. "There's nothing for me in Brooklyn, Goose. Dad's life is his work. My friends all moved to Jersey and Long Island. Dennis and I are done."

"Oh, I'm sorry, Moose. Dennis? Damn. I'm really sorry. But there's nothing for you here either."

"You're here. I want to be near you."

There was something enormous hiding in all the little words he was saying. For a moment, no words came. I tapped the rain from his beard.

"Fine." I broke the silence. "Stay until the storm clears, and then you can go."

"Why are you being like this?"

"Something awful happened this morning." I didn't want to reveal much more.

"What?" he pressed. "Tell me."

"One of our priests is dead, and the other is missing. I have to find him."

"Let me help! I'm trained for this stuff."

"Really hope I don't need a medic. Again. Don't be a big shot like Dad."

"Emergencies are my sweet spot. Put me to work." He stood tall and smiled, as if his own poise surprised him. "I want to help you."

"Fine. You can sit with my students until one thirty. Class has already started. Just make sure nothing blows up on my side of the classroom while I investigate. Shelly will give you a day pass and tell you where everything is."

"Roger." He nodded, grabbed his water bottle from his burgundy backpack, and drank.

Moose wanted to see my new life, and I handed him a backstage pass. If he could stitch blown-up bodies back together in the desert, he could chaperone my silver-spooned kids. Glad that Prince Dempsey was truant as fuck. He would have made Moose jump through hoops.

I had to trust Moose could handle it. I needed to find Father Nathan and track Father Reese's killer, even if the two men's fates were linked.

And maybe Moose really did want to help. But seeing him reminded me of the damage I had done, to Mom, to our family. Like a fracture that didn't heal right, pain reactivated when you leaned on it. The sharp ache and strange relief of realizing your whole life has been a lie.

Something had to give.

Shelly led Moose upstairs to my classroom. I didn't want to be there to introduce him to Rosemary. Didn't want to ask Sister Honor for permission either. Shelly could deal with the logistics. And fallout.

After they disappeared into the stairwell, I sat at Shelly's desk and called Riveaux's cell phone. It was the only number I knew by heart. Funny that *by heart* actually meant *by memory*, taking up real estate in the head. Which was lucky because my heart had no vacancy.

"I'm free a bit early," I told Riveaux.

"Let's investigate the priests' rectory, then head back to the river. We're gonna find something." Riveaux's voice was a distant rhythm through the receiver, energy traveling along invisible waves.

"Amen. You'll never believe who showed up at school," I said.

"Father Nathan, question mark?"

"I wish. It's Moose. My little brother, Gabe. I call him Moose."

"Aw. Goldsmobile family reunion."

"More like *Family Feud*."

"Survey says y'all should print up T-shirts."

"I might owe him one. He's subbing my class."

"Didn't you say he was in the army?" Riveaux checked.

"He was. A medic."

She exhaled. "A nun and a soldier. Daddy's a police chief. Intense brood. 'After a certain age, the more one becomes one-self, the more obvious one's family traits become.'"

"Deep cut. Proust again?"

"My man Marcel," Riveaux said dreamily. "We all grow up to be our parents. Let's face it."

"Will get back to you when I grow up."

Ten minutes later, outside, I met Riveaux, who was poking the wet pavement with her cane. We walked into the rectory—the priests' convent where Father Nathan had tried to make sense of his duty-bound life while other people our age collected designer handbags, Instagrammed cocktails, and planned themed vacations.

We had to find him.

But whenever I thought I saw a clue, it vanished, like a foot-print stolen by a greedy tide.

1:05 P.M.

RIVEAUX AND I SPLIT UP in the rectory to double our chances of finding anything suspicious.

Our old priest had been dead for at least five hours, his soul somewhere or everywhere.

Father Nathan had been MIA since eight Thursday night, and, though I hated to admit it, was our most likely suspect. If chapter 11 of the PI manual, "Locating Missing Persons," had one shred of validity. Riveaux loved that chapter. I tightened the laces on my suspicion when promised easy answers and bullet-point takeaways. The truth lived in the haze, the burrows, the secret passages under theater stages.

Digressions led to the heart.

Riveaux searched the second floor—the beehive of offices, Father Reese's bedroom, and the two mini libraries. She was hyper-focused, intent on beating the cops to the punch on this case, restoring her good name. Or showing them up, making them pound sand. Grogan, Decker, and the squares downtown never deserved Riveaux. Cops brutalized people every day of every month of every year for forever and ever. They never championed Riveaux when she deserved it ten times over. She worked alongside them as a fire investigator for years—first and only Black woman at the helm. Fought for justice in this sick world. Fell off a ladder for it, wrecked her body for it. The authorities and all their badges, clearances, and pomp slowed her down at every turn.

This was our time to shine.

Or fuck up so magnificently we'd never work in private investigation again.

How many second chances do you get?

I searched the first floor, its two large bedrooms and regal en suite bathrooms. The rectory smelled like halitosis and delivered baroque corniness.

As I pushed through the door, the flash of swimming with Reese's dead body seized me for a moment. My bones trembled and leg muscles quivered, strained from inside out.

The rectory was gold, manufactured importance. Chandeliers with crystals, marble-inlaid floors. T-bone steaks in the refrigerator. Single-malt Scotch in a cut-glass decanter. The priests lived like kings while us nuns grew our own food, raised our own hens, and lived off scraps. Shocker.

Ferreting in the trash, turning over statues, flipping over photo frames to the steady drumbeat of tedium. But it was drudgery that gave me purpose. Repetition kept my mind alert and on track. I was apprenticing with Riveaux but still needed to hunt. Lone wolves were hungry. Wounded wolves required the most blood.

I tasted and tested cups of water on the edge of Reese's bathroom sink. No alcohol or poison, thank you, God. I squeezed toothpaste from the tube (Theodent Whitening with fluoride) and opened the bottles of pills in his medicine cabinet. Like a photoflash, temptation blinked. It would have been so easy to take the pain pills and kick back the Scotch, but I said a prayer instead. Rawdogging life, the nun's way.

I spotted a grip of unused Q-tips in the trash bin. One was snapped in half, four intact. No earwax.

My queer sleuthing method? Know that the goalpost will always move. Know that everything is up for grabs. There's no there there. Every door is a trapdoor. Every pit has a false bottom. Secret to sleuthing and to life: Stay curious but expect the worst. You'll never be bored or disappointed.

I ran my hands under the mattresses, searched every page of every book on Father Reese's bedside tables.

I dug through Father Nathan's dresser drawers. Unfolded and refolded white undershirts and white underpants. There must have been a dozen mothballs in each drawer. Everyone hated moths, loathed the antigravity creepers that munched through wool, but not me. Tiny things had much to teach us. In every cocoon is a changing heart.

Riveaux walked into Father Nathan's bedroom, tapping her cane with satisfying thuds.

"Sister Goldsmobile," she bellowed even though she was right behind me.

"What?"

When I turned, I saw that Riveaux was holding a framed picture of Sister Augustine. Must have been from the school's picture day the year before my new life began as her Sister, and also her daughter, of a kind. I grabbed the dusty frame in fury, wanted to punch it into a million pieces and then incinerate each piece.

"Where was this?"

Riveaux was taken aback by my reaction. "Upstairs in the office."

"They must have forgotten to put it away."

"Nah. Maybe they wanted to keep it visible," she grumbled. "To face her, and forgive her."

"I can't forgive her and I don't want to see this." I put the picture in a drawer.

"Take it from me, not addressing stuff won't make it go away. It'll catch up to you."

"I'm a fast runner."

A vision of Moose sailed into my mind's eye. Knowing he was only a few yards away felt wondrous and treacherous.

I tried on Father Reese's bathrobe, which smelled strongly of industrial soap. His robe was stretchy, like the skin of an elbow. Wearing it, feeling the weight of it, I tried to imagine Father Reese, how he moved about his bedroom and upstairs den, all self-important, but it didn't work. White dander on the robe's collar made me feel weird, like I was violating his personal space, which I was. We had to work this case, go the lengths. I put the robe back on the door hook.

Riveaux slid a tennis racket from behind a bookshelf and held it up like a trophy. "How about a match sometime?"

"I'm terrible at sports."

"Except blood sports." She pointed to her left canine then tightened her ponytail. She moved over to the door and took a whiff of Father Reese's bathrobe on the hook. "Boy musk. Guys smell different." She drifted. "Been a minute since I smelled such offensive cologne. Was Rockwell's calling card."

"You're too good for him." I was sure I was screwing up the active listener routine. When you don't know what to say, after you realize that everything is probably fucked beyond repair, you still need to say something. Anything. "Glad you don't have to deal with his manipulation anymore."

But Riveaux nodded, her violet eyes widening. "Rock put the *man* in *manipulation*."

"He's basic. Basic people overcompensate."

"So why do I miss him so much, question mark?"

I sighed. "We don't always want what's good for us, but it doesn't mean we don't deserve better."

She blinked behind her smudged glasses and said—"We"— then stopped. Like she was reaching a moment of easy bumper-sticker clarity she knew wasn't true.

Ache yoked us, me and Riveaux. I was glad. Not because I wanted us to hurt, but because it meant we had a wordless way to talk. Pain either brings people closer or it cuts a moat between them.

Riveaux smiled. "Rock made me laugh a lot. He was crazy about me, and maybe I liked that, being the source of someone's fixation. I lost a lot," she said. "I lost too much."

"It's not fair. I'm sorry."

She tightened her ponytail. Despite her mom jeans and *Miss Congeniality* vibe, Riveaux had an advantage very few people in the world possessed: self-esteem. She seemed to enjoy her own company.

I opened another drawer, and noticed, within a stack of folded pajamas, a subtle yet crucial difference in the fabric, like shifting from lowercase to mixed case. Something was in there.

A box. No, a book.

Riveaux saw it, too. She dug her hand into a set of silk pj's, probably more expensive than all the Sisters' Guild blouses put

together, and pulled out a notebook. It was an old-school com-
position notebook, the kind in which you scribble song lyrics
and love letters and smutty poetry when you are not a nun.

We both sat on the hardwood floor to look through its pages.
Riveaux took her time descending, her left hand bracing her
lower back. Her wrapped arm obviously sore. Riveaux had the
goods and willpower to craft a solid life for herself, balancing
the realities of phone bills and mortgage payments with obses-
sions like investigating mysteries and perfuming. Though her
concoctions all smelled the same to me. Riveaux was determined to succeed in her next act. As hard as I tried, my second
life seemed as cursed as the first.

"Dang." She exhaled.

"Whose book is it?" I pressed.

"Calm down." She pointed to an *N* scribbled on the front of
the book, camouflaged with the black-and-white paisley.
"Father Nathan's. Looks like a log."

The notebook was overflowing with ink. Page after page of
notes. Each line, every margin, was filled with scrupulous
details about Father Reese. There were lists and lists of lists.
Times of Father Reese's boring-ass Masses, dates of his pathetic
book tours, receipts for his fineries from the Guild.

He conducted a background check on Reese. Searched his
public records, court documents, and financial statements.
Nathan was physically surveilling Reese, tailing him on foot.
Every obsession has a root you can trace. Why was Nathan
meticulously scrapbooking Reese's every waking moment?
Was he trying to gather evidence? Of what?

But there were inconsistencies. "Some of these entries don't
add up," I said.

"Tell me more."

I pointed to the top of a particularly full page. "This section would have been during Nathan's history class."

"So, unless he was cloning himself, he had a helper," Riveaux said.

"But the notes are all the same handwriting," I said, flipping through the pages. "See?"

"Stop for a second. Damn. You realize this means Nathan is probably involved."

"Why would you say that?"

"Smoking gun, Goldsmobile. Receipts." She held up the notebook. "Open your eyes."

But I stood firm. "I've seen setups firsthand. I lived through one, remember?"

"Vaguely rings a bell," Riveaux teased.

"The notebook's evidence," I conceded, reluctantly, "but not definitive proof of anything one way or another."

"We don't know Nathan's alibi. He's been missing for more than half a day, and now we know that he was spying on Reese."

"To what end? We need the whole story."

"True." Riveuax raised her left eyebrow into a high arc. "But it almost sounds like you want him to get away with it."

"Of course not."

"Then stay objective."

Riveaux was right. I wanted to trust Nathan, but that impulse should have made me distrust him even more. The logbook. The surveillance. The fact that he was missing. Not painting the best picture.

I had heard about plenty of missing persons cases from my old man back in Brooklyn. My favorite detective novels loved the trope. The police were brought in to investigate, their efforts yielding no results. As time passed, their theories always became increasingly outlandish. But I couldn't discount mine. Not that it was fully formed yet.

Did I know Father Nathan at all?

When you don't know yourself, you can't begin to guess what's inside another person.

The known and unknown were locked in an infinite loop, a duet, a song that made me cry for no damn reason. Everything worthwhile—prayer, sex, memory—fuses knowing and not knowing. But I still needed answers.

1:33 P.M.

"SISTER HOLIDAY! NOW!" Sister Honor had interrupted our search.

Her voice, like her personality, was a nauseating blend of buzzkill, killjoy, and the old-world confidence of the TCM noir movie marathon that Moose and I used to watch every Christmas Eve. We'd fall asleep on the sofa to Spade and Archer's banter, until Moose's nightmares jolted him awake. His feet tangled in the blanket as our cat Marple unspooled and hightailed it.

The storm-cloud scowl of Sister Honor was flanked by Rosemary Flynn, grumbling with the bent annoyance of an underpaid personal assistant. Both women were wet from the rain, every fiber sopping, like they had just scrambled out of a dunk tank. What I wouldn't have given to throw that ball.

"We need you to look at this immediately!" Sister Honor barked. "Stop fiddling around!" She held an envelope to her chest, but not too close.

Riveaux wasn't having it. "How did you know we'd be in here, question mark?"

"Basic common sense"—Sister Honor laughed—"something you two 'detectives' seem to lack! I inferred that our school sleuth would be in the rectory. You think you are the only people in the whole wide world who can put two and two together to make four?"

"No, but I—"

"Quiet!" Sister Honor held up the strange envelope. One drop of rain escaped from a corner of the thin package. "This arrived at the convent a few minutes ago."

"What is it?"

"It is addressed to *you*, Sister Holiday. There is not an address of return!"

I stretched my arm out. "Give it."

Sister Honor placed the envelope on my gloved palm.

"What is it?" Riveaux hobbled closer to see.

"Could be anything," I said, holding Sister Honor's eye. "Why are you getting lathered up and making a personal delivery? It's probably student work or a letter from my ex, or my brother." I imagined Moose sulking around the school office, waiting for me after he dismissed my students.

"We must open this in the presence of the police," Sister Honor clucked. "It could be a BOMB! We must call the police now!"

"A bomb?" I asked. "In a flat envelope?"

"It could be anthrax," Rosemary said. She was unusually animated. "I met your brother, by the way. Really interesting gentleman. Thanks for the notice." Her arms, usually assertively folded, were flailing.

Was Rosemary Flynn involved in this wretched case? Her flirting that morning was peculiar. I had never seen her remotely undone before. She rarely showed emotion. Never let a blouse untuck itself nor one strand of her red bangs grow past her eyebrows. Besides chalk on her cardigan, which I found annoyingly alluring, she was always buttoned-up.

I didn't know Father Nathan well enough, and I didn't fully trust Rosemary Flynn, Sister Honor, or Riveaux. Not yet.

The power went out in the rectory, and Rosemary gasped. "My stars!"

Even her expressions were nostalgic.

The rain pulverized the world outside. In the dim room of a stormy afternoon, the room steamed.

Riveaux pulled out her phone and dialed numbers. "Detective Grogan, please. Yep, I'll hold."

"I bet you already opened it."

Lit by the eerie glow of Riveaux's phone, Sister Honor looked like an old painting of a demon. Doomsday eyes and skin like melted wax.

"That's why you are freaking out, asking for the cops. You already know what's in there."

The rectory lights returned, seemingly brighter and more ominous.

"Let us go to the office this instant!" Sister Honor demanded.

"I'm not done searching Father Nathan's things yet," I said.

"Whenst your selfishness and impropriety endeavor to teach you nothing, truly nothing, about respect and safety, there is not one thing you can learn!" Sister Honor grabbed the envelope from my clenched hand. As easy as choking a lit match. I let my guard down.

"That's mine! It's addressed to me!"

Her babble was strategic—look here!—a clown flower to squirt me in the eye, to fool me. Fuck that.

"As your principal and Mother Superior—"

"*Acting* Mother Superior," I clarified.

"I never should have given it to you in the first place. And leave the belongings of Father Nathan alone. Stop meddling, for once!"

Was Sister Honor running interference to protect Father Nathan? Why?

I'd hunt down the truth. I always did. With reckless abandon, bloody knuckles, and as many Hail Marys as it took.

"Okay, okay, we opened your mail," Rosemary Flynn admitted.

"We had to! I am sorry!" Sister Honor's usually hammy voice was sincere. "I sensed the presence of the devil in there, and I, as usual, was correct!"

"What the fuck is going on?" I snarled. "What's in here?"

2:00 P.M.

RIVEAUX HELD HER BREATH and I didn't blink as I slid a smaller envelope out from the larger. She had tweezers and a gallon-sized ziplock freezer bag ready to go. Riveaux was like a cat laser-locked on a sound behind a wall. Her focus was an extra motor for me.

It was a nesting doll of envelopes, five in total. I was glad to be wearing gloves. Honestly, I would have worn the gloves, the scarf, a full balaclava, and a bag over my head if asked. What did I care. It wasn't about me.

It was only about the truth.

Or a truth.

"We really must go to the office now and wait for Detective Grogan and Sergeant Decker. Let us go together! I do not trust you!" Sister Honor declared like it was headline news.

"Cool it," Riveaux rasped, her voice as low as a shadow as I opened the final envelope.

Inside was a Polaroid. I hadn't seen one of those in years.

I examined the back of the photo first, then carefully turned it around, and we all saw Father Nathan.

Our new priest, my friend.

He was shirtless, his face swollen, reenacting the tenth station of the cross. "Jesus is stripped of his garments."

His sweaty body. Hunted eyes. Terrified. A distinct tremble in his cut lips.

The same scene was represented in our stained glass, Jesus's robes ripped away, with soldiers and onlookers watching.

Father Nathan's humiliation made me feel stripped too.

I swore I could see his face twitch in the photo. The cross next to him, a promise of something far worse.

Mary—Holy Mother, my silent pilot—was told that our collective soul was stabbed when the nails pierced Jesus's palms and feet, when the sword cut his side.

As I studied the photo again, I felt my knees buckle beneath me. Father Nathan was somewhere alone, abused, naked, and scared. I couldn't hold the thought. Tried to blink away the image, like a camera in reverse. Delete, delete, delete.

But I couldn't unsee it.

Every passing minute made it less likely that we would find him. I stumbled to the wall.

Needed something to hold me up. Every creaking floorboard made me jump, imagining the worst possible scenarios. The air thick with old myrrh and frankincense. The clock on the wall ignored me as I willed time to either rewind or speed up so that I could see Father Nathan again. Back to normal or on the mend.

Why was the Polaroid delivered to me? Didn't feel like I was being framed this time. Was it a catch-me-if-you-can provocation? Or a warning? A direct threat, saying *you're next*?

While studying the photo, the biggest clue we had, tunnel vision squeezed me.

I fainted. Out cold.

When I came to, Rosemary Flynn was on her knees, yelling into my face, "I think Sister Holiday is exhibiting symptoms of an acute trauma trigger."

Sister Honor agreed. "She is the one who found Father Reese in the Mississippi River!"

I grabbed Rosemary's wrist, held on to it. "I am right here. Talk to me directly. And help me up."

Rosemary guided me, my hand on her shoulder.

"This is not good," said Riveaux.

"No shit, Sherlock." My reply was cliché, sure, but warranted. "What kind of sick fuck would do something like this?"

Sister Honor smacked her slab of a tongue in her awful mouth. "Sister Holiday, must you exploit this, the most fragile of moments, to feed your indulgence in curse words, in vice? Father Nathan needs us now."

"Sister Honor," Riveaux said, "give her space."

Rosemary said, "Poor Father Nathan. This must be very hard for him."

"Yep," said Riveaux. "I'm pretty sure nobody's jazzed about being kidnapped, tortured, and held against their will."

"He was a real germaphobe, though," said Rosemary. "Washed his hands twenty times a day. And that was just in the teacher's lounge."

Maybe Nathan wasn't the only stalker on campus.

The rain continued its hellish music as Riveaux called the cops on her cell phone again to speed them up. Sister Honor begrudgingly rang the Diocese—the trio of clerical chumps who owned our school, church, and convent—from the rectory phone.

We kept losing power in the gaudy rectory, so Sister Honor, Riveaux, Rosemary, and I planned to meet the Homicide Squad

in the library to hand over the ungodly Polaroid and diminu-
endo of envelopes.

The lights went out two more times before we left to brave
the storm. Sister Honor carried the bagged envelope under the
awning of her tunic as the four of us walked to the school, powering through rain and lightning wands. The city was soaked,
sweating inside and outside.

No sun. No moon. Eternal twilight.

In the library, Sister Honor and Rosemary Flynn talked with
Alex Moore, and I photocopied the Polaroid and some pages
from Father Nathan's logbook. I couldn't copy everything in
time, but I needed my own versions. Riveaux and I could study
them, devote ourselves to them, merge with them. That fuck-
head Grogan would be none the wiser. The sweet-talking,
slick-suit-wearing, tobacco-chewing detective probably
wouldn't find anything useful in the originals anyway.

"Ahem," Alex Moore said, loud enough that the entire state
of Louisiana could hear. "Ms. Flynn, would you like to accom-
pany me next week, to the Mahogany Jazz Hall to see the
Tuxedo Cat Washboard Jazz Company perform live? If it's okay
with you, Mother Superior"—he laughed—"may I take a colleague out on a date?"

Alex's timing was astonishing. Made me want to stab. Asking
someone out on a fucking date the same day Reese's corpse
bobbed up? Moments after seeing a photo of our colleague in
peril?

"I do not see how an event such as the enjoyment of local
music between a consenting *man* and *woman*"—Sister Honor
replied, holding my eyes—"would be an impropriety. We need
Godly favor and beneficence, considering all the tragedies
today. You have my blessing."

No fucking way.

"Um," said Rosemary in a small voice, "I don't—"

"Well, okay then!" Alex pounced before Rosemary finished her sentence. "It's a date. The Tuxedo Cat Washboard Jazz Company is my favorite, so I know you will love it."

But Rosemary was already slinking out the door.

My first instinct was to punch Alex in his left ear—with quick efficiency—and watch him fall hard.

My second was to torch the remaining wings of Saint Sebastian's to the ground and roll around in the ashes.

My third? Grab the photocopies and the originals, and army crawl out of the library to hide in a hole forever. I needed to toss back a whiskey, smoke until my throat bled. In my bedroom I had one delectable, imported cigarette confiscated from the irritant-savant Ryan Brown. But with the insane rain, a quick escape was impossible. I missed being drunk. Getting lit was euphoria, it hijacked the port of my brain that needed connection. The baby-and-mother fantasia of wholeness so heavenly our bodies drove us to keep reproducing. Or trying. Chasing the dragon.

Biology was a blueprint, and, like religion, like any template, it could be misread and misused.

Although Father Nathan played innocent, he was an obsessive, like me, and he was hung up on old Reese. Tracked his every movement using all the tools at his disposal. That notebook was not a cute look, more stalker than concerned citizen. He had tried to identify irregularities in Reese's behavior. *Why?*

Then Reese ended up dead in the river with his face carved, and Father Nathan was being tortured by some psychopath.

Could it be a Saint Sebastian's student with a score to settle? Or a parishioner? If Nathan was even partly connected to

Reese's death, could the bishop and his Diocese henchmen have taken him hostage in retaliation, or to cover their tracks? Those gaslighting shitbags were responsible for untold atrocities. Were Reese's murder and Nathan's kidnapping just more line items? To what end? More power? Keeping mouths shut for good?

I was tracking them all, plunging into the depths. How long would I be able to hold my breath?

2:33 P.M.

ROSEMARY FLYNN RESURFACED, pulled me by the elbow from the ironically loud library into the hall.

"Hey," she said, her voice steady but urgent, "there's a situation in our classroom."

"School's over. It can wait."

She tilted her head. "This is something *you* need to tend to immediately. A family matter."

Moose.

I sprinted to my classroom where, an hour after dismissal, Moose was still holding court. Students glued to their seats. I noticed Jessie, one of my most devoted guitarists, melting down in their chair near the window. Sinister quake of a panic attack.

"Piles of bodies," Moose said, his big blue eyes swirling. "Body parts. Limbs. I saw arms and legs on the ground." He pointed to his big left arm and tugged his beard. "You kids really need to imagine that, okay. Listen and learn. We were trying to survive. So much blood it was an actual bloodbath. There were blood rivers in the sand."

Moose was entranced, telling my high school students lurid details about the battlefield, his tours of duty as a medic. War. Another elaborate lie, that shedding blood rights a wrong, helps people heal. He continued, "One time, a guy in my platoon lost his—"

"Stop!" I snapped and stepped in front of Moose to meet the eyes of my seven students, one by one. "Are you all right?"

Jessie nodded sheepishly.

The others said nothing, which I took as a hard *no*.

"Class dismissed. Happy Easter," I said. "Let's go, folks." I wanted to say *run* as the students shuffled out, dazed.

I pulled Moose to the side of my desk and squeezed his wrist. "What the hell were you doing? Taking them hostage?"

"I don't know, Goose," he replied. Blank eyes. "Kids need to understand how the world really is. This is not a good world sometimes." He started to cry and wrapped his arms around me. The ruthless, easy flood of Moose crying was cruelly familiar to me.

"I wish we could go back in time," he said.

"Me too."

"But not really."

"Me neither," I said.

Time is not a straight line—it's not straight at all. Time is queer. Doing whatever it wants, and just when you think you understand it, it surprises you.

My baby brother in rainy New Orleans. Why did I say *baby* brother as an adult? I had no memories of him as an infant. But in one of my heart's chambers, I felt like Moose's third parent. My need to care for him. The deep responsibility. The sickness from not being able to save him when I needed saving myself. And no matter how much we've changed, how disappointed we'd be in each other, we'd always be stupid kids. Goose and Moose. Making faces in the mirror and at each other. Letting toothpaste foam spill from our mouths, pretending to be zombies. Cracking each other up with our inside jokes in church.

Memories of our past selves live on inside us. Sometimes they get shoved to the front.

Even in the confused mess of it all, it was so right to hug Moose. We held each other as the clock hands stopped their relentless pursuit for a moment.

Then Bernard, essentially my chosen brother, appeared in the doorway. He carried two tin buckets, trying to battle the rain infiltrating the gym, boring holes through the storm-punched roof. He looked at my red face. "Sister, everything okay here?"

I stepped back and lifted my chest. "Bernard, can you show my brother around the school?"

"Your *brother*!" Bernard's eyes widened and his face glowed with an open-mouth smile. "Sister Holiday's famous brother! Hell yeah. Let's tour it up."

"That'd be great." I needed air, and space from Moose.

"All right, bruh. An army dude, right?" Bernard handed Moose a bucket. "Carry this. Tell me all about yourself."

"Too much to tell," said Moose, prompting a hand on the shoulder from Bernard.

They seemed like a good fit. At least that's what I told myself to fuel my return to the library.

I'd handed off my brother but soon there'd be a reckoning. I couldn't run from Moose forever. But I also couldn't slow down.

3:15 P.M.

AFTER I SHIPPED MOOSE OUT with Bernard, I ran back to the library.

The cops still hadn't arrived. Grogan and Decker were certainly taking their sweet time. Were they mainlining *Law & Order* reruns at some badge-kissing donut shop?

Riveaux and I stood in the corner and took turns studying the Polaroid and Nathan's logbook. I scanned for clues in the foreground and background of the picture.

The only good news from that Polaroid: Somebody other than Father Nathan was involved. Though he still could have been a key figure in a larger conspiracy. A pawn in a Satanic plot that went sideways. Maybe he tortured and slaughtered Reese before he was captured and put through his own hellride.

But Nathan looked so scared. His eyes were filled with genuine terror.

Like any formerly closeted queer, I knew a faker when I saw one. And this was legit.

I missed the tells in Sister Augustine because her psychotic logic had rooted so deep it altered her chemistry. And I wanted to believe. Recite a lie often enough, and the circuits of your brain will reroute to support it, hold it all together. Fantasy is the original mood-altering drug. Sister Augustine's story, the refrain she sang to herself again and again, was the only thing keeping her alive, so she clung to it. Until the fires she sparked ate the flesh from her bones.

"We have to put ourselves *inside* the photo and breathe it all in." She was staring at it, willing herself inside.

I rolled my eyes and played along, but after a second, I got lost in it, too. It was the strangest sensation, like entering someone else's daydream. I imagined reaching into the Polaroid, touching the wood of the cross (was it rough or smooth?), Father Nathan's ear, his nose, his clavicle. Needed to conjure him fully so I could shake loose any details about his circumstances. That nightmare chamber. His unknown coordinates.

"Bleak as fuck." Riveaux never minced words. "But could Father Nathan be *Gone Girl*ing us, question mark?" Riveaux dropped her voice and squared her shoulders when she asked me things, like she was lobbing the weight of her questions at my tattooed feet. "Staging his own kidnapping?"

"That's primal fear in his face." I tried to imitate Father Nathan's expression but couldn't. His horror was authentic. "And he's a good guy, I'm telling you. A real—"

"Don't get sentimental." Riveaux interrupted my train. "He could have been captured after he killed Reese. Maybe he was involved, got tangled in the net. Found himself on the wrong side of whoever is calling the shots, someone who decided to cover their tracks?

"The lighting is artificial, amber and cloudy, like an oven light." I pivoted, pointing at the wall behind Father Nathan. "That light is a clue. Off or something. Not natural."

My heart beat harder. When you had big feelings like I did, eureka moments were more like atom bombs.

"Could be a warehouse, a walk-in closet, a storage unit, something like that."

"No. It's underground."

Riveaux wasn't convinced. "Why you so sure?"

"Instinct."

Even though it was a photo—a frozen moment in time, a replication—I could tell natural light didn't permeate that space. "He is being held in a basement."

"No basements in New Orleans, Goldsmobile. They could have moved him to another city, farther inland."

"Potentially. What do you think it's like in there?"

Riveaux held the bagged photo with her left hand, her fingers both longer and more elegant than mine. She inhaled slowly, flaring her nostrils. Then she turned the picture over in the light.

"Smells like sweat, obviously." She lifted her eyebrows. "Like fear itself. Stress hormones like cortisol have a unique olfactory effect."

"Of course." Her scientific chops were notable, and I pretended to keep up.

She continued, "Probably reeks of dehydration. There's nothing left to ooze out. Salt crust. Ammonia."

"Good," I said. "What else? Smell the room."

"At the exact moment the Polaroid flash went off," Riveaux wound up, "it was like being inside a gym sock that fell into the water. Funky. There is so much humidity in this image."

"Aren't humidity and dehydration at odds?"

"Nah. In humid places, the body quickly loses fluid, especially if you're not replenishing." Riveaux said. "I wish I could hand him a jug of water right now."

"I wish I could buy him a beer."

"After the water." Riveaux grew still and closed her eyes.

A person's smell, like their voice, was unique to them, their chemistry and pheromones. How easily your voice breaks when telling a lie, how quickly your essence becomes feral when the walls of modern life fall away. Gel manicures. Hair dye. Fake tans. Crest Whitestrips. The hilarious ways we dress up the core condition of being a human animal.

"Look what the cat dragged in." Riveaux nodded her head toward the library door. "Rats."

I whipped around and saw them walking into the library, the Diocese. I was expecting the cops but even the unholy trinity beat them to it.

Hail Mary, full of grace. Help me check myself before I wreck these fuckfaces.

I had pulled Reese from a watery grave. Father Nathan was being held hostage in a bunker or closet somewhere. The Polaroid was a message, but I couldn't read between its lines.

3:46 P.M.

LOOKING DOWN AT THEIR EXPENSIVE, high-polish shoes, I mumbled, "Hello, Bishop. Hello, Vicars."

As usual, they didn't acknowledge me.

I wanted to stomp on their shiny loafers, scuff their glossy things.

The sound of rain interrupted my inner rampage. *Dear Lord, please keep the water at bay.* In Genesis, after the flooding, God commanded the water to stand down. *Back the fuck up.* God shamed the flood.

Detective Grogan and Sergeant Decker finally appeared a minute later. Had they discovered something, tracked a lead? Or was the Redemption PI Agency the only dog in this fight?

"Where's the photo? The notebook?" Grogan asked. He picked up a library book and tossed it. I wasn't sure if he was angry or play-angry, like an oiled professional wrestler riling up the crowd before a pile driver.

"Relax, Detective," Riveaux said. "Breathe in for a count of five and exhale for seven. Maybe you'll find inner peace while you're at it."

"Ain't got time for your woo-woo nonsense," he said. "Let's cut to the chase."

"The photo and journal are right here." Riveaux reached into her bag. "Be careful with them."

"We won't let you lose the evidence this time." He tried to tame his curly blond eyebrows, but they were too unruly. Nose hair grew past his nostril line.

Riveaux stepped closer to Grogan, her face a whisper away from his arrowhead of a nose and chew-packed cheek. "You do remember hiring us this morning, right?"

"You do remember getting *fired* from your department, Maggie, right? Or were you too strung out to notice what was going on?"

"She broke her back, for the love of God," Decker said. How effortlessly folks invoked God in their words, wishes, regrets. "Leave it be."

With a quick spin on the balls of his wing-tipped feet, Grogan left to chat up the profane trinity. Was he questioning them or simply sucking up?

Riveaux gave Decker a blink of gratitude. "Let's get to work," said Riveaux. "Let's all get to work."

I dropped my voice, and with my molars grinding, said, "Grogan would give his right arm to turn the clock back on us."

"You don't have to tell me," Riveaux said. "He clearly wants me in the back of the bus."

"And me in the closet," I added.

"What he'd really love is to see us all in the kitchen fixing him a sandwich," said Decker. Her barb was most unexpected and most welcome.

Grogan was a piece of shit. I loathed his pompousness, his casual yet consistent racism, effortless misogyny, and overt homophobia. The patriarchy punished all people, but, come on. Men got away with too much. Their kink was never ceding ground. Grogan was suspicious of me during our last waltz, the arson-and-murder festival at Saint Sebastian's, because he could not categorize me. He couldn't find a box my size. I'd used that suspicion against him and the so-called authorities. I knew what levers to press and when. Like crying crocodile tears to play a rookie cop and avoid paying a speeding ticket in Brooklyn.

The Homicide Squad stood shoulder to shoulder, all nice and cozy with the Diocese. Decker held an evidence bag with the Polaroid sealed inside. Grogan carried the notebook.

After Grogan, Decker, and the Diocese left, Riveaux leaned into me and said, "We need to do this aboveboard and by the book. Grogan doesn't trust us. He never liked me. They only hired Redemption to speed things up, to fast-forward to handshakes at the press conference."

"If they're looking for a quick solution, they need to pick up the pace on their end. Besides, we outed Sister Augustine. *We* did it. Not the world-famous Homicide Squad. I solved the case, and you apprehended her."

Riveaux laughed. "We found the culprit, we lost the culprit, and then the culprit went up in smoke, so it wasn't exactly a slam dunk."

"Probably shouldn't put that in our agency brochure."

With Nathan's notebook and the Polaroid in the cops' grubby hands, Riveaux and I wanted to scour the school library for any old catalogs, newspaper clippings, or books about Father Reese. But it was a disaster. Books everywhere. Nothing was organized.

"Running a library seems like a big job," I said to Alex Moore to play with his mind, build him up so I could knock him down. "How'd you learn the ropes?"

"Me?" Alex pointed to himself with both thumbs and laughed. "Well, I studied comparative lit at Dartmouth. I don't have a library science degree." He scratched his cowlick. "I wing it here, the library part."

Wing it. Queer people fight impostor syndrome every day, and Alex didn't have any business running a library but did it anyway. Go figure.

Still, we had to keep working, keep prowling. Refocus.

I wanted the clues to form a clear picture, but it wasn't developing fast enough.

We had the Polaroid of the missing priest. The logbook. The key was intriguing but God only knows what it was for.

The RENEW meeting would start in the church community room in a few hours. With zero priests, Good Friday Mass was off. My grounding exercises from Dr. Connie worked for about ten seconds.

Then memories flooded me. One after the other. The summer Moose and I stayed so late at SplashTown in New Jersey that we missed the last bus back to Brooklyn, had to be picked up by Dad, and shivered on the way home in the police cruiser. Moose's birthday party in the animatronic purgatory of Chuck E. Cheese on Flatbush, where he hyperventilated, thinking he was drowning in the ball pit.

I shook my head, trying to erase the images behind my eyes, like clearing an Etch A Sketch. Ghosts of what came before always lingered.

"Riveaux, let's get back to the riverbank and see what we can find."

4:28 P.M.

SOGGY HEAT SETTLED THICKLY in Riveaux's pickup as we drove downtown. It rained so hard we couldn't see, but we needed to revisit the crime scene. Comb for any clues. See if anyone was hanging around.

"I hate the rain." Riveaux still fiddled with her rearview mirror even though visibility was zero.

"I like it," I said. "Why does it bother you?"

"Because you like it." She grinned.

"We bicker like a married couple."

"That your way of proposing?"

"I propose we get to the bottom of this shit. Whaddya say?"

"I do."

The only benefit of the incessant storm was that it forced lead-footed Riveaux to drive marginally closer to the speed limit.

Ten minutes later, she parked at the entrance to Pier 11, behind the wet smear of a police car. Riveaux reached back into the cab, grabbed her cane. One umbrella for her, and one for me.

For a moment we sat in her truck. I watched the Mississippi swell, its ferocious water rising. *May the flood of water not overflow me, nor the deep swallow me up.* Psalm 69:15.

In a case like this, you could get in too deep too fast. Even the most seasoned diver can get their lines tangled.

Riveaux fished out a pack of American Spirits, tipped one loose. "Want one?"

"Can't let you smoke alone, can I?"

She passed me a cigarette, and I held it under my nose. Dear God, the tobacco smelled good. Like freshly split wood and the cracked leather jacket I wore for a decade, the one I gave Nina when I moved. In my mind's bloodshot eye I could see the jacket, slung low on Nina's strong shoulders. Over a skintight white tank top. Over my name inked in cursive on her collarbone. A tattoo that didn't exist. Imagined in a place I knew would hurt. Nina never went all in with me.

Riveaux and I sat for a minute, engine and AC running, windows cracked enough to let the smoke escape but keep the water out. We listened to our own exhales. Breath of embers, the baseline of rain. I readjusted my gloves.

"Your truck is one percent less shitty after they fixed your AC."

"You're a thousand percent more annoying now that I'm off the pain meds."

Sobriety was a sour pill. But living a life that wasn't yours was far worse.

We butted our cigarettes in the truck's ashtray and set off to wrestle the rain. At the forensics tent, a long-necked crime scene investigator and crew of cops put Riveaux and me through the paces, even though they all knew her. Worked with Riveaux for years.

"Officer Smith, Officer Duncan, good to see you two again," Riveaux said in a tone so matter-of-fact it could only be sincere.

The two men blinked. The taller cop, Duncan, cocked his head, which was bulged in points like a bag of nails.

"Maggie," he said, "the infamous investigator Riveaux." I couldn't tell if he was mocking or praising her. "Running your own private detective firm now, I heard, in Carrollton or some such?"

"Was ready to be my own boss years ago," Riveaux replied. "Change is healthy."

"I prefer the devil I know to the devil I don't," Duncan said.

"How about *no* devil at all?" I lobbed.

Ignoring me, Duncan said, "Glad to see you didn't throw in the towel after getting canned. We all vouched for you, you know, Maggie? How's my boy, Rockwell? He's a legend, that guy. Really loves you, you know?" His smile morphed into a frown. "Haven't seen him in months."

Keen to let the air out of his monologue, I interrupted. "We have a missing priest to find."

Riveaux held up her PI badge, rolled through her script about being hired by Grogan to help the NOPD search for missing Father Nathan. What a joke. Another waste of precious time, thanks to the cops. Anyone who wore a uniform in New Orleans knew Riveaux, but these impotent yahoos made her perform anyway. Shooting at the ground to force someone to dance the tarantella. They were playing to win, but I was ready to smash every game piece and flip over the board.

After they begrudgingly let us enter "their" tent, I cornered one of the lanyard guys. His ID read NEW ORLEANS CSI.

"See anyone around since I left this morning?" I asked.

"Not a soul." He gestured to the tent full of people and stepped backward.

"Was Father Reese killed and then dumped in the river?" I readjusted my scarf, moved closer. "Or did he drown?"

The investigator hesitated. "The coroner has to do a full pathology exam and report, of course." He looked at Riveaux, the PI badge in her hands, then back to me. "But I heard there was no fluid in his lungs," he said.

Reese was dead when he hit the water.

4:58 P.M.

"PULL ANY FINGERPRINTS?" Riveaux asked the beady-eyed examiner. "DNA?"

"They are working on it, but it's unlikely." Water hides stories, even in death. "The stiff was in the water for hours," he said.

Stiff. Apparently, sensitivity training wasn't mandated for the CSI unit. Though I surely had called Father Reese worse names in my mind, where every transgression began.

I thought of all the death I'd seen in my thirty-four years on this planet. It's the one thing that we cannot change, death. The one thing we mortals cannot bargain or charm or wisecrack a way out of. It united us. An expiration date.

"You think dropping the body in the water was intentional to wash away DNA, question mark?" Riveaux asked the CSI guy.

"Of course." He swooped his big, gloved hands. "Getting rid of evidence is the primary reason to dump a body in the water."

Water, a blessing when it cleanses, quenches, and renews. A curse when it erodes, erases, and razes.

"Maybe they got methodical and clever after the fact." I turned to Riveaux. "But whoever did this really went to town on old man Reese. Totally lost their shit."

Stillness everywhere except Riveaux's eyes let me know she was scouring the details, working through possibilities in her mind.

"This is an intimate crime," she continued, "a purposeful mutilation. There's meaning to it, planning, execution. The killer had to know Father Reese."

"Personal vendetta? You think it's too elaborate to be a total rando?"

She nodded. "Who had an axe to grind with Reese?"

"Could be anybody."

I pictured Father Nathan the way I used to see him every Sunday at Mass: easily confident but gentle, like Moose. Taller than me by a foot. Towering over the pulpit, magnetic, inviting. His big, ridiculous laugh, like Cookie Monster's. He was the kind of wholesome good guy I didn't understand in my old life because vice was my default.

"Whoever it is must be strong," I said. "Nathan's at least six three. Alex Moore is tall too."

And Moose, I thought but didn't say.

Three skyscraper guys, each distinct. A cool priest. A wannabe librarian who didn't know shit. And my gay medic brother recently discharged from the army for mysterious reasons.

Two months ago, while I was sitting outside the church taking a breather from Prince Dempsey's bullshit, Father Nathan found me.

"Hey, Sister," Father Nathan said. "Got a minute?"

I nodded and gestured to the step next to me. "Sure. What's up?" I chewed on my pen. Sad substitute for smoking but it took the edge off.

"I'm in a difficult place right now, and you seem like the type who's been there before," he said.

"What type is that exactly?" I looked at my gloves, leather stretched over ink.

"I lost my mother a year ago today."

"That's a place I know too well, a place I hate. I'm sorry."

Father Nathan frowned. "She was . . . I can't get used to it. She was back home in Abilene but I talked to her every day. The distance would melt away. Now I can't find her at all."

"It's so hard. The flick of the switch, and the irreversibility of it."

"True, true." Nathan nodded, wiping away gluey tears. "I'm on this righteous path of knowing but I can't find any comfort."

"Grief doesn't leave much room for comfort."

"I feel so alone."

"You're not." I leaned closer. "God is with us, always."

"Amen," he whispered.

"I do have an idea that might help."

"What?"

"Bernard has an extra bass in his garage. It's probably in rough shape, but we should play sometime. If you can keep up."

Nathan grinned. "*I'm* in rough shape, so it sounds perfect. And I should have known you'd have a better grip on solace than Father Reese."

In a snap, Grogan's honeyed voice splintered my conjuring, bringing me back to the present. "Time to move along," he said. "We hired Redemption to find Father Nathan, not to muck up the crime scene. You're not so good at following orders, are ya?

That's why you got eighty-sixed the first time, Riveaux." Cops never make it easy, but they didn't need to. Riveaux and I'd solve this ourselves.

I stepped closer to Grogan and said, "Thank God I'm a nun."

"Why?"

"I won't have to see you in hell."

Riveaux elbowed me as the cops and forensics team looked at each other.

Grogan, along with Decker—whom I held a sliver of empathy for because she had to deal with macho posturing all day—worked on high-stakes cases. I remembered how the pressure ate away at my dad. Danger could be around any corner, any day. Couldn't let your guard down. Ever. Even at home.

"Access," said Riveaux. "We need unfettered access, Grogan."

"Why is working with women such a headache?" he asked. "Can't you do your job, stay out of our way, and stop bellyaching?"

"But I'm so good at doing *your* job," I said.

"Watch that mouth, Sister," Grogan said. "Maybe this case is too much for y'all. This ain't no tea party."

Riveaux looked quietly enraged. "Let us do the work *you* hired us to do."

"I'm not in your way. Find Father Nathan and save your whining for someone who cares, honey. Good luck."

"We don't need luck. We need evidence and we'll find it."

Grogan laughed at me before rejoining the so-called experts who couldn't find piss in a diaper.

My insides churned. Riveaux and I walked back to the truck to the soundtrack of Riveaux's cane and my muttering. *Hail Mary, full of grace. Let the afterlife be a lesbian separatist commune. Amen.*

She lit two cigarettes with the same flame. She handed one to me.

"I have to head back to Saint Sebastian's," I said, exhaling a trembling ring of gorgeous gray smoke. "Can you give me a lift?"

"Yep. Hit that button on the right." With Riveaux's refurbished police scanner, we could troll the airways to glean more details about Father Reese's murder and the investigation. I pressed the button and the scanner whined. "Can you manage it as I drive?" she asked.

"I'll break it."

"You can't break what's already broken."

"Watch me."

5:36 P.M.

RIVEAUX DROPPED ME ON CAMPUS and sped off so quickly I forgot to borrow an umbrella.

I had hoped Bernard was still keeping an eye on Moose. Needed a moment alone before the RENEW meeting. Maybe I was dreading it. After the grisly events of the day, leading a support group for sexual abuse survivors didn't exactly sound like a party.

I took shelter under the leaves of the magnolia tree. The storm cloaked the convent garden in a hum of algae green. Eerie light, like opening your eyes underwater, or seeing through night-vision goggles. I imagined Moose wearing those nocturnal eyes, crawling across the surface of the earth a world away.

That's when I saw Prince Dempsey and his dog BonTon, an ice-white, one-eyed pit bull. BonTon was as intimidating as she was cute. In the menacing rain, the dog and her human stood still. I walked to them and tried to take cover under Prince's umbrella, but he quickly stepped back. He held the red umbrella over BonTon, letting us people soak.

Prince was lurking around campus but skipping class. Why?

"Where've you been?" I asked through the rush of rain, trying to snake my voice through the columns of water. "Haven't seen you in weeks, Prince."

"Got things to see, people to do." He looked down. "You know how it is, Sis."

"Sister Honor said—"

"That fucking bitch better keep my name out of her whore-ass mouth."

"Hold up," I shouted. He was at an eleven. Always an eleven. Not that my dial wasn't similarly tuned. "She said that unless you get your act together, you're getting kicked out of school. You're a senior, Prince, for the second time. Stick it out a few more months and you'll graduate."

"Ooh. Let's all throw hats in the air," he singsonged. "School is complete bullshit."

He wasn't wrong. Our schools, our grand social institutions, our healthcare, housing, and justice systems failed the people who needed them the most. The top guns were quick to throw vulnerable kids out and keep them locked away. Prince had stopped coming to school after Sister Augustine's death. She was his second mother. Mine too.

A week earlier, Sister Honor had held a conference in the teacher's lounge about Prince. Nurse Connors said Prince's diabetes and PTSD symptoms were getting worse. Guess watching your favorite teacher/principal burn to death in front of your very eyes will do that. Sister Augustine was a liar and murderer, but even liars and murderers can put a hand on your shoulder when you're crushed that your mom forgot your birthday. Prince scratched BonTon's head.

"The only person I could stomach at this shitty school turned out to be evil."

"What has been ruptured can be repaired," I said, and almost believed it.

"That's bullshit. It's all bullshit. *You're* bullshit."

"I miss Sister Augustine, too."

Prince said, "Don't talk about her! You're as bad as she was. You don't know shit."

Hail Mary, give me strength so I don't explode on Prince like an M-80. Amen.

I cleared my throat. "None of us are all good or all bad."

"I'm sick of everyone telling me what to think and what to do. What's the point? Trick question. There is no point to *anything*. Except my girl here."

BonTon looked up, slow-blinked her black eyes in adoration, and nosed Prince's skinny calf. His jeans had more holes than fabric.

"BonTon's the only thing that matters. The only real thing in this punch-you-in-the-dick world."

I tried to cut through his foulness. To reason with him. "If BonTon bit you, you wouldn't kick her to the curb."

"Hell no. She's my girl! She's my everything!"

"It's the same with God."

He laughed an ugly laugh, so hard he almost fell. "You think you've got me all figured out, that you can connect with the 'troubled youth' because of your stupid gold tooth. You have no clue."

"We will continue to make mistakes, you and me both." I barely heard myself in the downpour. "We are imperfect, but there is perfect love for us, even if we keep fucking it up."

"Wrong again. Love is not real."

"God doesn't exist for the pious alone. God truly serves fuck-ups like us. Jesus was punk. A misfit. He turned over gambling tables in the temple."

Prince pulled out his crucifix necklace from under his white T-shirt. "That guy seemed all right, but look where it got him."

I touched my cross, too. "This is not a cross to bear; it's a cross that can hold our weight, our bullshit. Come back to class on Monday."

"No fucking way. I wish Sister Augustine torched this whole place to the ground when she had the chance."

If I couldn't see a path for Prince, he sure as hell wouldn't find it on his own. Faith isn't only about God. It's about faith in yourself. That you aren't just capable of redemption, that you're worthy of it, too.

Prince had proved to be all bark, no bite before, but despite myself, suspicion itched inside my vessels like cyanide. Sister Augustine had played me, preyed on my weakness. My need. No one was getting the upper hand this time. Prince and I were cut from the same ratty cloth, the troublemakers, the bad kids. *Bad* as in damaged and dangerous. *Bad* as in hardcore, hard up, devil-may-care. Was Prince involved in what was happening now?

I walked over to the church meeting room. Inside, I was shocked to see Moose.

6:02 P.M.

"THE BURNED PART OF the school is terrifying, Goose," Moose said. "I can't believe you lived through all that and still want to stay here."

With Moose's voice behind me, I walked quickly to the pantry to retrieve the paper cups and pre-ground chicory coffee.

"Bernard showed you the east wing?"

"Yeah." He bit the nail of his left ring finger like it was the tastiest snack in the world.

I looked at him, but only for a second. His big blue eyes were too much. "I know it's intense, but I like it here."

Moose moved closer to me, but I kept backing away. "Bernard dropped me off, said you were leading a support group, and that I should check it out."

"Yeah. Not sure how much I'm helping, but it feels better than doing nothing."

The power flickered, on and off. The storm was in a mood. Elements, like emotions, were difficult to wrangle. Jesus walked on water and Moses tamed it, but God used water to power wash the world to oblivion when people screwed up.

Which they did, a lot. If only I had that power of persuasion. "You never told me why you were discharged."

Moose inhaled. "You wouldn't understand."

My brother was a medic, a fighter, but there was more to the story. Anyone was capable of anything. Sister Augustine taught me that. Hell, I taught myself that.

"Try me."

I added the grounds to the urn filter plus a pinch of salt to balance the coffee's bitterness. With one match I lit five prayer candles: for Mom, Sister Augustine, Sister T, Jack, Voodoo. I missed them all. So much. Grief is the reverb of loss. Lost love. Lost hope. Like any echo, grief can distort and confuse, lead you right off a cliff.

Moose softened his face and lifted his left eyebrow high. It seemed like he was about to say something unpleasant. Instead, he asked, "Remember our stupid game when we were kids?"

"Which game? They were all stupid."

"Baller."

I laughed. "Baller. The game where we gathered up all the kids in Bay Ridge to throw half-deflated basketballs against the graffiti wall on Eighty-Third Street for no reason."

"Did we even keep score?"

"No! How did we have so much time to waste back then?"

When I looked at Moose I could see the kid inside him. Crying at age seven, when Mister Softee ran out of rainbow sprinkles. Hurling basketballs at age ten. Practicing skateboard tricks at age fourteen. Wiping out epically. Laughing it off. Getting back up. Falling again. Shredding his knees and hopping back on the board for more pain. Like a true punk. I should have helped him, picked him up every time. It was all my fucking fault.

After his attack, and my big swing at vengeance, Moose learned how to lie and lie well. So skilled in deception he could pass a polygraph test. Like me. But the thought of him being discharged from the military didn't fit. Though the heave-ho meant that Moose was back with me. Not that I was any safer than the battlefield, despite my designation as a Sister of the Sublime Blood.

I wanted to flag it, say it, own it—my failure—while I had Moose in eyeshot. But the members of RENEW showed up. Two by two, Noah's Ark, 2.0. They gathered in the center of the room, in a circle of dented folding chairs.

After Sister Augustine's death, I needed to start something, raise life from her ashes. She did what she did, she descended life's sewer, because she was set on a course of destruction. The broken continue to break unless the cycle itself is interrupted. So, every Friday night at six we met. And on Good Friday we needed each other even more. Me and RENEW. *Repair Engage Nurture Empower Win*. Because we were going to beat the odds. Or at least endure them.

I ushered Moose to a chair. He was extremely resistant—I could feel it in his body—but he sat anyway, his large frame spilling over the chair.

"This group is helping people. It might even help you."

"I didn't ask for help."

"Please stay," I urged him.

"What is this? Like AA?"

"It's not anonymous, but it is a support group."

"I'm not like you, Goose. I'm not a talker. Let me make my own way and do my own thing."

"You don't have to talk. Sit and listen."

"And you're one to talk," he whispered. "You should be *in* a support group, not leading one. You're fucked up, too, you know."

"Oh, I definitely know it."

There were usually nine RENEW members, but that night we were eleven in total. Besides Moose there was another new face in the group. A tall, lanky white woman.

"Hi. I'm Susan. Susan Everett-Decker. Call me Sue." Her eyes were creamy green, the color of absinthe adorning the counters of the bars I walked past in the Quarter.

"Good to meet you, Sue. I'm Sister Holiday."

"I'm a math teacher at Holy Cross. I think you know my wife, Ruby. Sergeant Decker."

"Oh! Glad you're here."

Decker's wife. Surprisingly not horrible. Why was I shocked? You simply can't judge people. After everything I had been through, I should have known better.

I was the facilitator, but the members led the show. Sometimes you think you're teaching a group, but you're actually the one getting schooled. The members—Beverly, Crystal, Bryce, MK, Sonny, Ella, Kareem, Sue, Carlos—had different stories of pain and growth, lists of survival tips. Routes from ruin to return.

"Whoa!" Sonny yelped as the power sputtered on and off again. The rains were closing in. In the levees designed to protect us, a crack was forming. There's only so much pressure a wall, a building, or a person can stand before giving out.

I stood at the front of the room, my gloves on, scarf unkempt, and hair a tricky mess after a sad bleach job. These people deserved to be seen and surely weren't half as messed up as I was. But they looked to me for guidance.

"All right, you know the drill," I said. "Introduce yourselves with your first name only if you'd like, et cetera et cetera."

As the members took turns speaking, I kept my eyes trained on them. Somewhere, someone was holding Father Nathan captive. But I couldn't let myself think about it. At least for that hour. The group deserved my full attention.

Ella was earnest but spouted off clichés like they were hard-won truths.

Kareem was an art-school type, with a studded leather jacket that made me tantrum-level jealous.

Decker's wife, Sue, cried. She confided to the group that she was abused once, by a priest at a religious summer camp. She was only fourteen. It was thirty years ago, and it still held tremendous power over her. "I am ready to heal," she said. "I need to heal."

I extended my hand to her, but she did not accept it and stared at me with fear, as if I were radioactive. I prayed for her, in my heart.

One of the tall prayer candles dripped wax onto the cheap linoleum floor. The incense I took from the sacristy filled the room with pink fog. As the meeting went on, and more people spoke, something inside Moose began to shift. I could tell from the way he dropped his shoulders, turned his head, and rubbed his eyes. He was listening. Maybe it was the sincerity in everyone's words. The shared struggle.

The fluorescent lights hummed. At the front of the room there was a small podium and a microphone I never used. The simple chairs had straight backs and no armrests. My lower back ached. I listened, too, really listened. And when Beverly couldn't find the right words, I didn't try to fill in the blanks, as I would have done a decade ago. Instead, I leaned forward, rested my elbows on my knees, and offered a tiny word of encouragement. When Carlos abruptly stopped talking—a flash of rage on his face—I pressed my hands together, in prayer position, and held his eyes.

It was a strange sensation—compassion. I didn't like it. But I couldn't ignore the way it made me feel, like maybe there was more to life than my own misery.

"Thank you," I said to the group. "Healing . . . why sugarcoat it? It's fucking brutal." A flinch from MK suggested that they weren't yet used to my colorful language. "But it's real and it's doable. We have to feel things to heal them," I said, knowing better than anyone how hard, how desperately I worked not to feel, for so many years. My words as sharp and small as saw teeth. "Fear, happiness, anger—take it all head-on. If you numb your pain, you'll mute your joy, too. Get your stubborn ass to therapy." I stared at Moose, who crossed his arms. "Be with people who don't judge you, or throw words at you and try to fix you like you're a leaky sink."

"The way you are talking *at* us now?" Moose mocked me with his eyes, but I knew I had him. He didn't run away.

Hail Mary, have mercy on us. Hold Moose close. Don't let him go no matter how much he squirms.

"We have to be patient with ourselves and each other," I said, glaring at him. "Healing's a process, not a quick fix, and it will work if you give it time. I promise."

Making promises I couldn't keep was basically criminal behavior, but I wanted to believe. Not that desire made things so. I wanted to find Father Nathan. To help Moose. To undo the hurt. I wanted a lot of things.

"Sometimes it feels like I'm lost at sea," Sonny said without looking up.

"I'm lost too," Sue said, then pushed her hair from her eyes.

"That's why you found this group. Because we can be lost together," I said.

After the group disbanded, I started stacking the chairs. When I turned, I saw Moose looking spaced out, fidgeting hard. He picked at his skin, twirled his arm hair. As I watched my brother unravel, my face and hands went clammy, too. When I reached for another chair, I tripped on my own feet and started to fall. My clumsy body relearning the law of gravity.

But Moose jumped up and caught me before I hit the floor. "I've got you. You're safe."

"Don't be so sure."

We hugged each other, and I felt him relax. The tender, bitter relief of two bodies trained in holding defensive positions.

"I forgive you for being a hypocrite," he said. "Fix yourself before telling other people to get help."

"I never said I was perfect," I said. "And if caring about you is a crime, I'm guilty as charged."

"Lock her up, bailiff," he said. "Throw away the key."

"Just don't throw me away."

"Never."

"I'm sorry," I said. "For all of it."

Maybe one day, we'd look back on this moment and laugh, like characters in some kind of absurdist play that Nina would drag me to in the Lower East Side. Where I had to get buzzed on whiskey and Sudafed before taking my seat. Where artists tried to extract meaning from a viciously beautiful world that makes no sense. But for one moment, one forgettable, quick moment, my kid brother and I had each other, and that was enough.

7:10 P.M.

MOOSE AND I SAT in silence in the convent kitchen and shared a biblical dinner of bread and fish that he steamed with tarragon, Meyer lemon, and shallots from the garden. Fruit for dessert. I was calmed by the symmetry of my satsuma. Small miracle.

I watched each tick of the giant clock. Time was time travel. And a trick of the light—day into night and back into day.

"Look." Moose pointed to the garden, where the wind had tipped over a birdbath.

Hail Mary, Mother of God, time to pull the fucking plug and drain this shit out of here.

Would levees always rupture? What doesn't flex will eventually fracture. Too bad the Vatican never got that memo. People wanted a foundation and hungered for community but were denied because starfuckers and power holders—at the top, at the altar—refused to evolve. Nasty things were going to happen again. God doesn't cancel out all the badness. But real faith reminds us that we aren't in this dumpster fire alone. The story is bigger than any of us.

Father Nathan and I understood. We knew what people thought of us, inside the church and out. I'm no saint. Surely Nathan wasn't either. To be human was to make mistakes. Now he needed help, and Riveaux and I had to find him.

Sister Honor walked into the kitchen quickly, with the quiet revulsion of a massive roach, one I'd never crush because it had just as much right to exist as I did. She sneered at the sight of Moose, who was sitting at the table. As if God were punishing her for her annoyingness, another power outage plunged the convent into darkness so lush it felt like cashmere.

"Are all storms this scary in New Orleans?" Moose fretted. "This one's for the almanacs."

With our convent's shaky power and clues yet to be discovered, I had a crazy idea. Maybe I could convince Sister Honor to go for it, since she was being uncharacteristically quiet.

In the wash of dark, I asked out loud, "Where was Nathan before he joined us? Ascension Parish, right?"

"That is correct." Sister Honor seemed impatient.

"Do you know the Sisters of Ascension?"

"I did know them, years ago," she said.

"Would they let us crash with them tonight? We can't stay here with no power."

"No," Sister Honor said. "We will be fine. And the Sisters of Ascension should not be bothered at this time of night."

"It's only seven," Moose chimed in.

"We need to evacuate," I lied. "Bernard mentioned that it really isn't safe for us to stay here."

"Oh?" Sister Honor inquired.

"Right! Something about the roof." Moose tagged himself in. "Didn't he say it's *caving in*?"

"Oh, dear." Sister Honor's voice deflated slightly. "Well, the Ascension convent should have plenty of empty guest rooms at this time of year. But however will we make the journey?"

"Let me handle that," I said.

Sister Honor let out an agitated "fine," seemingly displeased with herself for agreeing with me. Too bad. It wouldn't be easy, with the blasting rain and an hour-long drive out of the city. But we had to try. Riveaux would be keen to drive us anyway, and together we could snoop around Ascension Parish. Clues were hiding somewhere, everywhere. But I needed to know where to dredge and dig.

"We should start heading over there now. Our candles are burning out, and we don't have enough flashlight batteries to last until tomorrow."

Across New Orleans, water was rising. Water was falling. The threat was as visible and invisible as the insects that buzzed in my room and tormented me as I slept.

With the landline still operational, Sister Honor called the Sisters of Ascension to request refuge from the storm, while Moose helped me wash the rest of the dishes by candlelight. We cleaned and stowed the dinner dishes and items used during the RENEW meeting—coffee cups, creamer carafes, spoons used to stir.

"Where does this live?" he asked, holding up the water pitcher I had dried. Tag-teaming chores, like when we were kids.

"Up there." I pointed to the cabinet above the fridge. The candlelight made the convent feel smaller.

With barely a lift in his feet Moose slid the pitcher onto the olive-green shelf. I had to move a chair to reach up that high.

Thunder rumbled, flexed its rage around the walls of the convent.

"Keep calm," Moose said as he lit two of the last candles using the pilot light, which was still on. He filled the tea kettle and started to boil water. I picked up the corded phone on the wall and dialed Riveaux's cell phone.

"Can you drive us to Ascension Parish tonight?" I asked her. "We can learn more about Father Nathan."

Riveaux cleared her throat. "Of course."

"Great," I said.

"Great *what*? Is she in?" Moose asked.

I shushed him.

Moose yelped, "But I want to know!" His voice was laced with the fury of a kid being left out.

"There's flash flooding forecasted in Orleans Parish for the next six hours, at least," Riveaux said through the phone.

"Then we should go *ASAP*. The power is out here, and they've agreed to put us up for the night. We will be safe there." I was vamping for Sister Honor.

I hung up, called Bernard, and asked him to come fetch Moose, like my brother was a puppy that needed a kennel. I had no other choice.

Moose resisted at first—"You've got to be kidding me!"—but then gave up and said, "Whatever. I'll have more fun with Bernard anyway."

In the bag I used to carry supplies to post-storm fundraisers in the school's auditorium, I packed a fresh change of clothes. Clean socks, underwear—a far cry from the lacy thongs Nina used to buy for me. An extra pair of gloves. A new scarf. The elegant, precious cigarette confiscated from Ryan Brown. I rolled the cig in an envelope and would savor it before sleeping in a new bed in a new convent in a new city.

As I brought our bags outside, Bernard's car sailed up and splashed me with rancid water. Bernard waved Moose in, then sped off like he'd stolen the beat-up Toyota. I worried about Moose—generally, always, every minute—but knowing that Bernard would be looking after him calmed my nerves. For a brief moment.

Riveaux helped Sister Honor into the passenger seat, leaving me sandwiched in the middle. Like a fucked-up family road trip, Riveaux, Sister Honor, and I sat in the front of Riveaux's truck. Sister Honor prayed the rosary loudly as we drove, with awe and anxiety as the torrid rain growled. Riveaux—bless her—sailed over two speed bumps and fishtailed but quickly recovered. Her reflexes were sharp.

"Investigator Riveaux, the speed limit is sixty-five," Sister Honor said, "and you are going *seventy-three*."

"A speed limit isn't an actual limit," Riveaux said, her glasses slippery on her sweaty nose. "A speed limit is more of a *suggestion*. A starting point."

She had to drive fast. And I had to speed up our investigation, think quicker, piece things together more efficiently. Father Nathan was locked away somewhere, and I had a Polaroid to prove it. And we were no closer to the person or people behind the crimes. Riveaux and I were on the back foot, racing to catch up.

"If I could turn back time!"

To my bewilderment, Sister Honor was belting along with Cher on the radio, braying operatically. Hearing her trying (and failing) to harmonize was as perplexing as it was invigorating. Dare I say fun?

I thought Riveaux would be dying, trying to contain her laughter. But she was nodding along eagerly, close to banging her head, humming with Cher and Sister Honor, and biting her bottom lip hard. Then we were all singing furiously.

Fifteen minutes later, after a trio of country radio catastrophes, Sister Honor proclaimed, "I spy with my little eye . . ."

And it didn't stop. The road trip to Ascension lightened her up in a way I never thought was possible. Was it the car ride, a rarity? The companionship? Something else?

In the dense rain and fog, the normally one-hour drive to Ascension Parish took ages. Sister Honor squeezed my arm and almost cursed—which I would have applauded—when we hydroplaned. Riveaux cackled after she righted the vehicle, as if she'd defeated a worthy foe.

She parked in the church lot after we arrived. I wasn't sure what I expected to find in the new parish, but we had to keep looking.

The stones of the pathway leading up to the Ascension church were slippery. I peered into the windows, but it looked empty. Reflections from the stained glass soaked the pews and altar in tumbling tides of green fire.

9:01 P.M.

THE ASCENSION CHURCH BELL clanged nine times, each ring a wavelet amplified by yearning.

Like Saint Sebastian's, Ascension was a holy constellation: a school, a church, a convent, and a rectory. So many people had passed through these walls, leaving behind their dreams, prayers, grief. Sister Honor was strangely silent as we walked to the convent door.

I clanked the heavy, owl-shaped metal knocker.

In the foyer we met Sisters Maria, Laurel, and Helga.

"Praise be!" Sister Honor marveled.

Sister Maria waved quickly with one hand in front of her chest, like she was trying to trigger the sensor of a paper-towel dispenser. She smiled at the sight of my gloves and scarf. "Welcome to the cataclysm slumber party."

Sister Maria was the most sarcastic of the crew, which meant I liked her the most.

Sister Laurel was tall, with reddish-brown hair, a subtle smile, and fun eyes, like she was buzzed on low-grade brandy.

She exuded a lazy confidence but still looked excited to see Sister Honor and me. I couldn't imagine the sight of Sister Honor inspiring joy in anyone, but clearly she did in these new Sisters.

"Well, here she is," Sister Laurel said to Sister Honor. They held hands. Laurel was a close talker and immaculately put together. Her habit was crisp and ironed. "It has been so, so long. But you haven't aged one day," she said to Honor.

Sister Helga planted her feet on the floor, arms high, ready to hug. A cross between a beloved diner waitress and Dolly Parton. She was a tell-it-like-it-is oracle I didn't want to mess with. Within seconds, Sister Helga launched into her life story, tales of her hard-knock childhood and deer-hunting, beer-drinking family.

In their presence, Sister Honor let a big smile brighten her usually dour face. The four Sisters caught up, gesticulating as they recounted the stories of their pasts. They were absorbed in one another, mostly oblivious to Riveaux and me after a few curious questions for "the young nun." I took the opportunity to nose around the foyer as we made our way into the living room.

"Those first years in the convent were something else," Sister Helga said. "We were fearless, the young Sisters of Ascension. We passed notes to each other in Mass, writing in code to avoid detection by our head priest at the time."

"Father Stephano never did catch on," Maria relayed.

"I still have some of our notes upstairs," Helga said.

"Oh, my!" Sister Honor exclaimed. "We must look at them in the morning. I too was quite the rabble-rouser in my day."

"You? Sister Honor!" Laurel clutched her habit. "A bona fide wild child in our midst?"

"What frivolous antics I pursued during my high school years in Baton Rouge," Honor said.

I was physically unable to hide my shock. "*You?* Antics? No way. Like what?"

Sister Honor readied herself to speak, a wistful smile on her face. "*I* put a whoopee cushion on my teacher's chair."

"Ice cold," said Riveaux, leaning on her cane with excitement. "Keep going."

"And I once dressed up in the mascot's bumblebee costume and told the opposing team to suck an egg."

"Dang." Riveaux whistled.

Sister Helga was so aghast, it was like Sister Honor just confessed to a triple murder.

Whoopee cushion? Bumblebee-driven insults? What a rebel.

I had my face cracked against the roof of a police car for spitting at a cop, and I blew up my mom. But hey. We all break bad in our own ways.

The Sisters laughed, and I laughed, too, most unexpectedly, until my sides ached. It had been more than thirty years since most of them had last seen each other, but their connection was strong. As was their shared regret. Whenever Sister Augustine's name was mentioned, all the Sisters blessed ourselves.

The tonic of it—I missed that warmth. There used to be four Sisters of the Sublime Blood. The smell of Sister T's high-octane coffee. How Sister Augustine hummed as she washed dishes and I dried, sitting on the step stool next to the sink after we'd finished. The residual sounds and feelings of a family, of a life lived.

Most of the people I loved eventually left. Or I left them.

Moose had found me again. And I couldn't stop pushing him away.

Nina wanted to find me. But I wouldn't let her.

I waited for a lull in the conversation. "Did you all know Father Nathan? He said he was here for a bit before joining us in New Orleans."

"What a smart man!" rejoiced Sister Laurel. "You're so very lucky to have him."

Sister Maria added, "A treasure!"

"We are all big fans of Father Nathan, and he left a hole behind when he left for Saint Sebastian's parish," said Sister Helga, solemnly.

"Unfortunately, we know what you mean," Sister Honor announced to the Sisters of Ascension. "Father Nathan is missing. He's in immediate danger." She blessed herself as the women clamored with concern.

"Did Nathan have any enemies that you knew of?" Riveaux asked the group.

Everyone shook their heads, *no*. Their breath gently scratched the air of the room, like falling leaves.

Sister Maria was urgent. "We must get word to Father Taft in Shreveport."

Of course their priest was high and dry.

Honor updated the Sisters on the full situation, including Reese's watery end, as I excused myself to the bathroom, walking slowly, taking it all in. I motioned for Riveaux to follow so that we could explore the premises together.

We started in the rectory, the door was mercifully unlocked, cautiously searching through the first floor. We examined every inch, looking for anything that might lead us to Father Nathan. We looked for secret doors under the rugs. Behind sofa cushions. We tried the mystery key in every lock we could find. Nothing. Scrutinized the bad artwork on the dusty walls and the statues.

Nada.

We inspected the kitchen, rifling through the old pots and pans. Riveaux sniffed the spices delicately so as not to sneeze.

I searched the laundry room, sifted through the piles of old coats, checking every pocket and seam. Closing a drawer, I thought of Father Nathan trapped in that small sunless space. The suffocating stillness.

As we slid back into the convent, I heard the Sisters talking over one another.

Night rain blinked through the windows like sequins.

In the living room, I watched Sister Honor open a card box and grab a rosary, as if she knew exactly where it would be.

"Sister Honor, did you live here, too?" I asked. "In Ascension? You all seem tight."

"Sister Laurel and I have a long history, but I never took residence here."

"How did you two meet?" Riveaux asked.

Sister Laurel shrugged. "I was at Sebastian's, actually, only for one year, before I came to Ascension Parish in 1979. It's been my home ever since."

She said nothing more. Questions about Father Nathan brought us here—where was he, who took him, why?—but those weren't the only gears grinding. In the new convent, Sister Honor was a familiar stranger. A degree happier. But something troubled her, and she refused to tell me its name.

Why was Sister Laurel sent away from Saint Sebastian's after only one year? Was she a rebel? Or a pawn, like me?

The Sisters seemed very close. But you don't have to be friends to be family. And you don't have to like one another to love each other. We were all concerned for Father Nathan.

Needing him back where we could see him, back onto the mothership.

"Hey." Riveaux tapped me. When I turned around, I saw how tired she was. I was beat, too. That Friday was the longest year of my life. "I'm sleeping in my truck."

"Why?"

Riveaux steepled her hands. "Feels safer in there, I guess. I'll leave you nuns to do your nun stuff."

"Something's up. I need to keep questioning the Sisters."

"Poke at it and see what happens."

"That from the PI manual?

"First rule of sleuthing," Riveaux muttered, "get good at unlearning what people tell you. You gotta feel your own way out."

Riveaux was right, of course. Like faith, spirituality, punk music, or any art, the more people tell you *how* to do it, the less good you are.

As the Sisters prayed and cried in the convent, I walked outside and trailed the perimeter of the church. I studied the details of the building. The stained glass of Ascension reminded me of my church in Brooklyn. A place I loved and feared. Sacred space of incense, connection, shame. Exquisite ghosts. I thought about that Sunday in high school when Moose and I skipped Mass and went to Coney Island. We rode the rides, chain-smoked, cursed, didn't care. Dipped stale tortilla chips into sacrilegious orange "cheese" sauce. Rode the Wonder Wheel as it got darker. Before we got old, before Mom's cancer, before Moose learned how to dress other people's wounds. We were Moose and Goose, drinking warm, flat beer, melting time like Dalí's clock. He was my anchor, and I was his sail, and together we slammed into the rocks and sent our boat adrift.

Outside, the wind was a lopsided hurl, like rage swerving through the body.

I was tired and filthy, a million thoughts stacking. I needed to clean myself in the Ascension bathtub. A tiny baptism.

10:28 P.M.

"MAY I TAKE A BATH?" I asked Sister Laurel.

"Of course, dear." Something—worry? regret?—quivered on Sister Laurel's face as she showed me to my humble accommodations. Bathroom down the hall. "I am so very pleased you're here, Sister Holiday."

Sister Laurel was deeply kind, had the same brand of warmth as Sister T. She glided from space to space, with ease, like turning on a light with a dimmer rather than a switch.

In the bathtub, with one bar of old, crusty soap and a coarse washcloth, I scrubbed away the grease and grime of stormwater, tried to tear off the layer of oil and sin of funk.

I stared at my own feet in the water. Toes and ankle bones. Sinew, tendon, and joints interwoven. Countless steps I've taken in my life, mostly backward. My pale skin, tiny scars.

The bathroom's interior was a crumbling ruin. The paint on the wall was peeled and faded. Sad as an old calendar still hanging decades later. Rust rings stained the tub drain. I submerged, with only my nose telescoped over the waterline. I tried to imagine breathing through my skin.

Mermaid realness.

My little mermaid, Nina called me once. Did I like it while we were dating? Meh. Did I like it after we broke up? Maybe. *My little mermaid.* The word *my* ended me because Nina never committed. Never made me hers. Not that I asked—I was too scared. The *little* was a sore spot—I was four inches shorter than her, which didn't square with my punk attitude, though I loved her long legs. Every walk was a runway stride with Nina.

The year before I moved to New Orleans, before I lost my mom in the fireball, Nina and I walked in the Coney Island Mermaid Parade. My favorite day of the year. We always went to the annual bacchanal together. What a stylish mob. Hundreds of queens, transmermen, and debonair gentlethem. Like Nina's recently dyed hair, the sky was mermaid-blue. Bar owners insistently slid water cups into our hands as we walked with tridents down Surf Avenue. Punk mermaids with glitter gills. The art of queer rapture.

How convincing we were—to one another, to ourselves.

Nina and I ducked into an alley hunting for shadows, leaned against the wall to make out. The sleek machinery of her biceps. Her metallic sweat. My fake eyelashes tickled her neck. We left our imprints on the brick—a mess of glitter, gold sand, and blue paint.

After the parade, dehydrated and barely functional, we tumbled into the subway. Nina's husband was traveling, so we had their deluxe West Village condo to ourselves. Inside, it was as cold as holy water in a marble basin. In her gigantic bathtub, we watched our glitter and paint swirl. She made a beard of shampoo bubbles, raised her left eyebrow, and pretended to steer a ship.

She looked at me, and in an alto voice, said, "My little mermaid, caught in the net. I'll save you."

To which I replied, "A siren actually. Didn't you hear my song?" I sank below the surface, grabbed her leg, and pretended to pull her under.

In Nina's living room, we dropped green grapes into each other's mouths. Tore bread from Chelsea Market. Ate a wedge of cheese with thin veins of Icelandic ash. I burst pomegranate beads with my gold fang.

Wearing Nina's trashy lingerie and robe, I drank blood-warm wine and played guitar. She kept an Alvarez for me so I could play whenever I visited. The instrument was a dusty beauty, with a tiny forest of cobwebs taking up residence inside the sound hole. You're supposed to remove spiderwebs from a guitar. Keep the vibration and resonance pure or whatever. But I couldn't remove them. Life inside the music felt magical to me.

"One sec!" Nina called out as she bounded up and cut a sharp right to her bathroom. "Have to floss. Grape seed jammed."

She brought out floss picks and her laptop and placed an online grocery order with FreshDirect while she cleaned her teeth. I watched, held in the beam of her thrall. Even boring chores like grocery shopping and dental hygiene were sexy when Nina did them.

"When is Nicholas back?"

I hated saying his name, even recognizing his existence, but I didn't want him to stroll in as I was jackhammering his wife. But even if I were sitting next to her on their sofa reading a mystery, I would have given myself away. I never could and never would pretend I wasn't madly in love with Nina.

"Who?" She smirked.

To hurt myself and her, I asked, "When is your *husband* coming home?"

"Sorry. Tomorrow night. Please stay tonight, though. It's late."

"Feels like it's a hundred o'clock," I said. "Take off your robe." And she did.

Nicholas and Nina were a modern poly couple, which, ordinarily, I'd dig. Beats the depraved self-sabotage of forcing yourself to live in eternal sexual sadness because of the pressure of monogamy and stone-age marital expectations. But anything other than being Nina's wife offended me. I chose to keep myself a hot secret.

"Put your tongue in my mouth," she said as she sat on my lap. She spoke with an underwater voice.

I usually hated French kissing. It never turned me on because it was, like a flood itself, too much, too soon, too clumsy. A car wash of indelicacy. But Nina tortured me with her tongue, and I loved it. She didn't seem surprised when I bit the back of her neck, held her hips from behind, and kissed her spine. We relished each inch, each second. She turned around, fit her mouth around my ear. Women trying to swallow one another.

Wanting to be eaten.

We spooned until dawn broke and sound crackled through the windows. Her arms were wrapped around me, her little spoon. She breathed into my hands, kissed each tattooed knuckle.

Nina broke my heart when she got married, so I unplugged it.

If I broke Nina's heart when she came to New Orleans to find me, when she asked to try again, it was for the best. She didn't need me. She deserved better.

If I won Nina—not that one human can win another like a goldfish at some shitty county fair—if I fought for her, reached into space-time, that electric jelly, and fixed things, would our love have the same charge? Wasn't it easier to hold a dream intact, behind the waterfall? A wish you can never fulfill.

It was a favor, really, to leave.

A glorious gift card with a limitless balance. The promise of never disappointing someone. Never tiring of someone. Never losing the fire because you have rightfully stripped her of the chance to actually know you—the full you.

My little mermaid, caught in the net. I'll save you.

Mermaids are unsinkable, but there are other ways to drown.

11:11 P.M.

AFTER I DRIED OFF and changed, I walked into the kitchen to make tea. I would have preferred whiskey in a tumbler, but I needed to keep my hands busy. While I was bathing, the Diocese had called Ascension to announce that they would be holding a vigil for Father Reese at our church. Of course, Sister Honor and I were the last to know.

Sister Honor, standing quietly by the window, startled me. I rarely saw Sister Honor awake after dusk. The moment was pliable, I had to exploit it.

"Must be like a reunion for you here," I said.

"Such a blessing," she said, "to see Sister Laurel. So many years have passed, but we are Sisters all the same. We are praying for Father Nathan's safe return."

Panic crackled in me, and my muscles quivered, thinking about Nathan's terrified face in the picture and Reese's bloated body in my hands. My chest tightened. Would the past always break into the future? The body responds before the brain. Like a fever boiling the sickness out of the blood. The spongy wings of the lungs. All the breath we take without thinking, all the sorrow we don't exhale.

"Is Sister Laurel asleep?" I asked.

"She retired to her room a while ago, yes." Sister Honor's voice and spirit were peaceful. She picked up an obsidian rosary from the window ledge, admired it lovingly, and returned it to its place.

"So, Sister Laurel . . . What's her story?"

"What do you mean 'her story'?"

"Why was she only with us—well, our Order—for a year? Why didn't she stay longer?"

"That is not information one is able to divulge without the permission to share said information."

I leaned in. "Was she sent packing? Or did she leave on her own?"

"It was all Father Reese's fault. All of it. That man . . ." Sister Honor looked down, her face suddenly so small. She closed her eyes. "Father Reese was a vile man. He was not a true man of God."

Father Reese. Vile? Our priest who led Mass. The skinny, drab man who presided over hundreds of weddings, funerals, confirmations, christenings, and baptisms. From birth to death, he waved his hands over each parishioner, their thirsty souls.

He was a bore, sure, but what was Sister Honor unable to say? Is that what led to his murder?

"What are you talking about?"

"You know all you need to know."

"This is important. Tell me," I pleaded. "Maybe it's connected to his murder!"

Sister Honor blessed herself and said nothing more. She abruptly left to go to sleep, or try to, in another empty guest room down the hall.

What in the fuck did Father Reese do? Did he hurt her, betray Sister Laurel? Is that why Sister Honor had been so appalling since the day I met her? Because she was so sick and tired of it all? Numb from eons of men's bullshit. Fighting off the choke-hold of the Diocese.

Meanwhile, the storm caught up with Ascension Parish. It looked like a wave had splashed through the window. Raindrops snuck inside the convent, seeping in through invisible cracks.

The Lord says: "See how the waters are rising in the north; they will become an overflowing torrent." Jeremiah 47:2.

Desperate to get back to New Orleans and search for clues, feeling like we'd reached a dead end in Ascension, I grabbed an umbrella and dashed outside to tell Riveaux about the cryptic revelation from Sister Honor. I knocked on the window of the truck. Riveaux unlocked it and pushed the passenger door open.

"The YMCA called," I said. "It wants its sauna back."

Riveaux blinked her wet eyelashes. "Did the AC break again, question mark? I can't tell anymore."

"How many times can we try to fix the unfixable?" I picked up a candy bar from the cup holder. It was almost completely melted. "White chocolate?"

"Only thing left at the gas station."

"What is white chocolate anyway? Tastes like nothing," I said, chewing the sloppy candy.

She added, "The way white noise sounds like nothing."

"To whiten something is to ruin it. To excise its soul," I said.

In a role reversal, Riveaux said, "Amen."

"Finding faith?"

Riveaux laughed. "Yep. Faith in myself."

"Listen. Sister Honor spilled something important. To find out more, I need to press her and Sister Laurel."

"What'd she say?"

A gust of wind hurled fallen leaves at the windshield. We were safe inside. Protected from the elements. In the heat of the truck, feeling friendship (or something like it), and with the metronome of the rain on the roof, I let my shoulders loosen.

Crack.

Quicker than sin, a twisted branch snapped off an oak tree and impaled my passenger window, sending knives of glass into my arm, head, and ear.

The shatter and rain of glass. Flames of dark light.

"Holy fuck! Goldsmobile!" Riveaux was shocked by the intensity of her own voice.

The pain was fast, sharp, and close. It skinned me. A hurt so exact it was sweet, like a nectar-dipped tip of an arrow shot from a shadowy perch. I howled and panted, making it worse.

The will to live meant to survive your own pain.

The next thing I knew, Riveaux was patching me up in the empty bathtub of Ascension. The same basin where I had cleaned and tortured myself less than an hour earlier.

The inside of my cheek felt stringy. Bitten hard. Couldn't feel blood flowing but I tasted its copper brine as I spit.

"I've never done this before," Riveaux said.

"Been nice to me?" I groaned. The ache was like a fried amp, smoky and singed.

"Picked broken glass from someone's hair, smartass."

"Moose will know what to do. Call Bernard's phone."

"Already did. It went straight to voicemail."

We hovered at the edge of the tub. I knelt and Riveaux sat on the ledge next to me, sifting through my bloody hair. Small candle flames on the windowsill drenched the room in soft red light. Riveaux used her fingers, then tweezers, to pinch the glass shards big enough to see.

"Ow! Go easy, damn."

"Breathe, quit moaning, and keep your eyes closed, Goldsmobile." To flush the rest, she dripped water from a mug. Water rolled behind my ear, along my jawline, as she poured. "Almost done."

"Thank God."

"You should thank *me*. So, wait a second. What did Sister Honor tell you?"

"She called Father Reese 'vile.'"

"Specifics?"

"Not yet."

"Well, stay on it. I'll crash in one of the empty rooms here," she said. "After I tape up my window with a trash bag. My truck can't catch a break."

"And yet it's always broken."

I should have added: *I'm grateful for you, my friend. And I will pray for us.* But I stayed silent.

"Get some sleep," Riveaux said.

My head throbbed and my arm cried blood. Upside down, I watched glass dust and tree splinters and leaves and blood collect at the base of the tub. I didn't know if Riveaux was injured too, couldn't tell whose blood was whose. Like water itself, like these bodies we tattoo and touch and kidnap and kiss, these bodies of stardust and Genesis spells are not ours alone. Our blood is ours, but we don't own it. The sacred can never be owned, let alone tamed.

SATURDAY

6:29 A.M.

I WOKE UP FISH-MOUTHING the air, suffocating in the breath of my own dream. Confused. I didn't know where the fuck I was. My heart and head couldn't agree on my coordinates or my purpose or anything.

I worried about bleeding through the meticulously ironed sheets, and anxiety had nudged my subconscious all night. The layer under the layer, like a river paved to build a downtown. My scalp and arm, the same arm singed by Sister Augustine's curtain call, burned. When I finally drifted off for ten minutes, it felt like I'd slept for a hundred years.

The Ascension Parish convent was solid and simple, as most are. I wondered about the five years my mother spent as a nun in Staten Island. Was her room damp or dry, drafty, steamy? Was her bed narrow? Lumpy? Thin? And what about her Sisters? Mom didn't let the emphasis fall on that period of her life. Never shared details about the chapter in which she was young and devout and fierce, afraid of nothing. But even if she had, I was too netted in my own drama to hear it. Mom had a previous life. She called a different home *home* before she left her Order. Before she met Dad in the deli line at Foodtown. I took the opposite path. Up the down escalator. Or down the up? Too soon to tell.

Wrapped in the sheet, cocooned in a thought loop, I made a mental list:

1. A client requested to meet at Pier 11 on Friday morning, but they never showed.

2. My Saint Sebastian's Fathers were gone. Reese was cut up and dumped in the Mississippi River. Nathan held in a dank shithole by some foe.

3. Sister Honor said that Reese was "vile." But what did that really mean to her? Given her bumblebee confession the previous night, that accusation could be as vanilla as an unpaid parking ticket.

4. Nathan had been spying on Reese, tailing him, before all this went down. Though it broke my heart, I couldn't rule out the possibility that Nathan had something to do with Reese's murder.

5. A Polaroid was slipped under the door, addressed to me, carrying no other words, only a dire vignette of Nathan. The tenth station of the cross.

6. Moose rolled into town, mysteriously discharged from his calling as an army medic. He was currently crashing at Bernard's. But Riveaux couldn't reach them.

7. Good Friday's lunch interrogation yielded weak alibis that would be nearly impossible to double-check.

8. Prince Dempsey was spiraling hardcore. He was one yellow slip from getting kicked out of school. Could he somehow be involved?

Riveaux had a good camera, an elegant cane, and a powerful mind. But our first case as the Redemption Detective Agency was heading south in record time.

With a Hail Mary, I heaved myself out of bed. Ascension's bathroom mirror shocked me. And not just because it existed. The glint of a gold fang and a gaunt stranger blinked in the glass.

7:00 A.M.

I FORCED MYSELF DOWN THE STEPS, aided by the pull of percolating coffee. The steps were cool beneath my feet. Scarf on, gloves on, blouse buttoned. What did people see when they saw me? A nun. Another white woman. A lesbian. A private detective in training, cutting her teeth on a case that was tanking fast.

Riveaux was in the kitchen, looking as rested as a hot-wired car with Red Bull running in the engine. She sat at the nun's table, eating Rice Krispies without milk in a large green bowl.

"No milk?" I asked.

"Nah."

"Edgy." I poured orange juice into small glasses and chugged mine. "Why use a spoon? Why not dump it into your mouth?"

"Social graces."

"Why would we start using those now?"

"Take time to enjoy the simple pleasures of life, Goldsmobile, or no one will enjoy you."

She placed one Rice Krispie on her spoon and ate it. Then another. And another. Barely audible snaps, crackles, pops.

"This cereal smells exactly like fresh notebook paper and dextrose. Here, take a sniff."

Riveaux held up the bowl. She was always comparing one smell to another, as if that made things any more interesting to me. I waved the bowl away. Needed a smoke. Needed to get my mind right before we left for the bishop's self-indulgent service for Father Reese.

"Power is back on at the convent," Riveaux said.

I poured coffee into a mug and lifted a napkin from a plate of fresh scones. A tentacle of steam escaped. "How do you know? Feel it in your bones?"

"My bones have a whole mess of feels. But Bernard called." She pointed to her cell phone with its fleur-de-lis case. "Said you needed to call him back ASAP." Riveaux took a long sip and recited "ahhhh" as she wiped her mouth, like she was in a juice commercial.

"What now? A body in the library?" I joked until I saw Riveaux's exceptionally flat expression. Her lavender eyes unhelpful.

"No idea. Seemed urgent."

The hair on the back of my neck itched. *Moose.*

I grabbed Riveaux's cell phone, punched the last number on the call list.

"Hey!" Bernard's voice boomed. "Private Eye Riveaux!"

"It's Holiday." He cleared his throat. "What the"—I dropped my voice—"fuck is going on?"

"Gabriel's gone."

"What?"

"He must have split at, like, five a.m. because I walked past the living room at five thirty, and the Murphy bed was on the wall. Didn't say anything before he left."

"No note?"

"Nothing. But his backpack and pajamas—which are epic, I mean, a full matching pj set—are still here. And it is still raining buckets out there."

I sighed into the phone. "When you hear from him, please call."

"You know it."

I hung up and took a long sip of good coffee.

Sister Laurel walked into the kitchen, her long hair a tumble of loose red curls. I needed to talk to her, ask her more about Nathan and Reese. But Sister Honor swooped in and took up all the oxygen in the kitchen.

"Time is of the essence. The bishop needs us back immediately," Sister Honor chided. "We must leave now or we will risk being late for the vigil."

In the convent foyer, Sisters Laurel, Helga, and Maria said their farewells. Laurel and Honor walked to Riveaux's truck arm in arm and exchanged looks. The eyes told the most important shorthand, but I couldn't decode it. Pain, love, loss? All the above?

We made our way east, to New Orleans.

"Sister Honor," I said quietly, afraid of what words were to follow. The middle seat of the pickup was cramped. No console, only a seat belt keeping me in place.

"What is it *now*, Sister Holiday?"

"Last night, you said that Father Reese was a—"

"Can you not see that I need peace right now, Sister Holiday? I hardly slept a wink."

"But—"

"Can you not allow me one small moment of rest?" She wiped her mouth with the back of her papery hand.

"Fine."

Smokeless. Radioless. The sky was as dense as packed ash—a ceiling of trapped prayers. Sister Honor fell asleep for a few seconds and snored herself awake as her veil brushed my left shoulder. Riveaux didn't blink as she drove, the rain ever stronger. We fishtailed for an instant before she straightened the truck and whispered, "Yeehaw."

The day my brother arrived, Father Nathan went missing. Then Moose vanished. Where the hell were they?

First rule of private-eyeing: There were no coincidences, only circumstances. Fear slithered through my body. Under the bandages. Under the blood and ink. Behind my blue eyes and goth dark circles.

Sister Honor's fits and starts of snoring hit the unmistakable rhythm of deep sleep. No small feat considering the trash bag whipping next to her blocky head.

I opened up to Riveaux. "I'm worried that Moose could be wrapped up in this." I spoke quickly because I didn't want to hear myself say the words.

Platinum clouds plaited the east. The storm was getting worse.

After a stretch of silence, Riveaux replied, "You know him better than I do, so stay objective. How does your brother have skin in this game?"

Evacuation traffic thickened. We hugged the outer lane of the roundabout, closing a satisfying and scary circle, like a grenade ring twirling around a finger. Sister Honor was still asleep, her hands folded gently in the lap of her black tunic.

"Maybe I'm worrying about too many people."

"Private Investigator Riveaux!" Sister Honor woke abruptly and pointed to the street sign ahead. "Are you embarking upon an intentionally circuitous route? We will be late!"

"This is the only open route into New Orleans." Riveaux motioned toward her phone to indicate her traffic app. Rain and flash floods were rewriting the map, restructuring the story, as acts of God tended to do. "And call me Maggie. I'll keep insisting."

Sister Honor pouted as Riveaux stayed steady through the storm. Windshield wipers worked overtime to keep up with the deluge as we dove in headfirst.

9:03 A.M.

THERE THEY WERE, right on cue. The Diocese, a trio of thugs in expensive robes.

The bishop and his two vicar cronies had arrived to exploit our congregation, ask for more money, and expertly capitalize on yet another tragedy. They were rewarded handsomely for their greatest skill, shaming people. Rubbing our noses in our imperfections. Frailty. Humanity.

Fuck that garbage.

"In the name of our fallen brother, Father Reese, we pray." As he projected, the bishop opened his mouth so wide I could see his full set of teeth like the killing edge of a broken bottle. "In the name of the Father, we pray. In the name of the Son, we pray."

They were at the helm, telling us what to pray for, whom to pray to, and even *how* to pray.

But my prayer was a force they could never see, let alone control. It wasn't a recipe of words. Prayer was a place. And the map that got me there. Father Nathan and Moose were the focus of my prayers. I wanted to catch the killer. But Father Reese's soul was God's problem now.

Incense flooded the church with luscious musk. The flowers from Palm Sunday were still supple. Lilies, daffodils, and tulips burst along the aisles. The church held on to its taut elegance, but torment seeped through the corners. Beyond the stained-glass windows, heavy clouds were held up by a mysterious design. I watched rain travel the length of the tallest window. It was easy to forget how far raindrops had to fall. It's a long, long descent from the world above the world.

Sandwiched between Riveaux and Sister Honor, I was still stuck in the middle. A sweaty mess.

A ragtag crew sat in front of us: Rosemary Flynn, Alex Moore, and Bernard Pham. Where was Moose? Why did he leave Bernard's so early?

Riveaux retrieved a tin from the back pocket of her mom jeans and handed me a mint.

"Thanks," I said, with my eyes on the bishop, wondering what twisted role he might have played in crimes.

It was a memorial for our dead priest. And a gathering of suspects. Riveaux studied the room crazily. Staring down each parishioner. Practically sniffing their hair.

Every time the congregation stood, Alex Moore put his goblin hand on Rosemary Flynn's lower back, as if guiding her to the light, which enraged me to no end. What was Rosemary thinking? Why was I thinking about Rosemary?

Sister Honor was next to me but in another dimension. Deep in prayer. One of the few things we shared that I deeply respected.

Rosemary gazed at me over her shoulder and didn't blink. I stared at her leering at me. Her lipstick was the color of a fresh love bite.

"Stop looking at me," I whispered. But I didn't want her to stop.

"Stop looking at *me*," she countered.

"All you have to do is look away"—I leaned closer—"but you can't. Can you?"

"You're impossible," she replied with a grin like cursive handwriting.

We were both impossible, unavailable women. That's probably why we were pulled to each other. Or maybe it ran deeper. A vein so vital it had to stay buried.

Rosemary exhaled, faced away from me, to the front of the church.

With his demonic fingers, Alex Moore removed a tiny ball of lint from Rosemary's right shoulder.

I needed to get the hell out of there.

"Be right back. Need to stretch," I said to Riveaux, eliciting a nod. I grabbed a random umbrella from the silver bucket in the church entryway.

Outside, in the parking lot, I saw the Bishopmobile. The expensive black sedan that ferried the Diocese around their kingdom. I knew they were dirty, and I needed proof. The car could be my ticket. There had to be something inside.

The passenger door was unlocked, to my surprise. Inside it smelled of stale smoke and old money. I ran my hands over the upholstery, then the whole car, feeling for anything out of place. Again, my gloves were ever so handy. Besides the insurance card and registration, I didn't catch sight of any receipts or documents.

I popped the trunk. Empty. Spotless. I slammed it closed. As I kicked the tires I felt the key in my pocket. The one I found in Father Nathan's classroom.

As a parting gift, I dragged it across the surface of their shiny sedan, delivering a sketchy line into the car's exterior. *RIP Patriarchy* would have taken too long to spell out, so I had to keep it abstract.

Riveaux waited for me on the church steps. She'd watched it all go down. Didn't feel her eyes on me. Her gumshoe skills were sharp.

"Guess the key turned out to be useful after all," she said.

"They deserve it."

"Find anything? See anything?" she quizzed.

"Another dead end."

In the church a few minutes later, Prince Dempsey and BonTon claimed the pew across the aisle. He let BonTon trot in first, then slumped down. His arms draped across the back of the pew, his wiry frame taking up as much space as possible. Seeing Prince willingly show up to Saint Sebastian's was as unexpected as a drag show at an alt-right rally. Prince's tatts were not covered, as mine were. He packed his Camel Reds on his thigh. Out in the open for all the world to see, a showcase of his rebellion. What was Prince Dempsey up to, attending Reese's vigil, trekking into a house of worship on the weekend?

I locked on the bishop's every move, tracked his shifty eyes, seized every word about "eternal life" for followers of "the penitent path." It was flat as fuck, but Alex Moore wept uncontrollably. His theatrics were suspicious. Rosemary offered no comfort, which I appreciated.

During Communion, I watched the faces of the Diocese twist into masks of piety. Duty. Contemplation. But I knew better. They were no angels. No one was.

Me least of all. But God needed me. And I needed God.

"We take Communion to remember His body . . . broken for you, and His blood . . . shed for you."

There was a zero on Redemption's scoreboard and I was desperate for a point. Had to find the motherfuckers who took Nathan.

The rain clamored as the service crawled. Sister Honor phoned it in as she sang the hymns. Alex Moore dropped a fifty-dollar bill into the collection basket. What high school English teacher in Louisiana had that kind of extra dough? Was he on the take? Who was doing the giving?

With Father Nathan and Moose still missing, the bishop's hollow words were like the peppermint schnapps I stole from my old man's liquor cabinet when I was thirteen, punishing and fake. Both made me want to fistfight. Made me thirsty for revenge.

11:00 A.M.

AFTER THE BISHOP'S dog and pony show, I ungloved my hand and dipped naked fingers into the holy water. Took a moment to let my body soak in a blessing. Any blessing that would have me. My cuts from Riveaux's shattered window stung.

Outside the church, the crowd scattered quickly. I had hoped for a break in the storm. But it only intensified. Rain came down in slabs, the kind that could knock people out cold. The light was a wincing gray. One color but deceptively complex, like breath as it freezes.

Riveaux and I sloshed across the street to her truck for a quick smoke. The doors were wide open in the downpour. Grogan and Decker leaned into each side.

"They better not be searching my truck," Riveaux mumbled.

The presence of cops was like a nosebleed. Never fun, never well-timed, always left a mess.

Grogan looked at us and closed the driver's side of Riveaux's junker. He spat chew into the rain, his essence now part of the storm. "Fancy meeting you here, Maggie."

"We really need to stop meeting like this, with you all up in my shit," Riveaux said. Her umbrella barely kept the water out of her eyes.

"You know the drill," said Grogan. "If we get a tip, we have to—"

"How about you get a warrant?" I hit back, my fists clenched at my sides.

"Simmer down, Sister." Decker tried to defuse the situation, but it would have taken a whole bomb squad.

"Just being thorough. This is a very serious case." Grogan's voice teetered on something sincere.

It was obvious that the cops suspected Riveaux. Maybe me too.

"If you find anything in there," Riveaux said, leaning on her cane, "I'll make sure everyone in New Orleans knows it was planted. A setup."

"Don't get ahead of yourself. Let us do our job and you do yours," said Grogan. "Stay in your lane."

Riveaux laughed. "Kinda hard to stay in my lane when you're inside my vehicle."

Point for Riveaux.

The Homicide Squad left empty-handed. But they had given us a gift. A reminder. We weren't on the same team and never would be. They wanted a quick resolution. We wanted the truth. All we had to do was catch one person in a lie—one little lie to shake things loose—and the pieces would snap into place.

Sitting in the truck in front of the church, the seats damp from the Five-O's violation, Riveaux and I each smoked a cigarette. I stared out at the blur beyond the windshield. Rain drummed the plastic-bag passenger window. "Do we have thirty-nine more days and nights of this shit or what?" I opened my mouth, contorted my lips, and blew a perfect smoke ring. One of my many worthless talents.

Riveaux tapped on the glass of her smartphone—the modern oracle. "Storm's supposed to finish by Sunday morning."

"Easter miracle."

A triple knock on the doorframe shook us from the moment. "Open up!"

Riveaux clutched her cane and nodded at me. I cracked the passenger door.

Moose. Soaked from the crown of his head to his feet.

When I saw him, I swung the door open. Rain beat my right leg.

"Where the hell have you been?" I shrieked, anger and relief swirling in my voice.

"I went for a run." Moose stood in a puddle, his wet beard flat against his cheeks. He tried to duck into the truck for cover. I scooted over and let him inside.

"In this storm?" I glared at him. "You ran in this rain?"

"I run nine miles every day no matter what. I can't sleep at night if I don't move during the day."

"But Bernard said you've been gone since five this morning."

He looked down at the rainwater pooling on the rubber floor mat. "Yeah. I wandered around after."

"Where did you go?"

"I don't know. Around."

Yes, running means going somewhere. It also means leaving something behind.

"Couldn't let me know what you were doing?"

"I don't have a phone. Neither do you."

My skin pickled under my gloves, my scarf soaked. The rain-water was slick as blood. It awed me, how water could hurl us right off the face of the earth.

"Do you have any idea how worried I've been?"

"Sorry, Goose. I didn't mean to worry you."

"Not like you gave me a choice," I said through gritted molars. "It's all about you, isn't it? I never asked you to come here."

"Where am I supposed to go? You're my *sister*."

"I'm everyone's goddamn *Sister*."

Despite the whiplash of anger, I savored the brief comfort that Moose was okay. Our family was fragile enough. I didn't trust Moose, but I wanted to. I'd split in half if anything happened to him.

"Blood is thicker than water, but it's not easy to look at up close," Riveaux piped up. "Remember you're in the fight together."

Moose nodded, chewing his pinky nail with passion.

Riveaux was saying things I should have been saying. Why are the people we care about the most the hardest to talk to?

"Just be careful, Moose," I said. "I need you to be responsible. No chances."

Riveaux exhaled a puff of smoke that Moose waved away.

The truck stank of cigarettes, wet hair, and Moose's Old Spice deodorant. I held my brother's big baseball mitt of a hand in my gloved one and said something not useful but true, "I need you to be okay."

Moose let go of my hand but rested his head on my shoulder. He had to scooch down to reach me.

The softness of not fighting, the brief calm didn't erase the fact that he had been missing for six hours.

And the timing—Moose showed up as Nathan went missing, the day I pulled Reese out of the river.

And why was he discharged, less than two years into his military career? "Don't Ask, Don't Tell" was over, but that didn't mean some homophobe hadn't forced him out. He lied so frequently, could I even believe him if he told me the whole story?

What kind of sister distrusts her own brother? What kind of nun?

Whoever loves a brother or sister lives in the light and will not cause anyone to stumble in his faith. 1 John 2:10.

Cain became a fugitive after killing his brother, Abel, in a jealous bender. The first children of Eve and Adam set a low bar for sibling dynamics.

Thanks, Genesis, for that pro tip. For the reminder that the need for love is powerful, and anything powerful is dangerous. That we're still little kids desperate to feel safe, to be told we're enough.

12:00 P.M.

RIVEAUX OFFERED TO DRIVE MOOSE to Bernard's.

I dried off in the teacher's lounge with a roll of brown industrial paper towels. They felt awful and smelled like decay. As I crammed the wad of foul paper into the hallway trash, I spotted Decker and Grogan in the school library. Decker scanned the space while Grogan leaned against a bookcase, looking down. He was staring into his Styrofoam cup like it was some fine single malt he was nursing with great care.

"Too bad you didn't have time to plant anything in Riveaux's truck," I said, studying him. Had to signal that he wasn't going to steamroll us. Cops whine and whine about backing the blue but they are paid by the city to protect us. To care for us. To fucking back *us* up. "Your little grudge against Riveaux is getting in the way."

"Grudge?" Grogan's eyes bulged. He reeked of cheap chew juice and arrogance. "The only grudge you should be worried about is the one riling up the psychopath that's taking out priests left and right. This is serious."

"Don't you think I know that?"

Grogan wiped his bottom lip. The pack of chew bulged in his pressed shirt pocket.

"Listen. We need to meet the members of your little group here."

"What group?" I asked, trying my best to sound convincing.

"Heard y'all put together a group for rape victims. RENEW." He held up the brochure that Bernard had designed and printed for me.

"Sexual abuse *survivors*," I corrected. "They are survivors."

"Use whatever words y'all want. I ain't here to start shit. I get up every morning thinking about the victims of crime. I do what I do to make it right for people who've been wronged. Make psychos pay."

I was surprised to find myself nodding, agreeing with Grogan. I banged on about him but God kept reminding me I had to work on my grudges, too. Still didn't like him.

Grogan ran his hand through his wavy blond hair. "Here's the deal, Sister. You're going to provide the list of names in that group. And we're going to ask them some simple questions."

"All RENEW members are anonymous," I lied. "Couldn't share names with you even if I wanted to."

"Help us out."

"Riveaux and I agreed to find Father Nathan. That's it."

No way I'd hand over their names. I'd learned my lesson. Selling out my friend John to win cred with the authorities. It broke him. Wouldn't make the same mistake again.

Decker grumbled her way over to us and took a swig of her coffee. "Well, tell us this. Any of these RENEW folks targeted by priests? Always hearing about it in the news. Same song, different verse."

"I can neither confirm nor deny," I said, and thought of Sue, Decker's wife. Had Sue kept the group a secret? "Abuse is a huge problem in the church. It's not only priests who abuse. It's everyone. One in four women will be sexually assaulted in their lifetime. One in twenty-six men. But numbers can't measure—"

"Must make you pretty irate." Decker cut me off.

What was she insinuating? Casting suspicion on me? Wouldn't be the first or last time.

"That's why we need your help. They've been through so much. We just need to ask them a few questions. They trust you."

Trust? My resting state of distrust was so thick and alive I could snake-charm it at the fair and charge admission.

I cracked my knuckles. "You want me to exploit their trust? Help you entrap them? Hard pass."

Grogan smiled. "'Entrap.' Listen to you, Perry Mason. Studying up for your private eye course, huh?" He spat into his cup. Chew juice. The whole time I thought it was coffee.

"The real world isn't always so cut and dry," Decker said. Her body was squat and round, tight as a bomb. There was no space for ease in her rigid frame. I couldn't imagine her dancing with her eyes closed at Jazz Fest or bopping down Frenchman Street in a second line.

Grogan stepped in front of Decker. "All we want to understand is what happened here, so y'all can find Father Nathan and we can put Reese's killer in the cooler."

"Same." That and the sweet, sweet vengeance of bringing some predator down. I wanted the murderer on his knees after Riveaux and I caught him, like an altar boy praying.

Grogan's finely tailored suit was neither brown nor red but somewhere in between, like a sepia photograph come to life. His starched shirt blazed with a fancy check pattern.

"If we don't get answers soon"—Grogan held my eyes with his—"someone else will get hurt."

"Is that a threat?" I asked.

"It's the truth," Grogan said.

And with that, he planted a seed of doubt in me.

He walked into the hall. Decker stood next to me in a quiet corner of the library. The rich silence of a place saturated with books.

"If you don't drop the RENEW thing," I said, "it might hit too close to home."

"Say what you mean."

"Literally too close to *your* home."

She narrowed her left eye, and the whole left side of her face twitched. "I already know. Sue didn't mention joining your group, but I'm glad she's finding people to talk to. Even if it's you."

"Thanks?"

"Help her, okay? I don't know what to say half the time."

I wanted to help everyone in RENEW, but I also couldn't vouch for them. Couldn't account for their whereabouts. Not even Moose. People I've trusted have hid things from me. I hid plenty. But God needed me to be brave and clear, and I was no closer to the truth of any kind.

Be strong and courageous. Do not be afraid; do not be discouraged, for the Lord your God will be with you wherever you go. Joshua 1:9.

No way in hell I'd give them up. I took matters into my own hands, where most matters belonged. Called a RENEW meeting in secret to question them myself, let them know the cops were sniffing around. Three p.m., in our usual meeting spot. I called everyone from the prehistoric phone in the convent kitchen, mostly leaving vague messages. Including one on Bernard's phone for Moose, a message I wasn't sure would be heard.

If I was on the right path, why did I feel so lost?

TWO PRIESTS WERE GONE, and I needed to question RENEW—and Moose. Needed to keep them safe by putting myself squarely in the middle.

My moral code was neither moral nor a code.

But my sleuthing method was a heat-seeking missile.

I squeezed the key in my pocket, hoping to channel Father Nathan. "Where are you?" I said into the air, see-through pressure, the invisible grip around my neck.

"I'm right here." Moose walked through the door of the convent, startling me.

"You're supposed to be at Bernard's."

"I didn't want to be alone." He cleared his throat. "Riveaux waited while I changed clothes, then she brought me back."

But he was alone all morning. Didn't make sense. I watched him closely, studying his every move. My brother, the enigma. His darting eyes. He was lying about something big, but what? The PI part of me wanted to push. The sister side of me hesitated. Deception was a family trait after all. Was Moose to blame?

"The NOPD is investigating RENEW," I told him.

"For what?" His head bucked back with the question.

"Don't know if you've heard, but there's a dead priest and a missing one."

"What do they think?" Moose's blue eyes caught the light of the room. "That they all linked arms and did crime together?"

"The cops don't think. That's part of the problem."

"Don't remind me," Moose said.

A moment of silence, of dread, hung between us, long and billowing, like a bedsheet we couldn't fold cleanly.

"I still need to meet with everyone in the group and let them know what's going on." I sighed. "That means you, too."

"What?" He slammed his foot against the leg of the kitchen table so hard I worried he broke a toe. "Just because you forced me to go to *one* meeting doesn't mean I joined the group."

He sunk into a red chair by the window and stared at me with scared, disappointed eyes, like I was sailing away in a lifeboat, leaving him stranded on a sun-stroked roof.

He pointed to the crown of thorns tattoo on my forearm. "I remember when you got that tatt."

I didn't realize that I had rolled up my sleeve, quickly pulled it down. I needed answers from Moose but still had to conceal myself.

"Meet with me and the rest of the group at three. The cops are out for blood, looking for easy answers. But I'll protect you."

"Whatever." He walked away, his broad shoulders barely fitting through the doorframe.

Pulling any sort of truth out of Moose would be like nailing a shadow to a wall. Challenge accepted. No other choice. Had to figure out what he was hiding before Grogan did. Not that Grogan could find a clue even if it was handed to him in a box with a neon sign flashing *CLUE* in big, loud letters and animated arrows. That guy probably didn't even skim one line of the notebook *I* found.

I only had a few pages copied, but you have to work with what you've got.

As I flipped through them again, in the wake of another scuffle with Moose, the entries during Father Nathan's class stood out.

How the hell could Father Nathan jot down every little detail about Reese while teaching his own class? He never once called in for a substitute, so he wasn't skipping out. How was he documenting it all?

I ran through some of the entries. Reese eating a croissant at his desk. Shredding paper. Taking a nap in his cushy, ergonomic swivel chair.

The logs during Nathan's class solely focused on events in Reese's office.

Then it punched me like a rifle's kickback.

Nathan wasn't just recording stuff about Reese in his notebook, he was goddamn *recording* him. The guy must have hid a camera in the old priest's office to keep an eye on him.

From the convent phone I dialed Riveaux's cell. "Where are you?"

"Gassing up at the station on Napoleon. It is *nasty* out here. Raining so much—"

"I'm going back into the rectory," I interrupted, "to Reese's office. I think Nathan installed a secret camera."

"*Dang,*" Riveaux said, taking her time with the word. "A covert op. It actually makes sense, Goldsmobile."

"Meet me in Reese's office."

"Hold on. *Do not* go in alone." The rain was so loud Riveaux had to yell, as if her voice was being swallowed by the storm.

"But I'm one second away. I'm going now."

"Wait. I can be there in five minutes. Working in pairs minimizes risk. Remember chapter six of—"

"If you're not outside the convent in five minutes, I'm going in." I hung up.

In the convent foyer I waited. Prayed. Looked through my own ravaged reflection as I watched the rainy street, scanning for the telltale red of Riveaux's truck. My mind wandered to Father Reese's eyeless face in the Mississippi.

The river was a mirror.

A grave.

Holiday Walsh and her watery grave. That's how Hannah referred to that one show in Brooklyn where we literally brought the house down.

Original Sin was playing a basement club off the N line where the bathroom amenities included missing toilet seats, a stall door swinging on its last hinge, and very cheap coke. A steep staircase down to hell led to a door guarded by a zombie bouncer. He waved the lucky ones through, not with words, but a knowing nod.

Around midnight, the basement was packed. Another venue with no stage. Only a corner where we held court. The falling-apart bar sold bottom-shelf booze and warm cans of beer that went flat the moment they were opened. We played our set in the sweatbath while bodies thrashed around us. People shouting over the power chords. So many cigarette butts, too many to count.

Nina looked extra gorgeous that night, with a gold sheen and smeared eyeliner. In her own world on her bass. Seducing the crowd. Driving me insane.

Then, suddenly, there was a loud split. A rupture shook the basement. Water poured down from the ceiling. A busted pipe.

Smiles, Hannah, and Nina stopped playing immediately and stared up in total shock, unsure of what was happening. Then the squeals of fear. Panic. And the crowd rushed to the only door.

But as the ceiling collapsed and water gushed, I continued to shred. Why not?

Never performed a better show before or since.

"Holiday! Stop! You're going to get electrocuted!" Smiles gestured at the amps, mic stand, and audio cables spooled near my feet. "It's not worth it!" She grabbed her vodka and dashed for the door.

Cold, sludgy water seeped into my boots, as I struggled to keep my balance. But I kept playing.

With another loud crack a massive section of the ceiling came crashing down. I ducked as plaster and water rained. A chaotic wet mess.

I finally said *screw it* and managed to splosh my way to the door and trek up the steps, shivering even though it was sweltering summer.

Dozens of people were standing outside, dripping and miserable, when a fight broke out. Maybe it was the hour. The coke comedowns. Itchy wet denim. Who knew. It started with a shove and a shout on the sidewalk, by the entrance to the stairs. Then, the fists started to fucking fly. I dodged elbows and duct-taped Doc Martens, trying to escape the dense, manic crowd. Had nearly managed to squeak to the street and look for Nina when a bottle smashed into the side of my head.

What I needed: light. But my vision went dark as I staggered, slid down fast.

When I came to, Nina hovered above me like a promise. I lay on the gritty pavement like I owned it.

My guitar had a broken neck. Glass scattered everywhere, refracting and reflecting Brooklyn light. The strange twinness of that moment and its warped image as a memory. The flattened Dasani water bottles, the dog shit, the torn KFC bag. Idling trucks and sharp tang of exhaust.

As I crawled on the ground, I found an emerald ring. Didn't ask around to see who it belonged to. Nina and I pawned it the next day, used the cash to buy a new guitar. As if it never happened.

"When will you learn?" Mom asked over and over again whenever I staggered home with a bloody cheek or a broken instrument. "Why don't you *listen*? You're going to get yourself killed."

Who was I supposed to listen to? My bandmates, my parents, God?

In Numbers 14:22, God said to the people, "Again and again they have tested me by refusing to listen to my voice."

I listened to Sister Augustine, and it almost ended me.

All the effort and orthodoxy of the Church. This life. The Papacy, the rules, the sacraments, the vows. Was Prince Dempsey right? Was religion a vestigial organ? Still inside us but no longer needed. And prone to rupture."

The mystery of faith. We say *hold space for the mystery*, but space is something that can never be held.

Riveaux's truck splashed to a halt as she parked in a rush. As fast as the rain fell, the mist rose. A cycle of descending and ascending, an infinite circle, tight as a throat closing.

2:01 P.M.

INSIDE THE DANK FOYER of the rectory, Riveaux said, "Smells like teen spirit."

"Nirvana fan?" I was mildly surprised. Grunge didn't seem like her vibe.

"They're all right. I was always more of a jam-band gal myself," she said. Fortunately, she didn't notice my extreme recoil. "What's your frequency?"

"X-Ray Spex, Bikini Kill, Le Tigre, Sleater-Kinney."

"Are those bands or the names of torture devices?" Riveaux asked with genuine confusion.

"Uncool people might say both." I sat down at Reese's desk, turning in his expensive, ergonomic chair, trying to make sense of it all. I didn't know the angle, but Nathan's notes suggested the camera was focused on that point.

I jumped up, inspected every surface. Ran my fingertips along the walls and shelves. Scanned every saint statue and lamp. On a bookshelf between a stack of file folders and drafts of his old manuscripts was a tiny camera. Its lens pointed directly at Father Reese's desk. I grabbed the camera and started examining it.

Like most expensive things, the camera was small, wireless, the size of a Communion wafer. The techier the model, the more it shrinks. Soon technology would be as thin and transparent as contact lenses.

"Riveaux, get a look at this."

"Well, well. I'll be damned." Her right hand was outstretched gently, like she was waiting for a butterfly to land in her palm. Saint Riveaux of Assisi. I placed the camera in her hand. "This is a good one," she said. "Maybe even military grade."

The camera was so sleek and buttonless I had no idea how to turn it on or off.

She slowly input the long model number into her phone. The camera, like the all-seeing eye of God, dared me to blink at it. I felt lightheaded and started to see cameras everywhere, in every corner of that offensive gaudy rectory. Behind every framed picture of Reese. Like I was being watched, judged, punished, tested.

In Exodus, Moses said to the people, "Do not fear; for God has come to test you."

I was wondering when the tests might stop. But I was strong. As pure as black tar heroin. And just as bad for your heart.

"Why don't you keep nosing around while I figure out how this thing works," Riveaux said.

In the closet, I rechecked every pocket. I felt inside each shoe on the shoe rack, hoping to find a roll of cash. A map. A password scrawled on a caviar receipt. Something. Anything.

I sifted through the trash again, piece by piece.

All that sleuthing made me want a smoke. Even lighting a match would have scratched the itch. I remembered the just-because matches Father Nathan handed me the day we met.

The deck of cross cards.

The peanut butter fork.

I jogged to the kitchen. In the pantry, the peanut butter jar was half full. The lid oily and crusty from sloppy hands. While there, I dug through each shelf, rifled through bags, shook every can. Beans, soup, tuna. On the top shelf of the pantry, pushed to a far corner, was another jar of peanut butter.

At first glance, the jar appeared full, but upon lifting it, I discovered a strange weightlessness. Inside the empty jar, a brown manila envelope was intricately curled into a cylinder. And inside the envelope were strands of hair—human hair—tied together with minty dental floss.

Human hair tied with a bow.

Was this a trophy? Whose trophy?

"Got an evidence bag?" I yelled to Riveaux.

A moment later, Riveaux walked into the pantry and placed her cane against the wall. "Oooh, what have we here?"

I showed her the thin tassel. The hair was about three inches long and a generic shade of brown.

"What in the fresh hell is this?" Riveaux whistled. "Every time you think a case can't get creepier, here comes the sick-as-fuck keepsake."

"Whose head did this come from?" I asked.

"That's for the lab to determine." Riveaux called Grogan and told him about our newest discoveries.

Hair. Such an intimate and ordinary feature, yet special. Personal. A new haircut can make you feel resurrected. A bad haircut estranges you from yourself. Holding someone else's hair in my gloved palm felt sinister but important.

By the grace of God, I would help make this right.

The logbook detailing sustained, obsessive stalking by Nathan. The camera confirmed it. And Sister Honor said Reese was a "vile man." Did Nathan dig up something truly awful from Reese's past? If so, what did the discovery set in motion?

I'd follow the clues wherever the hell they led. Including hell itself.

Riveaux held the camera in her left hand and the bagged hair trophy in her right. "Grim."

"You think there's a chance Nathan was kidnapped because he was taking on the Diocese, but doing it while eating the Church's steak?" I asked.

"Sometimes the only way you can truly fuck the system is from inside," Riveaux said. "But it's not easy. The master's tools will never dismantle the master's house. Audre Lorde, not Proust this time."

"If it's true, now we're doing exactly what Nathan did."

If we didn't find Father Nathan soon, would we be next?

Claustrophobia closed in. I was a tangle of live wires. Maybe Moose's nine-mile runs did make sense. Running the mad dog until it was too worn out to snap.

"By the way, I did some digging. This kind of camera stores its feed directly to the cloud." Riveaux looked pleased as she read product specs on the glowing rectangle of her phone. "But I haven't seen a charger, let alone a laptop or tablet."

"Clergy and clerics aren't supposed to indulge in personal devices. Not even cell phones."

"Poverty and obedience?" she asked.

"Close enough. The only computer available to us is in the school library."

"Didn't you check it out when you searched the database yesterday?"

"Yes, and there was something I couldn't get into. Maybe we can bust it open."

2:41 P.M.

WE WALKED ACROSS THE STREET to the courtyard. As we climbed up the steps, Riveaux's umbrella left a river behind us. I gave up trying to stay dry hours ago. The branches of my Tree of Life tattoo were flooded. In the library, we waited an eternity for the giant monitor to wake up. I kept clicking and pounding the mouse, trying to speed up the damn thing as it chugged.

"Sounds like the Hadron Collider," said Riveaux.

"What's that?" I asked.

"Particle collider looking for the Higgs boson—the God particle."

"Joke's on Higgs boson. God's in everything."

Riveaux rolled her eyes.

There. I moused over the desktop icon labeled OREGON TRAIL. *Hail Mary, full of grace. Please don't let this be a dead end.*

"Blast from the past," said Riveaux. "Let me have a crack at it." She took control of the mouse and keyboard. In profile she looked like a corporate tycoon, with perfect skin and big ambition. "Six characters, eh? Let's try an old standard." She typed in p-s-s-w-r-d.

No dice.

I said, "Try 'one, two, three, four—'"

"Yep. I get it." Riveaux punched in a few combinations, but nothing worked.

After another attempt, a pop-up warned, YOU HAVE THREE MORE TRIES BEFORE THIS APPLICATION IS LOCKED.

"Think or pray or something," she said. "We need this password."

I did pray. To Mary, to God, to Jesus, for Father Nathan. I played memory reels and revisited scenes with him. Nathan telling me about his mother. His bass playing. Being a loner in high school. His peanut butter fork.

"Try *peanut*," I said.

Riveaux tapped the clunky keys. "Nope."

Fuck.

His nickname. *Nathan's Famous Hot Dogs.*

Like with any detection, it was never about luck. It was a relentless need.

"Try *famous*."

"Bingo! He really should use a stronger password, though." We dug into the contents of the application. "No dysentery-ridden wagons on this *Oregon Trail*. It's the camera feed. We got it."

We watched the high-resolution footage of Father Reese at his desk. He was alive again. How remarkable it is to capture real movement, to keep someone in motion forever. The ghost in the machine. Seeing him come back from the dead was curiously sad. The recording showed him writing by hand on a legal pad. He filled page after page. He stopped to eat a sandwich, for lunch based on the light coming in through the window. He jammed his hand into his mouth and picked food from between his teeth. He scratched his scalp. He picked his nose. We watched that gross nonaction for ten long minutes.

"Can you fast-forward or something? I have to meet RENEW at three, warn them that the cops are sniffing around."

Riveaux tapped some keys and sped up the feed, but nothing appeared suspect. We compared the video's timestamps and recorded activities to Nathan's log. The accuracy was undeniable.

Nathan had planted the camera in Reese's office. But why store the feed in a public place? Was it a matter of access? Because the library computer was the only one available to him? Or did he hope someone would find it, the way I did? Did he leave a trail we could trace because he knew he was in danger? Or was this whole thing a trap, artfully set to lure us in—hook, line, and sinker?

3:02 P.M.

WHEN I ARRIVED AT THE CHURCH for my hastily planned RENEW meeting, I was horrified to see Decker and Grogan with all ten members of the group, including Moose and Sue, standing like they were in a dreadful lineup. Their backs to the wall.

My rage was instant and demanding. I needed to gut Grogan, flay him with one perfect slice. So his lies would have nowhere to hide.

Lord, forgive me, but you gifted us these bodies, these minds programmed to either kill or be killed. As seen in the Bible.

"Get out." I bared my gold tooth. "This is my meeting."

"Not anymore," Grogan said coldly. "We're taking this fine group down to the station for official questioning. We have ten POIs here."

"You're fucking kidding me." Grogan towered over me but I got right up against him. I looked him dead in the eye, my chin level with his crisp shirt pocket. "No! Question them here."

Decker's gaze was a switchblade, then she locked eyes with Sue. Like she wanted to apologize but couldn't. She was so stuck she shut down. Trapped. Knocked out in the cage fight between duty and family.

"How kind of you to round 'em all up for us, Sister," Grogan said, reveling in the moment like it was a well-chilled Sazerac. "We bumped into your buddy Bernard Pham when he was listening to the message you left for your brother. He didn't hesitate to spill the details."

Fuck. Bernard was so earnest, and I hadn't made it clear to keep this on lock. But it wasn't Bernard's fault. Grogan's plan all along was to double-cross me. Wait for me to lead him straight to RENEW. Do the work for him. Again.

I had strolled directly into their trap. Who would be their easy out for the murder and kidnapping? Or would they implicate them all? Pinning them like dissected bullfrogs in a science lab.

Dear God, not Moose.

"We have questions for them, nothing to get your hackles up about," Grogan said in his syrupy lilt. Decker stayed stone silent. "We ain't pointing any fingers—they all agreed to go with us voluntarily. This is all as routine as can be."

"Harassment is routine now?" I asked.

"Nothing to worry about. These folks will be treated to a quick round of basic but formal questions downtown. We'll take care of your brother. Let's go. Vans are outside."

"Don't they need lawyers?" I balled my hands into tight fists, the leather of my gloves melting.

"No need to lawyer up unless they're guilty," Grogan said.

Moose mouthed, "What have you done?"

As Grogan led everyone outside, I walked briskly alongside Moose. He refused to look at me. "I'm so sorry," I said, to him, and to everyone. "This is the last thing I wanted to happen."

"You're always sorry," Moose said, "and yet nothing ever changes."

I grabbed my cross, the one that Mom wore. "I've changed."

"But not for the better. This is a new low. You made me join your meeting and now I'm, like, a suspect?"

"They played me," I said.

I tried to explain, to prove that I cared, even when I said the wrong words or did the wrong thing. As always.

Moose looked away. I didn't blame him for hating me. I hated me, too.

Outside, they showed IDs to the Homicide Squad, gave their names. Moose, Sue, Beverly, Bryce, Crystal, Carlos, Sonny, Ella, Kareem, MK. Some nervous parishioners from the church; a former student; my brother, biting his nails raw; Decker's wife frozen, her mouth open, like it was mid-scream.

I stood in the rain, jammed my tongue into my gold tooth. My arm felt even worse, every inch sore, my body angry at itself. The rain was relentless. Enough water to fill a thousand Grand Canyons.

Grogan herded everyone in one by one as they got soaked. Clothes clinging to their bodies. The RENEW apostles split into two vans. Good people in bad hands.

Of course, they all showed up for me, at my request.

They'd been ambushed. Because of me.

I watched Moose look around nervously until the doors slammed shut behind him. I hoped it would all be over soon but worried it wouldn't.

Grogan's face was distinctly triumphant and expressive in the storm light. "You keep looking for Father Nathan," he said. "Think you can manage that? These folks will be fine. Y'all need thicker skin to be PIs."

As he slithered away to the cruiser with Decker, I turned, tried to light a cigarette at the crosswalk. Riveaux materialized out of the downpour, pinned her umbrella between her chin and shoulder, then helped create a barrier against the wind with her hands. Her cane rested against her hip as if by divine decree.

"Well, that was a damn disaster," I said.

"I caught the tail end of it," Riveaux said, "saw Grogan shove your brother into a paddy wagon. A special kind of clusterfuck."

"I want a special kind of right hook to knock Grogan's teeth out." Rain pelted my eyeball.

The rift in the sky kept opening as the tires spun and the dented vans behind us set off down the hill to the station.

As we sloshed to her truck, Riveaux's phone blared with a brassy tone, loud and evil, like an air-raid siren.

"What the hell is that?" I asked, my hands cupping my ears.

"Flash flood warning." Riveaux squinted.

"In what part of the city?" I asked, but it was too late.

A wall of water and debris tore across Magazine Street.

Monstrous. The surge tore down the hill, trying to take us with it.

Riveaux shouted, "Hang on to something," as the flood waters swept in at our knees, trying to knock us off our feet and toss us around like BonTon's chew toys. I hugged the side of Riveaux's truck as tightly as I could, trying to keep my balance. Contorting for a good look at the vans.

I only saw one at the top of the hill.

Then, I saw tires. Axles. The other van was upside down at the bottom of the hill. Overturned by the torrent. The driver must have swerved, lost control, and flipped it.

Dear God.

The flood turned the street into a rabid river. One van was safe, and one was trapped.

"We have to do something! We can't just watch. We have to help!"

Riveaux nodded, her eyes fixed on the flood. "But the water is too strong. We'll be wrecked in a second."

I imagined panic, shock intense enough to paralyze, even before the battering ram of water hit. Swore I heard fists pounding the windows of the submerged van.

Was it Moose? Was he in there?

Dear Lord, Hail Mary, please. No.

Thinking of their desperate attempts to escape, pure horror writhed inside me, as if the water had carried it over, injected venom.

Cruel. Why was water so *cruel*?

God gave us life. And Acts of God could take everything, and everyone, away.

And there will be terrors and great signs from heaven. Luke 21:11. What was God trying to tell me?

"I can't do this," I said. "We're watching people die."

"I need you to stay alive. Pray or something!"

Hail Mary, if you can hear me, please save them. I'll do anything.

Mary didn't answer, but I got the message.

As I stood there in the storm, water to my knees, waiting to learn if Moose was alive or dead, I learned what Mary learned the day Jesus was stripped and crucified. The only way to keep someone close, to really keep them forever, is to watch them get ripped away.

4:01 P.M.

TIME STOPPED. TIME BROKE. Time ran out.

A rescue team was dispatched for the submerged van, but as the seconds ticked by, the fate of its passengers was clear. I imagined the people inside. Upside down. Noses and cheeks pressed against the glass as they prayed, cursed, begged for help. Until they couldn't. Until the fragile clock of the body ceased.

Have mercy, Lord. May the souls of the departed, through your glory, rest in peace.

I watched a blur of orange-vested people race to the bottom of the hill. No words formed. Nothing made sense enough to say out loud. Even too terrified to scream.

A rope system weaved its way through the current like a mesmerizing strand of lights. One of the rescuers reached the door of the swallowed van, but it was stuck. My heart swelled then burst then swelled again.

Almost as quickly as it slammed the top of the hill, the water receded from higher ground.

"Look." Riveaux pointed. We watched as the door of the surviving van opened. Hands reached out to steady themselves against the trees across the street.

"Do you see Moose?" My voice was so guttural, I sounded like an animal mimicking speech. "Can you see him?"

She put a reassuring hand on my shoulder. "Not yet. Not yet." She repeated words as if they would get easier to say the second time.

I needed Moose to be in that van.

I almost tore my neck muscle straining for a better look, hoping to see my brother's face.

Finally. Across the flooded street, I saw Moose. And he saw me.

I let out a cry, a prayer, of relief. Moose was there.

Against all odds and zero thanks to me, my brother survived. Like Moses, he survived. Moose was strangely calm. Another battle scar for him. Another poison to eat him from the inside out.

"They're all gone," a rescuer's voice sliced through the rain, from the bottom of the hill. "A recovery situation here." A scene of retrieval, not hope.

Five people I was trusted to help were dead.

Before I could wade over and hug Moose, Decker was in my face.

Sue wasn't in Moose's van. Nor Beverly, Crystal, Sonny, Carlos. All in the second van, now gone. Their driver, too.

Lord, please keep them, grant them eternal peace. Give them everything I couldn't.

Decker and I were at the edge of the floodwater. My hands were in prayer position, in front of my chest. I was about to say,

"I'm so sorry," but I couldn't because she grabbed my arm and wrenched it behind my back.

Decker was fast and enraged—a lethal combo—and she landed a hard blow on the back of my skull. I couldn't fight back. I turned and she took another swing at me, sending me crashing backward into the water. She held me down underneath, then pulled me and sunk me again. The floodwater rushed into my lungs. The choking thick burn of it filled me up, dragged me lower. I tried to fight my way to the surface, but Decker held me down in the septic water. Not sure who was the more ferocious opponent, her or the flood, I struggled and thrashed. The current of her rage too strong.

"Sue's dead!" Decker pulled me up long enough for me to hear her scream. "It's your fault."

My eyes were clawing out of my skull when she pulled me up again. I felt a rib loosen, an appalling give.

"She's gone!" Decker howled. "It was your group! Your meeting. This is on you."

She pushed me back into the filthy water. I groped around, looking for a rock or anything to protect myself. I couldn't yell *help* or *sorry*. Couldn't say, *I was trying to warn them*. It's a bit hard to talk when you're getting your ass kicked.

The impenetrable force of it, trying to breath in wet cement.

Thud. Decker's boot landed a devastating kick to my left temple. A void so sudden, so complete.

This was it, I thought. Again. The end. I went limp and surrendered to the warmth, the darkness. Death shuddered through me like a bolt of dark light. A kind of desire.

I wasn't afraid. I wasn't even me. I was seeping into everything and nothing.

Then, suddenly, a hand on my arm. I opened my eyes just as Riveaux hit Decker with her cane, double-handed, like she was swinging for the fences.

"Ruby, I'm so sorry," Riveaux gasped. "But killing a nun won't help." She and Moose yanked me up from the surface of the thick water. "Everyone out of the pool."

As I choked, Riveaux patted me hard on the back as I stood. Was that love? Saving someone, being saved? Pushing through the invisible membrane of whatever world this was. Something elemental piercing the immaterial.

"You have a knack for pissing people off. We'll dry off in the truck," she instructed.

Riveaux's truck seemed impossibly far away. Moose helped me stumble through the water. Somehow, we made it. My ribs were bruised, my face was fucked-up. We crawled up into the pickup, our bodies lashed with rain and mud. I sank into the seat. Blood clogged my nose.

Sue and five others perished in the water. Again I taunted death. It was so close I could hear it breathe, could feel its cold heartbeat pulsing in my big toe.

My third chance.

The clouds blocked all light, hiding the sun, keeping it captive. All I could say was, "Oh, God."

Moose was silent as he clicked into triage mode. He pulled a first aid kit from his backpack and cleaned me up. His hands moved quickly, like he was casting a spell. "All right," he said. "Almost as good as new. Some of my best work."

"I'll leave you a five-star review on Yelp."

Riveaux laughed.

Moose laughed too. "You're lucky I'm here." For once, he wasn't lying.

5:11 P.M.

BACK IN MY QUIET ROOM in the convent, my ears rang. I touched one rib but even the gentlest contact made me scream.

I looked outside. The flash flood wrecked the street, and our convent garden was in shambles. Small trees uprooted. Roses and jasmine muddied. The statue of Mary lay on her side, as if she were in a deep sleep.

Storms were common in New Orleans. But this one felt like a focused wrath. I showered slowly and changed clothes for what felt like the fiftieth time that weekend, then slinked downstairs. My head and arm throbbed, the pain intimate. Sometimes I wondered if pain shadowed me or I followed it, rolled round in it until I was high. Like catnip.

A glass of lemon iced tea had been sitting on my dresser for two or three days, growing a thin film, but I drank it anyway.

Downstairs, I saw Moose sitting at the kitchen table. His leg bounced uncontrollably.

"Take a nap in my room."

"Ha. You kidding?" He tugged his beard and chewed his thumbnail, then his pinky nail.

"I can't sleep. Not now. No way."

"Lie down, Moose. Stare at the ceiling if you can't sleep. You survived something truly terrifying."

"That? That was nothing compared to . . ." He almost laughed but stopped himself. "Honestly, it was probably more traumatic for you. You okay?"

"No," I said, "but I will be."

"Me too."

Moose sighed his tall body upstairs.

Our convent kitchen was dimly lit. The windows were small and high up, letting in just enough light to see. The walls were painted a dull gray, their only adornment a faded picture of the Virgin Mary above the stove. Sure, I added a Bikini Kill sticker to it, no bigger than a dime, in the top corner where Sister Honor wouldn't notice, but it usually brought me joy. Not that day.

The steel counter lining the wall shone brightly. Moose must have cleaned the surface, buffed and polished it like Mom taught us. The kitchen air was thick with the perennial scent of bread and simmering soup. In one corner, a large industrial butcher block, and in another, a stack of old baking trays leaned dangerously against the tiled wall. Before Sister T died, we used to sing up a storm as she cooked. If Sister Honor butted in, told us to tone it down, Sister T gave her a withering stare that could strip paint. That's how she rolled. I fucking missed her.

A sound like *hello* reverberated in the foyer.

When I went to investigate, an envelope seemed to slide itself under the front door. I threw the door back but no one was there. No knock, no stamp either. The only words on the godforsaken thing were my name. As I stared at it, my body recognized danger before my brain, which began to hiccup under my skull like it was laughing at me.

Another Polaroid. It had to be.

I didn't wait for Riveaux.

I'd expected the envelope would hold another photo, but I still wasn't prepared for this grotesque descent.

My breathing was shallow. Could barely take sips of air. Even my eyes felt suffocated as I saw it.

The new picture showed Father Nathan, eyes covered with duct tape, acting out another station of the cross. Station one, "Jesus is condemned to death." His hands were bound in front of him. Razor wire for the crown of thorns. Bright blood running down his face. Molten red and fresh.

There was no message, no caption written on the bottom of the Polaroid. Nothing to demand ransom or point to a motive.

We had five dead RENEW members, one dead NOPD driver. One dead priest. One missing priest, two Polaroids of his dire circumstances.

The crimes had to be linked—but how? Why?

Was an unhinged Satanist trying to bring the church to its knees, one priest, one cleric at a time? Or a burned-out grifter looking for a payday? A vigilante tired of waiting for justice in a depraved world that can't deliver?

Who was bloodthirsty or wounded enough to hold another human being hostage?

It had been forty-five hours since Nathan was last seen. The NOPD would have to alert any known relatives soon. I knew little about his family, apart from the anniversary of his mother's death and the few stories he had shared.

As I studied the new Polaroid closely, I tried to read Nathan's face, but it was eroded by shadows. His eyes were covered, no expression to decipher.

My head pulsed with pain, from sorrow, after Decker's smackdown.

"What's up, buttercup?" Riveaux had walked into the kitchen. "What's that?"

"Another photo of Nathan. Even worse than the first."

"Damn. That is savage," she said as she looked at the new photo. "Someone's got their foot on our necks."

"Did you see anyone outside?"

"Nope," she replied.

As Riveaux took photos of the image and its envelope with her phone, I poured over small details. My sleuthing mind taught me to thread impossible needles while also seeing the whole tapestry. That's the miracle of queer tutelage, drag queens teaching dyke punks how to sew.

There. A unique pattern in the background. Not wallpaper but something repeated. A refrain. An order. Like the wood paneling in our den back in Bay Ridge.

"See that?" I said, pointing to the shadows on Nathan's neck. "The light is harsh. And concentrated. Like a flashlight or something shining at his face."

Riveaux thought for a moment and added, "The corner of the cross is touching the wall. It's a small space."

We studied the new Polaroid from every angle. We compared it to the photocopy of the first photo. We spun it around and looked at it upside down. I prayed over it. Riveaux brought it to her face and smelled it.

"Think, Goldsmobile, of cramped, wood-paneled, secret spaces with harsh lighting."

"Old-school pizza shops? A cousin's basement? The back room of a wack-ass bar where no queer person dare go?"

"Wherever he is now, he was moved," Riveaux said. "Someone might have seen Nathan—or *something*—while it was going down. Even if they didn't realize it at the time."

"Maybe someone saw a vehicle," I said.

"Yep. But we'd need a make, model, license plate—or a partial."

"And we've got nothing." I peeled off my gloves and dug under my scarf to wipe away sweat and attack a nagging itch. My dove tattoo was soaked. If we could sweat holy water, we'd be redeemed every day. But wasn't all water blessed by simply existing? Thirteen billion years ago there was no water. Only a vast infinity of unlight, then the Big Bang.

Hail Mary, share with me your divine vision, because I can't see a fucking thing.

6:01 P.M.

THE PHONE RANG in the convent kitchen, and I grabbed it before the second ring. "This is Sister Holiday."

"This is Bernard." He coughed. "Bernard Pham."

The sound of his voice, even his cough, made me smile. Bernard had inadvertently tipped off Grogan, but I couldn't be mad at him. Wasn't his fault. Synthy atonal music spiked in the background. "Tell me something good, or at least not bad," I said.

"It's a mess out there. Marigny is getting hit right now. It's not safe for Moose to come back over," he reported. Moose was still upstairs, resting in my room. "I wouldn't be able to drive over. Riveaux shouldn't either. And I doubt Ubers are running."

"It's wicked up here, too."

"He's going to have to stay with you tonight."

"Sure."

I listened to the dial tone, the confident music of it, then returned the phone to the green cradle.

It wasn't that I didn't want to hang out with my brother. I loved the kid. He also drove me nuts. He was an anxious time bomb and refused to get help. I had to watch over him. But I felt like I couldn't perform the role of a functional big sister when all I seemed to deliver was despair with a heaping side of disappointment.

I prayed for the RENEW members and Amy, their driver, whose souls escaped this plane while their waterlogged bodies remained trapped. I could still see the water swallowing the van whole. All I was left with was the heinous mix of guilt and memories. I should have been used to it after Mom, who I ruined. And Moose, who I couldn't avenge.

They were so different, each one unique. Decker's wife, Sue, the high school math teacher. Beverly, the veterinarian who was always early for meetings. Crystal, a software engineer who was always late. Carlos, a quiet guy with a love for bad poetry that he insistently recited at every meeting. Sonny wore vintage tweed blazers, and his hair was always coiffed, which suggested that he spent hours in front of a mirror. Who'd see themself in the mirror now?

So much potential vanished in that fucking water.

I had to make it right. But how do you make amends with the dead? Yell until your throat's raw? Turn the music up even louder?

Wish it were easier, wish it were all different. But empty wishes were a waste of time, so I didn't traffic in them. Action was more my speed. Going ninety miles an hour, and barely in control of the wheel.

6:09 P.M.

I NEEDED TO TALK to more people, more congregants, students, lowlifes. Anyone who might have dirt on the Diocese. But with the rain powering down and the wind kicking up, we were stuck. I thought of Moose upstairs in my modest bedroom, and I hoped he was asleep.

Riveaux went outside to secure another trash bag over her busted window.

In the convent kitchen, as she walked in with a chipped teapot, I confronted Sister Honor.

"I hate to tell you this, Sister Honor. I hate to be the bearer of bad news. Did you hear the sirens?"

"Speak plainly," she said. "Spare me your vexing hints and theatrics."

"There's been a great loss of life. A terrible tragedy."

"Whatever do you mean?"

"Six people were killed by a flash flood right outside."

"Are you certain of this?" she asked, probably thinking that I—the novice, the screwup, perpetual disappointment—had misunderstood, gotten it wrong.

If only. For once, I hated being right.

Blinking, trying to beat back tears, I said, "Five members of our support group and an officer all died. Drowned."

I couldn't handle the one-two punch of telling her about the Polaroid.

Without anger or sadness, Honor said, "Your duty, *our* duty, as Sisters of the Sublime Blood, is to tend to wounded and departed souls." Her face was absolutely blank. "One cannot help but feel overwhelmed by the magnitude of this tragedy, but it must not consume you. 'Eternal rest grant unto them, O Lord, and let light shine upon them.'"

"Amen," I said. "And help us find Father Nathan."

Sister Honor blessed herself and started an Our Father, but I talked over her. "The police think the motive is a grudge against priests."

She huffed. "I know nothing of *motive*, Sister Holiday. I do not play your hedonistic detection games."

"I'm not playing." I pulled my gloves again, taut. "You said Reese was a 'vile man.' Could that have something to do with what happened to him? To Father Nathan?"

Sister Honor exhaled as the power flickered off. I swore she'd grown an inch by the time the lights turned back on. She stood up straight. "What I can tell you is that this matter is much bigger than Father Reese."

"Tell me why Sister Laurel had to leave Saint Sebastian's," I pleaded. "You said *it* was all Reese's fault. *What* was his fault?"

"You do not want to know." Sister Honor picked up a fig, examined it intently, then gently placed it back in its bowl.

"You're right. I don't want to, but I need to know."

"Father Reese defiled her sanctity."

"Defiled?" I repeated. "Reese raped her?"

Sister Honor nodded with closed eyes.

Fury tore through me. I wanted to resurrect Reese so I could throw him against a wall, take a sledgehammer to his skull, make him beg for mercy.

Forgive me, Lord, but this shit's getting old. If there's a snake in the grass, mow that fucker down.

Why was abuse *always* part of the story with religion, politicians, society?

"That monster," I raged. "Don't men realize they can't control us?"

"That doesn't stop them from trying." Sister Honor hastily blessed herself and said, "Hail Mary, Mother of God."

The power in the convent flickered again.

I rarely interacted with Father Reese, assuming he was a garden-variety narcissist obsessed with his own BS. But Sister Honor revealed that he was an abuser. Why do those things go hand in hand so often? Ever since I joined the Order, the Sisters of the Sublime Blood had been deferential to Father Reese. Not because they respected him. Not because they were afraid. Because they *hated* him.

"How many Sisters did Father Reese hurt?"

She sat straight and lifted her chin, as if she were being live streamed to the Vatican, directly to the Pontiff himself. "Far too many. But even one would be too many."

"Would they want revenge?"

She unwrinkled her tarp of a tunic. "My Sisters know to seek solace where it is abundant, with the Lord, with the Sisterhood. Now give me peace. I have said enough."

Sister Honor made a shooing motion with her hands, like I was a slimy kid who'd kicked a ball into her picnic basket, upending the macaroni salad. She was a case study in the right and wrong of religion. A woman who had devoted her entire life to service, putting others' needs first, fighting for prison abolition, reparations, refugee asylum. She visited the children in foster care every Christmas, bringing them fresh bread and presenting religious toys—wooden Noah's arks—that they surely didn't want. But something was better than nothing. This woman was so shaped by servitude. Was her real self buried?

Maybe it wasn't Sister Honor's fault, how petty and mean-spirited she had become. Who was I to judge, anyway? I was careening on my own slick Slip 'N Slide toward the abyss. I griped more than anyone, yet I held myself in such high esteem.

"Please, Sister," I entreated once more. "Did you file claims? Call the cops?"

Sister Honor looked extremely upset but spoke. "I reported Reese's violations to the Diocese, but it did not help."

The Diocese. I knew it. I knew they were in this up to their gold pinky rings. "Bastards."

Instinctually, Sister Honor raised a finger to wag at me for my infraction, but she said nothing. She must have agreed with me, surprising herself.

"Sorry, Sister." I bit my lip, hard. "What happened after you reported it to the bishop?"

She sighed. "It took ages for the Diocese to act, and they only 'acted' by sending the women he targeted away. Sister Augustine said she informed the police chief, who was our parishioner. None of those 'godly men' chose to assist us."

"I'm going to call the news. Refile the complaints. The Diocese is done."

"Take a moment, Sister Holiday. I want you to *slow down*. Can you do that for me?"

"Why?"

"*Why?*" Sister Honor repeated. The power dropped and returned. The silence was broken by the hum of electrical circuits and the crackle of static. Shadows on the walls looked like hands reaching through a grave. "Because for as insufferable as you are, and indeed you are most tiring, I cannot bear to lose yet another Sister."

How grand it would be if our faith was built around sacrifice and compassion, and not forever warped by lonely, angry men. And, yes, women, too. People with the most to lose hold the tightest grip on the reins.

Because as always, abuse is about power. Power and control.

So who killed Reese? If it was Nathan—a massive *if*—why? Who took Nathan? Who sent the Polaroids, and why did they send them to *me*? Question marks burned under my eyelids, curved as bodies in the fetal position.

6:47 P.M.

WITH THE POWER INTERRUPTIONS, Sister Honor retired to her room. She said "slumber" was the most "practical" use of her time.

Moose, Riveaux, and I had planned to meet at the church at seven. I went early so I could pray and think in silence.

As I walked across the street to the church, I noticed the jasmine and phlox, usually vibrant and lush, weeping under the dark weight of the downpour. Rain was as common in New Orleans as the cheeky bachelorette parties traipsing around the Quarter with phallic-straw-adorned Hurricanes. But every storm grew heavier, harder. Loss and renewal. Moss and rust. The changing, wounded world was too much to think about. Too immeasurable for my wobbling mind, even with God's assist and monthly sessions with Dr. Connie.

I kept turning over the clues, fixating, trying to locate the spider silk connecting them all.

My primary suspects: the Diocese, with a long history of burying their problems instead of solving them.

My secondary suspects: Father Nathan was involved. The notebook, camera, and creepy hair trophy proved it. But what did he do? Sister Honor had been withholding information, and she had a motive, too. And the last time I overlooked a Sister of the Sublime Blood, I got burned. Never dismiss a Sister. Period.

The other suspects: everyone. Moose was holding back. With his bad timing and erratic behavior, he looked more suspicious than Saint Mary Mead during a scone festival. Rosemary was pulling my chain. Prince was Prince. Alex Moore was a moron. Bernard Pham had access but absolutely no motive. Sister Laurel from Ascension had plenty of reasons to want Reese dead. Perhaps some folks in RENEW did, too.

Did people's pain and faults and vagueness mean they were culpable, or even capable? Kidnapping, murder, and covert Polaroid drops took planning. Major muscle. I sensed that the bishop and vicars were connected, but I had no proof.

Not yet.

Five minutes later, Moose sauntered into the church wearing a placid expression, the space between sadness and relief. I thought of him that morning, running in this awful rain, dealing with Grogan's peacocking, the flash flood. He survived that violent assault, too, all those years ago, and became a hero. Who knows what he did on the battlefield? My students got an earful of it. If his recent brush with the afterlife riled him up, he wasn't showing it. Maybe his compartmentalization was so refined that he believed his own lies. Was Moose really fine, like, *actually* okay, and I was the one who was still drowning in the past?

Riveaux and her shrieking phone followed right behind Moose.

"Another flood warning?" I asked.

"A stay-in-place order, issued from the city. Can't get a break, can we?"

Moose glanced at me quickly, then looked away, saying, "At least we're together."

He was tough, wise, distant. Like Jesus, talking softly while kicking ass. Jesus had the strength—and goodness—to get resurrected. After resurrection, are you the same you? I'd resurrect every animal if I could. Every hurt thing. I'd bring back everyone that left this earthly realm too soon.

I walked to the basin of holy water, stared into the tiny pond blessed by some man I'd never meet. Maybe it wasn't sanctified to begin with, but every person who dunked their fingers graced it with their own wishes and faith. Maybe we were all consecrated by one another and we didn't even know it. Catholics didn't invent holy water. In religious practices ranging from Christianity to Sikhism, water is used in special rituals, for birth blessings, for spiritual cleansings, to pass essence from one plane to another.

An unexpected sight, Prince and BonTon blustered into the church.

"You're fourteen hours early for Easter Mass," I said.

"The streetcars aren't running," Prince said. "My car's impounded and my asshole mom won't come pick us up in the storm. I'm starving and I feel like shit. Is there any food in this hellhole?"

"I'm sure we can find something," said Moose. My brother's gem-blue eyes were electrified as he sprinted around. He returned with a stash of crackers and a few bags of almonds from the sacristy. "It's no charcuterie board, but it's something."

Our shitty Last Supper.

Riveaux tightened her ponytail. "We'll have to camp out in Club Jesus until the stay-in-place order's lifted."

"Great. A fucking lock-in." Prince's voice was cracking under anxiety or loathing, I couldn't tell.

I glanced at the faces in the church. Riveaux, smart and resilient in a world determined to crush her; Prince, dealt a losing hand from a trick deck; Moose, a survivor who deserved goodness and fun and the glory of a Fire Island tea dance; BonTon, a devoted service pup rescued from a tortured existence. I read fear and strength in all our eyes. We've all survived. What if we pushed harder for love, for each other? What if we all said *yes* more. More risk, more life.

"Let's play Two Truths and a Lie," Moose suggested, clapping his hands, quickly stepping into the role of camp counselor. He seemed so young at that moment. If he'd pulled out a juice box and animal crackers, I wouldn't have been surprised. "We played it a lot in the army to pass the time."

"My name is Prince Dempsey, I rescue lil babies like BonTon, and I'm so happy to be here."

"No, no, Prince. You clearly don't understand the rules. You have to say two truths and one *lie*." I liked razzing Prince.

Riveaux's three offerings were next. "I have a pet snake, I can speak three languages, and before my accident, I bungee jumped off a Kentucky bridge."

I blessed myself at the thought of diving into nothing.

Moose narrowed his eyes and held his breath. After a moment, he said, "I know! The snake is the lie."

Riveaux chuckled and nodded. "Oui."

"This game sucks," said Prince. "You all suck."

It was Moose's turn. He chewed his thumbnail and said, "I've seen twenty-one firefights, I recently developed a tremendous love of yacht rock, and I used to steal MREs and hoard them even though they were super gross."

"Yacht rock?! BLASPHEMY!" I started laughing. Back in Bay Ridge, Moose listened to Depeche Mode and the Cure morning, noon, and night. "Dear Lord in heaven, *please* let the yacht rock be the lie."

After a few seconds, Prince asked, "What the fuck even is yacht rock?"

"I get it, I get it. Michael McDonald is a beautiful man," Riveaux said, nodding so hard I was worried. "Not as magnificent as Luther Vandross, not by a mile, but still, five stars. No notes."

"What alternate universe has this storm unlocked?" I couldn't stop laughing, which felt good and wrong after the death and pain of the past two days. But isn't that more reason to take a beat? One moment to feel a life-giving lift.

"You got me, Goose. You know me too well."

"Thank God." I blessed myself again.

And yet there was a Moose I didn't know.

Space between us despite our closeness. What was he hiding? I had to find a way to break through Moose's wall. Wish we had some booze to loosen things up. Like the old days, when I snuck into our father's liquor cabinet and siphoned undetectable amounts from every bottle—Jägermeister, peppermint schnapps, birthday cake vodka (the only alcohol Mom ever drank)—and mixed it all into one empty Snapple bottle. The result was a revolting hallucinogen that ensured a stomachache and an apocalyptic hangover.

Then I remembered. There *was* booze. Holy wine, the blood of Christ.

THE COMMUNION WINE was easy to find.

"I have to use the bathroom," I announced, and snuck into the sacristy. Opened the Eucharist cabinet and there it was.

Plying my brother with wine to shake the truth loose, breaking my vow of stability. My pledge to stay sober. Not a great look. But sometimes we have to dive into the gray area to find the light.

I walked back with the wine and two glasses and sat near Riveaux, who was scratching BonTon's chin. I glanced at Prince. He was muttering something to himself, or to BonTon. I could have sworn it was a prayer. We were all tired but in the same broken boat.

"Is that what I think it is?" Moose asked, his eyes brightly following the jug of wine.

"How else are we gonna pass the time? Want some?"

He nodded, and I poured him a big cup.

"Hey! Where's mine?" Prince asked.

"Water for you two," I said to Prince and Riveaux.

Riveaux replied blankly, "Never been much of a drinker."

"Come on!" Prince ordered. "I'm an adult!"

"But under the legal drinking age?" Moose asked sternly.

Prince sulked, but once we settled in, the light cast a strangely cozy hue on all of us. The church felt alive. It was one of those places that felt happier with people in it. As the body encodes muscle memory, maybe buildings—blueprints brought to life— also remember human moments. Do the churches and schools and homes we build long for our movement? These are the ghosts of religion. Altar by altar, edifice beside edifice, each inch alive with who came before and who would come after. I poured Moose another cup.

"I'm not going to drink alone," he said. "Have some."

I filled my glass, toasted with Moose, "To Father Nathan and RENEW." I shouldn't have had a drop to drink, but I knew I wouldn't get much out of him unless I joined. We sipped in silence for a moment, then I asked, "Why are you here?"

"The stay-in-place order." Moose shrugged.

"I mean, in New Orleans. And if you're really moving here, where are all your things?"

"People have too much stuff these days," he replied. "I don't need things."

"When did you plan this relocation?" I asked as I slugged back more wine. The alcohol did little to break down his wall. I pressed ahead anyway.

"I thought about it for a bit," he said. A vague nonanswer. He pointed at the wine. "Can I have more?"

"Here. Polish this off. I'll go turn some water into wine," I said, though my dinner of almonds and cracker crumbs was already wearing thin.

The storm raged as Jesus—in his infinite joyful sorrow— stared at me from the wall. The crucifixion was the first murder mystery I wanted to solve. Not your typical whodunit, but the ending's quite a twist. The murder isn't the mystery. It's all about what comes after.

I drank more. Our second jug pillaged from the church's supply. The Diocese owed me that at least. The wine was a medicinal poison. Didn't realize how much I was putting away until it was too late. I downed it like Selina Kyle swallowing a whole bottle of milk after dying. Morphing into a new creature. Cat woman. Another species entirely. My buzz cocooned me, defeating the purpose of drinking in the first place. And in the fog I missed that Prince had been sneaking wine. Even a little could be dangerous for him. He was stumble-drunk. He sauntered over to the baptism tub.

"Water, water everywhere, but only wine to drink," he said.

"Prince, stop," Riveaux directed. "You need to drink water right now."

Prince knelt near the baptism tub, leaning over, gulping water from his cupped hands. I thought of Father Nathan begging for water. As Prince stood, he tripped, then regained composure.

"Hey, Prince, be careful," I said.

My hands were shriveled under my leather gloves. My head spun from the cheap drink. From Decker's penalty kick. My arm was still so sore from the shattered glass of Ascension.

"I'm fine!" Prince wore a drunk smile. "Chill, all right. You can all chill because—"

Prince tumbled headfirst into the tub. It was no deeper than a kiddie pool, but Prince was absolutely frantic.

"I can't swim!" His arms flailed. He was punching the water and hitting himself, as if searching for the key to escape. He wasn't in real danger, but when you've been hurt before, any threat could seem like mortal peril.

Prince yelped and BonTon barked, running back and forth at the tub's edge.

"Stand up," I shouted. "Prince, just stand! It's shallow!"

"Help!" he cried and thrashed. "Please!"

Moose leaned over and grabbed the kid out of the tub with a motion so confident it looked rehearsed. My brother, an outstretched hand whether you needed it or not.

Riveaux dug around and brought Prince a choir robe to replace his sopping wet clothes.

"Better practice your scales before morning Mass," she said as she handed him the purple robe. He grumpily grabbed it and went off to change. When he returned, it took all my strength and the grace of the most sincere and golden heart of Mother Mary not to completely lose my shit. "Well, well," Riveaux said smoothly, "look at that magical little Merlin. Abracadabra."

God, I cherished her. Friendship was a quick flash of holiness.

Prince sneered at us, but I caught the shine of something new in his face. A mouth tilting upward. A smile?

"Looks like you sobered up," I said. "Stay off the sauce. We need to get you swimming lessons, too. Pretty sure you baptized yourself over there."

"You gonna finish the job? Baptize me?" Prince asked. His words lacked bite, replaced by something softer. I blinked. "No joke," he said. "I mean it."

"I can't. And you've never seemed like the—"

"Like the *what*?"

"Baptism type," I offered.

"Maybe I'm not the type you think I am."

Prince's sudden shift caught me off guard. "I can't," I said.

"Why?" he asked, echoing the impulsive questions that drove most of my waking hours. My move to New Orleans. My provisional vow with the Sisters of the Sublime Blood. Prince held my eyes. "Baptize me tomorrow, on Easter, okay? Tomorrow at six. The marina."

"Maybe we could have a ritual in the . . ." I started an empty promise, but he walked away before I could finish.

What was Prince's angle? Prince Dempsey, young but not naïve. Damaged goods, like me.

Scanning the church, I counted the hidden treasures in the murals. Candlelight bounced off the stained glass, bled down the walls. The storm had spiked again with ferocity. Cascades of power outages and flooding around the city. Our neighborhood had been one of the hardest hit, but with our elevation, there was no safer place to go. Many queer people would consider a church a dangerous place, from so much alienation, so many years of brutality and othering. For me, the biggest danger was my own head.

At the altar, I prayed again, for Nathan. And Beverly, Crystal, Sue, Sonny, Carlos, Amy.

Beyond the stained glass was rain. Beyond the rain was what? Nothing? Everything?

My fellow campers lay still in their long pews, like arrows in a quiver before a battle. Anxious calm as the rain worsened. It made sense, taking my permanent vow. I could see it. A port in the storm. Light as a voice saying, *look ahead*.

10:28 P.M.

TOO RESTLESS TO SLEEP. Too tired to stand.

From the last pew in the church, as everyone else quieted in their preamble to sleep, I stared up at Mary's eye in the stained glass. Mother Mary, gracious and true. Badass protector. I studied the panels. The quiet drama. The garden. The snake.

Snakes always made me think of Nina. Not because she was a viper. If anyone was the snake in our relationship, if anyone had a poisonous bite, it was me. But we both looked for beauty in danger. Predation. We sent the snake emoji to each other when we were in the mood to screw around.

For my twenty-ninth birthday, we snagged matching snake tattoos. Our serpent ink, we called it. After the tattoo artist etched the scaled creatures into our skin, we karaoked "Livin' on a Prayer" and washed down kimchi dumplings with cold beer in Koreatown. After that, tequila shots with Tecate chasers at a neon-lit dive bar in the East Village known for an avant-garde roach infestation.

For the life of me, I couldn't remember anything about covalent bonds, the Pythagorean theorem, or the history of this wretched country's Constitution. But every moment with Nina held together like a movie I replayed in the cinema of my mind. Even our drunk-serious conversations could be transcribed with incinerating clarity.

I remembered her, us. Every second.

"What I can't put my finger on"—Nina beamed, years ago, in the ripped red-leather booth of the dive bar on that fateful birthday—"is the missing piece."

"What do you mean?"

Nina was knee-deep in her library science degree that year, loved to wax on about all things books. Mostly novels with titles I could barely pronounce, let alone understand. But she read some mysteries so we could have something to discuss. She was sweet like that.

"The best books are written with holes in them, so you can see yourself there, in the story, at the table with Nick Carraway, eating filet mignon with a fork and knife, and drinking lager as Gatsby's orchestra plays across the lawn."

I loved when Nina shut her eyes as she spoke.

What would have happened if I said *yes* to her, six months ago? What would Nina have thought of Sisters Augustine and T? Alex Moore? Rosemary Flynn? Riveaux?

I recall reaching across the table and holding her hand. The softness of Nina's fingertips. Her bronze hair, too cool for any and every school. Her fresh viper glowed under the plastic bandage over her bicep. Skin is the body's largest organ, the last border between the soul and the world. How fitting that we adorn it, test it, worship it.

We walked under the smoky moon—that spectacular trick rock—to the train. Back in Nina and Nicholas's apartment, she unfolded my fist and smoothed my hand out like a map. Her glossy nail polish was chipped from bass strings. Then she kissed me. She ran her hands up and down my back. She pulled her hair up into a messy ponytail and wrapped it around the pen she grabbed from her end table. I opened my mouth to tell her she looked amazing, but she put her finger over my lips.

"Don't talk," she said. "Let's be slutty and dumb."

"I have to say one thing, then no talking."

"Okay."

I kissed her chest and said, "You're driving me insane."

"Happy insane or asylum insane?"

I smiled. "Happy insane."

She ran her fingers through my hair. "Your hair is so gorgeous. Should I dye mine again? Mermaid blue?"

"No. I love your hair."

"It's half gray! It makes me look so old. I want to dye it."

"No," I said. "It makes you look . . ."

"What?" she asked, worried.

"Real."

She rested her cheek against my chest. "I want you to split me like a wishbone."

"Are we in love, or are we using each other for sex?"

"Yes and yes," she said, then kissed my neck softly, the way they do in movies, but it was real life.

With my cheek against hers, so I didn't have to look her in the eye, I whispered, "We were together before you and Nicholas." I choked on his name. "Why didn't you marry me?"

"He's the one who asked."

She was right. I never asked. But our love was real. We were real. Me and Nina.

"Are you wet?" I knew the answer but asked anyway.

"Dripping." She took my hand. "Feel."

The flood of Nina, the scald of her. I remember the way she stitched her eyebrows together in ecstasy, or pain. Her two-toned eyes. Her chest and the mysteries beneath. Inside the heart is what, exactly? A sigh, a volt, a God, a promise to keep beating? Nina licked her lips when they were dry, which made them drier.

Behind the storm, the full moon was drowning.

Nina said, "dripping."

And "my little mermaid, caught in a net."

And "I don't know how to let you go."

And "I can't give one heart to two people. It wouldn't survive the cut."

The heart is as monstrous as it is beautiful. Maybe that's why God caged it behind ribs. A sculpture, a blood pump, a furnace. *Hand on heart*, we say when we're sincere.

Nina used to touch the Sacred Heart tattoo on my chest. My ink that radiates divine fire, pierced by the lance, crowned with thorns, topped by a cross.

Love and faith and magic. They're all ways to beg for help, to say out loud, *I'm so fucking tired. Hold me. Please.*

Another reason to take my permanent vow, to live a life in which I'd always be held. By God.

Sometimes, when I held Nina, when I touched her the way I knew she wanted to be touched, I spoke directly to Nicholas.

"Guess what? Your wife actually wants me, loser. She loves me, not you."

But I was the loser.

I lost Nina again and again and again, every single time I remembered her.

11:19 P.M.

ON MY KNEES, I prayed for patience, for the lost souls of RENEW, for Father Nathan, for a cigarette.

Back in the pews, Moose lay awake, fidgeting. More nervous energy than I had ever felt.

As night deepened, he seemed to get more anxious, moving his hands, his fingers, like he was knitting. He held a rosary that I hadn't seen in years. Strange because he wasn't faithful. Never felt the call in any real way.

When I looked closer, I realized the rosary was Mom's. The glass prayer beads carried a buttery, iridescent sheen that caught the amber light with every movement. I couldn't stop staring at the beads. Needed to feel their cool comfort.

"Can I hold that rosary?"

"It's mine," Moose refused, clutching it protectively. "I found it in Mom's bed, after . . . I kept it with me there."

"Where?"

"Afghanistan. It was with me when I needed it."

"Unlike me?" I wondered aloud.

"I didn't say that, you did."

Moose bobbed his body as he spoke, cupping the rosary beads tenderly, like a bunch of ripe blackberries about to burst. Instead of wasting time getting defensive, I stole the rosary from his hand. Moose wasn't startled when I snatched it, but his anger was swift.

"It's mine!" he exclaimed.

As I slipped the rosary around my naked wrist and hand, I felt a familiar rush, like shoplifting a bottle of Bulleit and getting away with it. The beads were even more beautiful than I remembered. My knuckle ink, LOST and SOUL, writhed under their luminance.

"Goose! Give it!"

We fought, my arm gash tender, shoving as we argued over who had the right to hold the rosary. To claim it. Moose grabbed it hard, but I wouldn't let go, and it broke violently. Glass beads launched in a dozen directions across the red carpet and marble floor. They glinted luxuriously in the prism of stained glass. We stood still, sweating, surrounded by the shatter.

"Jesus, Mary, Joseph," I whispered. I wasn't sure if I was cursing or praying. "Jesus, our Lord and Savior."

"What have I done?" Moose chastised himself. "What have you done? No, no, no, no."

I knelt, tried to pick up the beads one by precious one. But there were so many.

"Put the rosary back together." Moose's eyes twitched and he bit his thumbnail viciously. "Save the beads. Every one."

"It's a Hail Mary storm." Prince grabbed a bead and flung it toward me. It would be impossible to catch, but I reached for it anyway. He threw another. Again I missed.

"Quit it, Prince," I said. "I need *help*."

"You can't tell me what to do. Help your fucking self, Sister Nobody."

He was even bolder when drunk, his body demolished by years of mistreatment and neglect. I was asking him for help—something he never had. If I weren't drunk myself, I would have caught him drinking. I was getting sloppy. Would have to chew three drugstores' worth of Tums to calm the acid from all that wine.

"*Nobody?* Takes one to know one. You don't have a single friend and it's obvious why."

"I know it's on theme and all," he said, "but why don't you stop crucifying me?"

Prince raised his arms like Jesus on the cross. BonTon was superglued to his side.

"Get up," Riveaux snapped. "We'll collect the beads tomorrow. You can't find them all now."

"Save them, please." Moose started to cry. "Don't let them escape. Save them."

To save or be saved. To find a missing soul. To remember. You have to take a blessing deep inside and believe it will grow.

I am in them and you are in me. John 17:23.

I grabbed one rosary bead off the marble floor, the shiniest and most perfect sphere of them all. I blessed myself with it and swallowed.

Two into one.

Not the body nor blood of Christ, but a glass bead holding the tears of Moose, Mom, Nathan, everyone hurt.

"What the hell?" Moose tucked his chin to his chest.

"What the hell!" Prince echoed.

Moose and Prince started laughing. Moose's laugh was so large yet so light you could bathe in it.

"Ha ha," Riveaux mocked. I was grateful that she had my back. "You're children, all of you. Let's get some rest. Or at least shut the hell up so I can."

Then Moose's laugh changed. He held his head in his hands and cried.

The rosary was a string of beads. It could be mended, but what about a family?

For years, Moose spun and fell. Like Riveaux, Moose tried to show the world he could take the punches. That he could get back up after each TKO. Threw himself hard into battle to prove that he could carry his own bloody body home. What is strength, anyway? Doing whatever it takes? Saying *fuck it*, sailing into the storm's eye, cutting shapes the clouds will never record.

The rain tried to wash us away that weekend. Or bless us, hold us under until the last breath. Every end a beginning.

EASTER
SUNDAY

7:00 A.M.

WHAT WOKE ME? Something new. Silence.

The storm had ceased. The tomb, empty. Easter's rebirth.

As my eyes adjusted, the sun through the stained glass was curiously blue. Aquatic light—nostalgic, yearning.

I heard a voice. "Wake up."

When I blinked and turned my wounded body on the hard slab of the church pew, I saw Rosemary Flynn. Her face was so close to mine, I could see her freckles, the color of cinnamon. In my infrequent but exceedingly detailed daydreams about sleeping with Rosemary, I never imagined it would be in a Saint Sebastian's pew.

"I'm awake," I whispered, only one-tenth as hungover as I feared I'd be. But I wondered if I was still asleep.

"Holiday"—she didn't say *Sister*—"the storm has ended. Everyone needs to get going." She touched my arm softly. A moment of warmth, something fluid under the shell.

I suddenly remembered the rosary glass in my stomach and lurched upright, accidentally hitting Rosemary's face with my face. My lips grazed her cheekbone, below her left eye. It was the quickest, strangest kiss in human history. The closest thing to kissing that I'd experienced in nearly two years.

"Fuck! Sorry!" I said, searching her gray eyes for a reaction. "You okay?"

She smoothed her red hair and said, "I'm fine." She didn't smile, but I caught a hint that she wanted to.

The pews around me held the stirring bodies of Moose and Prince Dempsey and Riveaux. BonTon watched the scene quietly, her paper-white chin resting on Prince's hip. The dog's shiny eyes were ringed in obsidian, like she was wearing the most on-trend eyeliner.

Now awake, Riveaux was on the phone, waving her right arm and up and down, then stabbing the air with her bony index finger. Moose was chewing his left pinkie cuticle. Beads from the RosaryGate sibling spar had vanished from the marble floor. One was hiding inside my insides.

As I stood up, I watched a shadow spill behind Rosemary Flynn. The lurking drip of a creeper. Alex Moore fanned his body out from behind her as if in a cheerleading routine. He wore expensive shoes and an a cappella–esque Ivy League bullshit bow tie. He stared at my face and neck, the tattoos laced across my skin. I rubbed my eyes and knotted my scarf. I pulled my gloves on tight.

"What the ever-loving fuck?" I whispered. "Why are you all here?"

"Easter Mass," Rosemary answered. "Sister Honor called us all in to support."

Bernard bounced into view with the hyper pep of a jackrabbit. "Whoa! What happened here? Weapons of Mass destruction?" He surveyed our mess and spoke a dozen decibels too high. His time onstage must've been busting his eardrums.

"It's seven." Sister Honor paced a triangular shape in the aisle. "Why, in the name of all that is holy, is it a blasphemous pigsty in here?" She pointed at the empty jugs of Communion wine. The puddles of water around the baptistry. Empty snack bags, cracker crumbs ground into dust. Prince's wet clothes draped over the sacred tabernacle. "The bishop is on his way with the vicars."

The Diocese, at it again. Another power move. Three fuckers like Hungry Hungry Hippos inhaling anything in their way. Hoped they'd cannibalize one another in the process. I didn't have evidence yet, but I was sure they were connected to Reese's murder and Nathan's kidnapping. But they were too wimpy and weak to knuckle up. Who was their muscle? Their fixer?

"The altar boys will be here at eight," Sister Honor continued. "Easter service begins at nine!"

"I hear you." I blessed myself. "We've got this."

Except we didn't. We didn't have a damn thing. The weekend days had melted into one another. Porous boundaries. Time was nothing—and everything to Father Nathan, trapped somewhere without light. No way to tell day from night. He was still alive. I felt it. But time was running out.

Rosemary scrunched her nose as she watched me bless myself, my hands moving up down, side to side. As I brought my fingers to my lips, she inhaled. Sometimes we kiss our own hands during blessings to say *it's okay* to ourselves. To make it better.

Rosemary said, with her arms crossed, "I presume the bishop plans to step in and lead Mass today."

"Obviously," said Sister Honor.

"*You* should lead Mass today, Sister Holiday," yelped Alex Moore, like a golly-gee oh-shucks sidekick in a fifties TV show.

One I'd rather regrout the convent shower than watch. "You'd be quite the draw."

"Thanks for the vote of confidence, Alex, but I can't lead service."

"Only holy men can lead Roman Catholic services." Rosemary sighed. "What a progressive institution you have here."

Bernard raced around with his supplies, rearranging flowers, dusting, swapping out used candles for new ones.

"Well, well. You have committed yourself, Mr. Dempsey," Sister Honor said to Prince. "Not only have you returned to the house of the Lord, you have joined the choir." She pointed to his purple robe. "Perhaps returning to *school* will be next on your list."

I moved closer to Moose, still in his pew, and hugged him. He didn't hug me back, giving me the teen-who-can't-be-seen-with-their-mom vibe. I was painfully aware of the lack of toothpaste.

Despite the chaos, I remembered that it was more than Easter. "Happy birthday," I said.

"You didn't forget."

"Last night sucked. I'm sorry." I thought I saw a rosary bead on the ground near the confessional booth, but I couldn't tell. Wasn't sure where they all ended up.

Moose cried silently, tears collecting in his beard. "I'm sorry." His long eyelashes clumped with wet. "We are all we have, Goose. Dad's given up and . . ."

Like the strange contagion of yawning, Moose's tears made me cry, too. Didn't care if Alex, Rosemary, Bernard, or Prince saw.

Riveaux was growing louder on her phone call, demanding, "Listen here, Grogan."

I shook off the crying as Moose wiped his eyes, stood, and stretched. He used water from his bottle to fill BonTon's bowl.

"Uh, thanks, Brother Holiday. Here." Prince reached into the choir robe pocket and pulled out a dirty sock. He handed it to Moose, who raised an eyebrow as he looked inside.

"The rosary beads," Moose exclaimed, peering into the sock. "Thank you."

"Whatever," Prince replied. He must have collected them from the floor in the middle of the night.

"If you don't want to stay for Mass, both of you should leave now, while you can," I advised.

"I'll stay," Prince said.

Moose shook his head. "Sorry. Can't do the Mass thing. Not on my birthday. This place creeps me out."

I leaned over to Moose and said, "You can sleep in my room, in the convent, if you're still tired. The door's open."

"Hang with me," said Bernard. "Let's get coffee and Peeps."

"Nothing's more hardcore than biting the head off a Peep on Easter," Moose said.

"Well, maybe coming back from the dead," I added.

"True. And thanks for the offer"—Moose smiled weakly at Bernard—"but I need to go for a run."

I looked at Moose's jeans, brown belt, and shirt, not ideal athletic attire for jogging. And how could anyone do anything before coffee? "Be careful," I said.

"You should be careful too." Rosemary Flynn touched her temple, and I touched mine. The swollen, tender bruise from Decker's fierce kick. I didn't notice Rosemary listening to us.

The church doors swung open, seemingly by themselves. Riveaux, who was still on the phone, held my eye. Then we both turned and looked at the bishop, vicar one, and vicar two as they floated inside. Going toe to toe with these "men of God" would be like taking a turn on a mechanical bull in a Brooklyn dive. You have to ride the beast to the edge of breaking. You'll embarrass yourself or snap a finger. But there's no glory without pain.

8:45 A.M.

CORRUPTION USUALLY FERMENTS under the surface. But the trinity's sick agenda was out in the open. No need to hide.

"Grogan's blowing up," Riveaux said. "They've been in a world of hurt since the RENEW tragedy. He's finally en route here, wants the new evidence."

"Grogan can freak out all he wants. My priority is Father Nathan," I said.

"We need an Easter miracle or something. If we don't find Nathan soon, well . . ." Riveaux trailed off. "I need a shower before Grogan arrives."

"If you don't mind a cold one, the convent door's always open."

"Even with a murderer on the loose?"

"Old habits die hard."

"Let's hope not." Riveaux tapped her cane on the marble floor and left.

Our slapdash glow-up had done the trick. Brilliant white cloth draped the altar. On either side, wooden crosses wore garlands of blue ribbons. The stained glass blazed as parishioners filed in, taking their seats.

"And may the Lord bless the chosen people and forgive all the sinners here today," droned the bishop. His face puffed grotesquely, his nose a red bulb from decades of drink. "Only the obedient are worthy of God's love."

Lies. God loved us all.

The pews were filled with believers and skeptics alike. Many of their faces were new to me. Father Reese's murder was two days old, and we'd had a vigil, but it wasn't a top story. Massive flooding stole the headlines.

I noticed a few folks nodding off, heads bobbing, as the bishop talked. Sister Honor was a tyrant, but even she could stir up excitement. Or fear. Despite her verbal sucker punches, Sister Honor knew God's divine love, and she knew it was real.

Jesus walked out of his tomb, flesh intact, wounds washed away. Then he levitated, right up to heaven. Can you imagine the feeling? Is it like dying in reverse? Giving birth to yourself? What I did know was that everything important—birth, death, punk rock—involved lots of screaming. So much pain to enter a new state of being.

The bishop babbled about the perils of sin. On the day we were supposed to celebrate forgiveness and new beginnings. I squinted, pretending to squish his grape-sized head with my gloved fingers. Might have been the sleep deprivation, but I forgot Sister Honor was sitting next to me. I braced for impact. But she joined in, covertly sticking out her tongue at the bishop.

But the good mood was punctured when I thought of Nathan.

I had stared at the Polaroids until my vision blurred. The sketchy light. Weird shadows. Confined space. Wood paneling.

I felt Nathan's energy touching mine, like human Wi-Fi, like a peanut butter fork reaching through space and time. The uniqueness of a person. Like the serrated teeth of the key in my pocket, the specific tiny details make us *us*.

There was a ruckus at the back of the church that I felt before I could see. My body reacted before my brain and I spun toward the last pew, closest to the door. Where Prince and BonTon had spent the night.

In the church aisle, I saw the backs of two men exchanging blows. A silhouetted tangle. Cursing. Moose was cleaning some guy's clock. Shocking precision of fists. The stranger cowered, trying to back away. My brother swung hard, landing a blow on the guy's butcher block of a face. And another. And another. Then I heard a crack like a pencil breaking in half.

I snaked my way down the pew, into the aisle, and ran to them. "Break it up!" I yelled, but the pummeling intensified.

Moose knelt to keep slugging the man on the ground.

"Stop!" I jumped on my brother, dug my knee into the middle of his back.

He instinctively reached around, pushed me off, and flipped me on my back. My shoulders bashed the marble. Moose's forearm crushed my throat. He ripped off my scarf in the process.

I hissed at him.

"Oh, no!" My brother suddenly realized what he had done. And who he had done it to. "Sorry, Goose!" He raised his hands, his anger drained. His body shrank like a stabbed tire.

Parishioners were stunned. Especially the ones who knew me, Sister Holiday, the new nun on the block. Their faces were striped with terror and confusion. Even amusement. Like they'd seen a flash mob with anger management problems.

The guy Moose beat up was a bloody heap in the corner. Thankfully he was whimpering and cursing, which meant he wasn't dead.

"The Walsh siblings know how to make an impression," I said. "What the fuck?"

"I came back. Tried to sit through Mass, for you. To support you. But I couldn't after the bishop said all that stuff about sinners. Making mistakes doesn't mean we're bad or going to hell."

"I know, Moose. I know."

"You *don't* know. How can you actually live if you only live in fear?"

"I need the structure. And God."

We sat breathless. Moose's face, knuckles, and shirt were splashed with a stranger's blood.

Grogan walked briskly in through the doors and stopped suddenly. By the grace of God, he missed the melee, but he was trying to add up the aftermath. He ran his hand through his thick blond hair with a signature blend of self-adoration and purpose, like he just rescued a swimmer caught in a riptide.

The bloodied parishioner rose from the corner and said, "That guy was muttering crazy shit. I elbowed him to shut him up and he lost it." Blood soaked his shirt. Furious inkblots of blood.

Grogan grabbed Moose by the collar, standing him up on his feet. They were the same imposing height. "Is that so?" Grogan asked.

"I'm sorry," Moose said, hanging his head. "Things got out of hand."

"I won't press charges." The congregant winced as he touched one of the many tender places on his face. "It's Easter. Good time to forgive and forget."

"I keep seeing you around, brother." Grogan brought his face close to Moose's. "First the RENEW debacle. Now this."

"I'm sorry, Officer."

"I'm Detective Reginald Grogan, second generation of Grogans in the NOPD. Say *I'm sorry, DETECTIVE*," he said, almost daring Moose to make a move.

"I'm sorry, Detective." Moose tried to wipe his nose, but his hands were too bloody. He used his arm instead.

My ribs ached. Grogan was enjoying the scene. I looked away and stared at the stranger's face instead.

Grogan let Moose and the pummeled congregant go with a warning that I knew all too well, "Stay out of trouble."

Moose hid in the hallway for the rest of the service. Not that he missed anything. The gift of the resurrection had to be personal or it was nothing at all. The bishop only offered one constricted pathway. But there were infinite roads to the light.

After Mass, I caught Rosemary Flynn before she could flee the building.

"That was quite a display," she said. Her generally no-nonsense manner melted into slight amusement.

"We need to talk." I put my hand around her upper arm, which was much stronger than I had imagined. Was she flexing? Or just uptight?

Rosemary paused. "About what?"

I let go of her arm. "You and Alex Moore are close, right?"

"*Close* is debatable," she replied warily.

"He asked you out, for God's sake."

"I respect his ethos." She pursed her caution-red lips. "Don't read too much into it."

"You have to help me."

Rosemary shook her head in what appeared to be exasperation.

I continued, "Ask him what he was doing Thursday night and Friday morning. Get the details, please. There's more to his story and I need to know if his alibi holds water."

"Ask him yourself." Rosemary's cheeks flushed as she rubbed her arm, as if to rid it of contaminants. "You're the *private eye*."

"Alex Moore likes you. You have an *in*. Do it for Father Nathan, if not me."

Rosemary studied her manicure as if seeing it for the very first time.

"Fine," she whispered before walking away, one delicate foot in front of the other. "It's not like I have a choice."

But she was wrong. We always have a choice. Everybody loves the parable of the boiled frog, how slowly turning up the heat eventually kills us. No way. We know when the heat is rising. We feel it and choose to stay anyway. We boil ourselves.

10:18 A.M.

THE BISHOP HAD A potato-shaped mole on his chapped bottom lip. Looked like a real fucking potato. I stared at its horror as he shouted at me after the church cleared out. Prince hung back, and for a second I thought I saw concern in his eyes, but then he whistled on his way out. Was he only there for the entertainment?

"How dare you," the bishop tore into me. "You've brought violence into our sacred house."

"I'm the one who broke up the fight."

"Unless you fall in line and stay in line," he snorted, "you will be banned from taking permanent vows with this parish. Regardless, your brother is forever banned from Saint Sebastian's Church."

"He'll be thrilled."

"I know who and *what* you both are." The bishop's lip potato danced. "A family of disgrace."

"Fuck you, bitchface," I whispered with the intimacy of an urgent prayer.

"What did you say?"

"Forgive me, Bishop."

"You will go to confession. You will behave." His eyes were the color of a red tie on a Republican during a pancake breakfast fundraiser. "You will pray for redemption. You will ask for forgiveness from Jesus Christ who is our Almighty Savior."

"I am familiar with Jesus. That's why I'm here, for God. Believe me."

"If you do not comply, you will be escorted from this campus within two weeks. We will also need to examine Sister Honor's role in all of this. She is your Mother Superior, and she has failed miserably in her oversight."

They found it, my weak link. By tying my fate to my Sister's, they knew I'd fall in line.

"I am truly sorry, Bishop. I won't let you down again."

The unholy trinity left, ferried back to their gilded lair by their personal driver, who had the awesome personality of an in-flight meal.

I'd gotten under their skin.

I felt like Riveaux and I were getting closer to defrocking those fuckers. Naming names. So when she finished with Grogan and said she had confirmed their alibis, I was furious.

We met outside, in the soggy convent garden. The storm had ended but left the sky hammered flat, colorless.

Riveaux pincered two cigarettes from her pack. She lit both, kept one, and gave me the other. "Here's the surveillance footage," she said. With the cigarette dangling from her lip, Riveaux held up her phone. It showed pixelated video footage of the bishop and vicars—Tweedledee and Tweedledumbass—dressed in full clerical garb, standing at a roulette table.

"The casino? What were they doing there besides losing money? No one wins at roulette except the house."

"The bishop held a New Orleans Diocese fundraiser there on Thursday."

"At the *roulette table*?"

"The casino theater. Some of New Orleans's wealthiest families were there. Two hundred witnesses."

"You're sure?" I took a long drag. "Couldn't this be spliced and diced or deep faked or whatever?"

"Casino security is top-notch and it's centralized, with multiple sources and feeds that route into one system. I got these images from Jerry, a tech at their surveillance center. We go way back. Played bridge together in high school."

"Bridge as in the card game?"

"I was old even when I was young." Riveaux let out a quick "ha." Not laughter, more like choking.

Sitting on the garden bench, I imagined Voodoo leaping onto my lap like she always used to. Purring and kneading the air. Even after all those months, her spirit was so brutally alive, it made the hair on the back of my neck spark. The dead never leave us. They just find different ways to speak.

As we fast-forwarded the recording into the next day, the trio was still there.

"Long night, eh?" Riveaux tapped ash from her cigarette.

Around the time I found Reese's body in the river on Friday morning, another familiar face came into view, and I pointed at the screen.

"Our dear Detective Grogan has a hobby." While I couldn't be sure, it looked like he was playing Texas Hold'em. A dwindling pile of poker chips in front of him.

Riveaux zeroed in. "Looks like our favorite cop can't resist the allure of easy money, huh?"

On the screen, Grogan nervously shifted in his seat as he placed bets, tapping a poker chip on the table. Absent was his cocky demeanor. Grogan looked like a man desperate to recoup some losses. A state I knew all too well.

There it was. The Diocese at the casino during Father Reese's murder and Nathan's abduction. My primary suspects must have had accomplices. And Grogan. Riveaux said his marriage was on ice. Looked like he was losing more than sleep over it.

I needed courage, felt the embers of my Sacred Heart tattoo fading. I had to listen to my gut. Even if my gut bled, burned, and ruined me from the inside out.

11:02 A.M.

I SLOSHED THROUGH THE puddles on campus, eerily quiet that Easter morning. No Easter egg hunts. No sugared-up kids. No parades of fine Easter hats.

"Rosemary told me everything," Alex Moore declared, having appeared out of nowhere, holding a box of heavy books. Science books.

"Told you what?"

"That you wanted her to ask me questions that I have already answered," he exploded. "Who do you think you are?"

"I'm investigating a crime, man. Cut me some slack."

"You should have asked me yourself."

"I'm—"

"Don't bother offering an insincere apology!"

Alex wouldn't let me explain myself, wouldn't let me say *sorry*, a word I should've fucking tattooed on my forehead for all the countless times I had to say it.

His ire surprised me, but the dork was right. I fucked up.

Rosemary walked out the main entrance of the school, carrying other books, texts I recognized from our shared classroom.

She set the box in the open trunk of Alex's Kia, which sported a Dartmouth bumper sticker. Spindly Alex climbed into the driver's seat and slammed the door with a flourish.

"You told him I wanted his alibi?" I said, my voice roiled with anger and the sadness underneath it. I cornered her. "You double-crossed me."

"You *never* should have asked me to breach someone else's trust."

"But this case—"

"I'm done." She closed the trunk of Alex's car. *"Done."*

"With what?"

"You, this job. I resign from both. You use people, Holiday. You don't *care* about me. You don't even like me."

It was the first time I had ever heard her raise her voice.

We stood in front of the same door where we'd met less than two years ago. Her loud lipstick. Her rose perfume, elegant, softer than mist. Taking in her mesmerizing scent as she yelled at me was like getting fucked by a sunset.

"That's not true."

"Really?" Rosemary asked, her gray eyes searched mine. "You sure know how to show it."

"I can't make a move—I'm a nun, for God's sake." I blessed myself.

"Would you, though, if you could? Do you want me?"

"Yes. I mean, I don't know. What does it matter?" I threw my hands in the air. "You're dating Alex anyway."

"Alex?" she scoffed. "He's harmless. Maybe I was entertaining his affections so you'd notice. I *like* you."

"You only like me because you can't have me," I said. I should have added, *Rosemary, I can't do shit about it, but I like you too.* The words were too hard to say.

"This place is falling apart. I bought these books myself because there's no budget. It's toxic. People have died here. People have done terrible things."

"You can't leave."

"Of course I can. I haven't taken a provisional vow, like you. This is a job that's beneath me, and I'm over it."

"But—"

She opened the passenger door and slipped in.

Alex Moore, with the righteousness of a tattletale, put on his wraparound sunglasses even though it wasn't sunny. Maybe he'd heard the whole fight, maybe he hadn't. I watched them drive to First Street, turn left, and then become invisible.

But Rosemary's perfume was still in my nose.

11:30 A.M.

ROSEMARY FLYNN WAS GONE. Father Nathan was withering away somewhere. Reese was on a slab at the morgue. The shifty bishop had basically said my ass was grass. Even with their alibis, I knew the Diocese were connected to the crimes. Though a direct link eluded me.

I had no appetite, but I needed the strength, focus. Hennifer Peck and Frankie seemed happy after emerging from their storm shelter. I could tell by their clucks as I gathered eggs for lunch. To my surprise, Sister Honor had given them extra food and water. As I tapped two eggs against the silver lip of the mixing bowl, their cracks both satisfying and sad, my brother walked into the dim convent kitchen.

"You okay?" He was showered and squeaky clean but looked weighed down.

"Working on it." I looked at Moose, really took him in. His army-cropped hair. The bruises on his arm. Some fading, some darkening. I had plenty of my own. From Ascension. From Decker. From him. His anger scared me. "A birthday for the record books."

He thought about what to say for a moment. "Let's not record this one."

"Tell me what's going on." I whisked the eggs lightly, tossed some salt and pepper into the bowl. A chill hit me in the musty kitchen.

"The thing is, I was let go from my duties," he said, finally, "but for a super unfair reason."

"What happened?"

"I was shot."

"Shot?" I dropped the whisk and blessed myself, leaning my hip against the counter to stay upright. "You were shot?"

He continued, "Shot, then discharged. Game over."

"Start from the beginning." I shut off the heat, moved the frying pan to a cool burner. A pop of hot butter landed like a wasp sting on my arm.

"Do I have to?" he whined. "You don't get it. I am not a talker."

"Please, Moose." I pulled two chairs from the table, and we sat. "Please level with me."

"I took chances, Goose. Too many chances." He rubbed his face. "I ran out onto the battlefield before getting clearance, before my commanding officers gave us medics the green light. I did it over and over. And, Goose, it worked. I saved at least ten guys that way! They would have bled out without me. COs are too cautious."

"You saved people. That's miraculous, Moose. Why the hell would they discharge you for that?"

"Disobeying orders. I kept disregarding them and putting myself at risk."

"Family trait."

"I tried it one too many times. After I grabbed Terrence, I got hit." He pulled up his shirtsleeve, revealing a gouged crater at the top of his bicep. The surface of the wound was purple and hard. I held my hand over it and prayed.

"Moose, I'm sorry. You never told me."

"Now you know," he said. "I get why you're doing this."

"Doing what?"

"The nun life." He pointed at my gloves and scarf.

"I'm a believer. Always have been."

"That's true, against all odds. But it's also to be closer to Mom."

"But why are you here now?" I pivoted. "What happened with Dennis?"

"I loved Den. I mean, I still love him. Really. He's so good, you know, in his heart. But he can't relax. Snapped at me all the time. That's how lawyers learn to talk, like everything's a damn trial. We started fighting over what kind of cereal to buy. What Netflix show to watch. And then everything that went down with Mom."

"It doesn't get easier, does it?"

The clock was ticking so loud I was surprised it didn't break.

"I still love Den. I wish he'd take better care of himself, but I couldn't do it for him. I've got my own stuff."

"We all do." I placed a small tea-light candle on a piece of buttered toast. Sister Honor's classic wheat. Excellent at baking, terrible at coffee, our Mother Superior. "It's not cake, but we need to celebrate. Happy birthday. Make a wish."

"Happy Easter." Moose smiled. "I wish for you and Riveaux to find Father Nathan."

"You can't say your wish out loud!"

"Why not?"

"Hello." A new voice joined the post-bloodbath birthday party. It was Riveaux. Her eyes were empty as she and Grogan walked into the convent.

12:31 P.M.

"Y'ALL ARE DISMISSED," said Grogan. "Redemption is no longer needed."

"What?" I didn't understand the words coming from the man who hired us two days earlier.

"The NOPD wants you to wrap up your PI services by the end of the next business day. That's tomorrow." Grogan spit chew into his stupid Styrofoam cup. "Everything you touch turns to trash or ends up dead. Y'all found nothing."

"What do you mean, 'nothing'?" I said. "The Polaroids are nothing? The journal? The hair? The camera?"

"For all I know, you could be manufacturing 'evidence,' maybe even be the ones holding Nathan hostage." Grogan's Adam's apple bulged.

"That's insane," Moose said. "You're looking for a scapegoat." Again, my brother and the homicide detective sized each other up.

Grogan laughed. "You've wasted our time, and now the clock is running out. I'm doing double duty with Decker out. So sad, that whole situation." He held my eye.

I stepped closer to him. I could smell his sour body odor and mint toothpaste under his chew breath. "You're the one who ambushed RENEW. And we know you don't have any more *chips* to play," I said, wondering if he was quick enough to catch my attempt at intimidation.

Unphased, he said, "Your contract's nearly up, so farewell," and walked out.

Moose chased after Grogan. A bad move, but sometimes any move was better than none.

Riveaux and I stood face-to-face in their wake. Her mouth was open, her eyes blinking rapidly.

We fucked it up.

She cleaned her glasses on her blouse. "I should have opened a perfumery, not a PI firm. It was a mistake to hire you."

"You didn't hire me, I'm apprenticing."

"Semantics don't matter, Goldsmobile. We let it slip away." She pounded the linoleum with her cane. "*You* let it slip away," Riveaux accused. "Getting drunk, fighting with your brother, acting like a child. You took your head out of the game."

I couldn't believe what I was hearing. "Like hell I did."

But she was right. After two days of searching and chasing leads, we weren't any closer to finding Nathan.

"Grogan is pulling the plug on us." Riveaux put her hands on her hips.

"You think I don't know that?" I unknotted my scarf, used it to sop up the sweat across my brow.

"Redemption Detective Agency, over before we began."

I imagined Father Nathan stuck, barely able to crawl in whatever shack he was being held. Walls all around him. He could be lying there for days longer, weeks, until he starved to death. I wouldn't let it happen. But Riveaux and I were stuck, pointing fingers at each other.

The door burst open. Moose, Sister Honor, and a familiar stranger appeared in the doorway. Sister Laurel from Ascension Parish.

12:49 P.M.

"SISTER LAUREL, what are you doing here?" I asked. Another Easter surprise.

"I joined the relief effort," she said. "A rescue team chartered a van of volunteers after our Easter service to help with the flood relief efforts. Do you have any news on Father Nathan?"

"Not yet," Riveaux chimed in.

"Oh, dear." She was deflated. "I haven't stepped foot inside Saint Sebastian's in decades." Her worried eyes roved around the convent's interior.

Sister Honor reached out and made the sign of the cross, blessing Sister Laurel. "We help our Sisters carry their burdens, each in our own way."

"And ever so many burdens we have shouldered," said Sister Laurel. "So many."

Was that why Sister Honor was hard on me from the jump, to protect herself from getting hurt? To prevent more heartbreak?

Sister Laurel looked through the window. Following her eyes, I could see the statue of Mary. Bernard must have placed her upright. "After Sisters Augustine and Honor reported my abuse," she said quietly, "the police chief talked to Father Reese directly."

"Was there an official line of inquiry?" Riveaux asked. "Was Reese ever charged?"

"No. Nothing like that." Sister Laurel took a breath. Though it's not one breath. It's millions of cells opening. "The Diocese moved me to Ascension and let Reese stay here, in Saint Sebastian's," she said. "I shared my enduring anger with Father Nathan in the confessional booth. Nathan said he would try to help."

Canonical law says priests can't take action about what they hear in the confessional. It's a sacrament. But that made me respect Nathan even more. We truly were cut from the same cloth.

Sister Laurel sat in one of our high-back kitchen chairs. "I fear that Father Nathan's capture—all of this—is my fault."

Moose slid down the wall silently, his forearms rested on his knees. His light-blue jeans needed a serious wash. "It's not your fault," he said.

"So, Nathan secured an appointment here to keep a close eye on Reese?" I needed to hear it all out loud.

Sister Honor was silent. Still. Like a dead bird.

Laurel nodded. "To ensure he wasn't hurting you, Sister Honor, or any of the children at the school."

I thought of Sister Augustine, burning down the school before giving it over to the bishop. It almost—*almost*—made biblical sense. In Sister Augustine's warped way, she was trying to protect her Sisters from "men of God" the only way she knew how.

Moose started banging the back of his head against the wall. Sister Laurel moved swiftly to him.

With her hands on Moose's head, she said, "It's okay. You feel so deeply. That's a good thing." She patted his hair the way Mom used to. She turned to me and then continued, "Before they moved me to Ascension, I learned that I was with child. I had the baby and was sent to join the new convent."

"You had a child?" I held my own hands. The puzzle pieces were starting to fit. "Like Sister Augustine?"

Sister Laurel nodded slowly.

We all walked outside. The volume of rain made New Orleans itself feel like a washed-up thing. The alleys were murky canals. Flowerpots overflowing. In front of Riveaux's pickup was the van that had brought Sister Laurel. RELIEF TEAM was printed on the side. A dozen rescue workers in orange vests fanned out. People of various ages, races, and genders. All focused. I was struck by the resolve on their faces. The volunteers picked up debris, set up stations for emergency supplies.

As Moose, the Sisters, and Riveaux talked in the garden, I walked to Riveaux's truck. Sister Honor had loosened her iron grip, but I still didn't want to smoke in front of my Mother Superior. The truck was unlocked when I sidled up to it, so I reached into its glove box and grabbed a cigarette from her stash. One day I'd repay her.

The dark street echoed with drips. In low spots, the water was ankle-deep where the drains and gutters had backed up. Birds had yet to reappear, still hiding among the oak branches and Spanish moss. The sky was lonely, holding only prayer-white clouds impaled by distant steeples.

"Sister Holiday."

I turned when I heard my name. It was Ruby Decker.

"What do you want?" I asked without looking up, too ashamed, too sad, too scared to look at her directly.

"You know what I want." Decker wiped her eyes. "I want my wife back." She seemed too exhausted to yell. "But I know that I was part of this. My job. Never questioning Reggie, ever. Backing the damn blue above all."

Authorities don't like being questioned. The Diocese, cops, principals, Mother Superiors.

I brought my gloved hands together, but as my palms touched, I felt nothing. Less than nothing. No spark of prayer. No Holy Spirit.

"I wish I could bring Sue back. I wish it were me instead. I'm sorry."

"You're making it worse," said Decker, her eyes wet.

Decker was, like me, someone who hurt people and who was hurting. Anyone who has loved and lost could tell you: She was at the first mile marker on the road of grief. A route with a destination but no ETA.

I NEEDED RIVEAUX. She was the only one I could trust.

"How are you?" I asked, hoping she didn't want to cane me to death after Grogan's gleeful dismissal.

"Me? Oh, I'm dandy as candy," Riveaux replied as she scowl-walked.

"You're upset."

"You really are a sleuth. Of course I'm fucking upset."

"I want to make sure that *we* are okay," I said. "We need to stick together."

"Doubt anyone else would have us." Her cane made music with each step.

I readjusted my scarf and smiled. "So it's a truce?"

She nodded. "How would you like to mark the occasion?"

"By finding Father Nathan. And baptizing Prince Dempsey."

Riveaux froze. "Baptizing *whom*?"

"I know. Just drive me down to the marina. I can do a quick river ceremony with Prince at six."

"Are you serious?"

"I know it sounds ridiculous."

"Remember, Goldsmobile, it's a baptism, not a waterboarding session."

"No promises." I blessed myself. "Before Prince's dip, we can comb over the crime scene again, since it's not pissing down rain anymore. I'll grab my brother and meet you at the truck in ten minutes."

I found Moose in the convent garden where he was feeding Hennifer Peck and Frankie.

"Troops are rolling out in ten," I said. "We're going back to the crime scene and uh . . ."

"And what?"

"I have to baptize Prince Dempsey."

Moose, even more surprised than Riveaux, said, "Interesting kid, that one."

"He needs help," I said.

"But when are you going to help yourself?"

"This isn't about me," I said.

But I needed a blessing too.

Sure, baptizing Prince was crazy. But it would be something good in a stretch of terribly bad. Nathan was still missing. Our first case was getting torn away from us. Baptizing Prince was the one thing I could do. It wouldn't *technically* be a Catholic baptism, but he didn't seem to care.

Then, a different kind of flood rolled in.

Grogan and two fucks in blue pounced on me and Moose, their grubby hands snatching my brother away. I lunged forward as Grogan pushed Moose toward the NOPD car.

"Moose!" I roared. "What the fuck is this?"

"Taking a little trip downtown," Grogan said, revealing his big set of teeth, which were as brown as the grease trap in a foul roadhouse bar where white men smoked, chewed, talked smack about women, and then drove home drunk as skunks. "Your brother is still a person of interest in the investigation. You know what that is, don't you, from your 'PI training'? We couldn't question him yesterday because of the accident."

Moose's eyes locked with mine.

"Goose, I didn't do anything," he said before they jammed him into the back of the NOPD cruiser.

"I believe you. We will wait for you at the station. This will be okay," I said, though nothing up to that point suggested it would be anything other than bad.

I watched, ready to unleash holy hell, as they slammed the door shut, cutting Moose off from the world.

Riveaux parked outside the police station. It felt like an eternity, waiting for Moose. I cycled through the radio stations until I found WWOZ as Riveaux made some calls. She motioned three times to keep the volume low.

I played with the dials of the AC and blew a stream of frigid air into my eye until I teared up. The garbage bag covering the passenger window still held together. Riveaux put her phone on the dash and blinked at herself in the mirror. She tightened her ponytail with the determination of a politician about to step on stage and lie at a Town Hall. I noticed her ringless fingers on the steering wheel and thought of Nina's wedding ring, how I'd watch it on her hand while she played bass, bought me a cup of coffee, or went down on me. I shut my eyes tight.

The silence disturbed me, so I broke the quiet. "You didn't wear a ring. Before, I mean. Part of the job?"

Riveaux cleared her throat. "Never had a wedding ring. Rockwell got me an engagement Key lime tree instead. He planted it in the backyard. Clever and creative like that, Rock. Like a little kid. They are the best limes you've ever tasted, too. You ever think about getting married? In your other life?"

"Once or twice." I stared at the ridges of the garbage bag.

"My mom wasn't too happy about my marriage," Riveaux continued, directing the conversation back into safer waters. "She said Rock wasn't at my level."

"Moms are right sometimes. What's she like?"

"Gwen? Ha. Ha." Again, Riveaux laughed as if it choked her. She selected a new radio station. "Gwendolyn Deidre West Riveaux. An oracular method of parenting. Nothing surprised Gwen. You can't teach her anything because she knows every-thing. A good quality when working with patients, I guess. Maybe that's why I'm a PI now, I want people to pay *me* to teach *them.*"

"You teach me plenty of things." I blew out a smoke ring and let my cigarette burn precariously close to the leather of my gloves. "Like how I should never let you select a radio station."

"Yeah, yeah." Riveaux sang along with the Doobie Brothers, and I plugged my ears.

"Patients? Your mom's a doctor?"

"Physical therapist and serial monologuer. She talks *at* you, not with you. Gwen is incapable of two-way conversation."

"Some people love to hear themselves talk," I said, convinced I did the same.

"And Mama Gwen loves hard history. Her 'lucky sweatshirt' is a Jack the Ripper Tour hoodie. First, who would buy that, question mark? Second, what kind of luck could a Jack the Ripper Tour garment bring, question mark? Illogical."

A moment later, Moose tumbled out of the goddamn police station, his face dripping with sweat. I flung open the truck door, and he collapsed into the seat beside me.

"Why does Grogan want to break me?" he asked, exhausted.

"What did they do?" I asked. "Did they question you?"

"They asked for my Thursday and Friday alibis over and over, looking for cracks. Questions about the priests. I was honest, but they make me feel guilty, just being there."

"Don't let them get into your head," Riveaux said before shifting gears and heading south.

Driving to the marina, we were the only vehicle on the road. I took in the world beyond the windshield. The jade, ficus, and jasmine. Neon grass after days of rain. Light and color can change your life, and give you new ways to see the dark. Saul into Paul. There were knots in the sky, remnants of the storm. Some clouds were itchy fists, writhing with lightning, not ready to die yet. The posters and multicolored calendars with horrendous stock art of Gulf pelicans and swamps never did justice to the elixir of Louisiana.

"Goldsmobile, Brosmobile, we got this," Riveaux said.

I felt our bond deepening, going in the right direction for a change.

6:05 P.M.

OF ALL PEOPLE to turn to the light, Prince and I were the least likely suspects. He wasn't kidding, the twerp. Prince wanted to be baptized. In real water.

"Old-school style," he'd said, pointing to a tattoo of a wave on his gaunt, scarred arm.

Of course, Prince Dempsey wanted to do things the hard way. Katrina almost killed him and his mother. He wanted to take power back from the water. With no authority and no right and not one lick of sense, I took it upon myself to baptize Prince in the water of the marina, close to Pier 11, where I'd found Father Reese two days earlier. We would feed two birds with one seed, as Sister T might say.

Riveaux and Moose stood along the railing, BonTon's leash in Riveaux's hand. I watched one-eyed BonTon watch Prince, dressed in all white. To match his dog?

We made our way to the water's edge. The steps leading into the river were as sturdy as wet paper. We stood in the light current, with the water only up to our calves.

"You know you could do this officially in the church, right? Use that tub you splashed around in yesterday. You don't seem to like water very much."

Prince's snark was instant. "We're doing this here, renegade style. Just us. You promised!"

"I'm still a nun, not a priest. It doesn't count."

"Counts for me."

Months ago, I attacked this greasy kid with Rosemary Flynn's ruler. He pushed me and I pushed back. Now I was about to baptize him. One fat raindrop fell on my nose as I began the DIY baptismal ceremony. Recited the traditional prayers and blessed the water. We can ask the water for miracles, but it chooses whether to respond. Anything can be sacred, but we have to invite it, to treat it right. A blessing is alive, too. A magic spell, a thought, the wind itself. Religion is a batch of stories. I happened to like the punk underdogs in the collection. The drama and grudges. And hope. As Prince knelt, I scooped up the muddy water in my hands, poured it over his head, arms, and body.

"Careful!" he said. "Damn! It's colder than I thought it'd be."

"Don't drink it!" Riveaux's voice dropped an octave. "Who knows what the flood did to that water."

Prince's white shirt and pants became transparent in the water, revealing his red underpants with some kind of character on the butt. Prince was wearing Spider-Man undies.

I continued, "This water symbolizes the cleansing of fear. This is the beginning of a new life in Jesus Christ, a brother to anyone who needs one." I looked at Moose, Riveaux, and BonTon. "You can lean on Jesus when you are scared. A North Star. But you are your own inner altar. Jesus will be a voice, a presence to say you are loved."

I said the words because I believed them, and I wanted to believe in them.

"Prince Dempsey, with this baptismal blessing, vitalized by sacred water, you will never be alone again."

With his eyes closed tightly, he said, "Thank you, Sister."

I couldn't say why, but Prince, when he tried to stand, couldn't. He collapsed inelegantly and quickly. Land legs in the shallow water. It was beautiful and strange. No tears streamed down Prince's face as he emerged. No words. Only a face wearing an inch less pain. We have to try to do some good in the broken world, right? After tragedy strikes, as it always has and always will, people say that time will heal. And time will tell. But it's what we do with the time. How we treat each other. That's what matters.

The wind was warm and wet. Like drawing a woman's breath into your mouth.

"Pier 11 is that way." Riveaux pointed up, which meant downriver. "Let's go. The rain is starting again."

7:26 P.M.

AS WE WALKED AWAY from the marina, the sky changed. Slashes of light on the harbor, fine as fish bones, blurred and darkened. Dusk settled in. The storm was coming back to life. Prince, Moose, Riveaux, and I said nothing. BonTon was quiet, too. My pants were still damp, and Prince was drip-drying too.

I pulled out the Polaroid photocopy from where I had stored it inside Moose's backpack and stared. Really let myself enter the picture, like Riveaux taught me. Father Nathan's face. The cross. The light. I'd thought that the pictures were snapped in a closet, crypt, or basement because of the odd light and worn wood paneling. But New Orleans doesn't do basements. Crypts don't do wall treatments.

"It's a *boat*," I exclaimed. "Father Nathan's being held in a boat. We need to search the ones here."

Moose cleared his throat. "There are hundreds."

"And there are a dozen marinas in NOLA," Riveaux added.

"We have to start somewhere."

"Here." Riveaux pointed to a long red houseboat, perhaps humoring me. "Try that door."

Moose tried the door, but it was locked. He spotted an open window on the second level. "Prince, give me a boost."

"You're like the Jolly Green Giant. No way," Prince said. He was still woozy from the baptism high.

"I'm always the *nunlikely* hero." I elbowed Prince out of my way, and with my gloved hands interlaced like a basket, I boosted Moose up, straining under his weight. "Almost there? You're ruining my guitar hands."

"Higher!" Moose gripped the ledge as he hoisted himself up and maneuvered through the open window, disappearing into the boat's interior. Thirty seconds felt like thirty thousand years before Moose appeared in the doorway, saying, "Clear."

We walked inside, into the heavy air, into the floating apartment. Peeling wallpaper clung to walls. Tattered cushions lined a love seat. In the nasty kitchenette were red plastic cups and paper plates. Empty potato chip bags littered the floor. Po'boy wrappers were balled up on the counter. The sleeping quarters, empty. Hauntingly void and musty.

We snuck onto a different boat, using two paper clips Riveaux nabbed from the marina office. Prince was our lookout as we worked the door. Inside, a new atmosphere greeted us. Rich bitches. Cold and sleek as an art gallery, probably owned by some academic bullies who tormented misfits like me in high school. Clean lines everywhere, tons of windows, polished surfaces. Stainless steel appliances. A neatly made bed in the bedroom.

Again, empty.

"Like no one's ever stepped foot in here," Riveaux said.

"We are going to get caught," said Moose, worried. "We can't search every boat. It would take days. We're pressing our luck."

"We'll be fine," I lied. "But we are running out of time."

A few steps later, walking north, I noticed the cursive words
Lez Boat stamped in curly letters into the side of a large houseboat. I tapped Riveaux's shoulder and nodded toward it,
smirking.

"Hey! That's Decker's boat." Excitement charged Riveaux's
voice.

"Their French is good," I said, the hilarity of it crashing
down. "*Lez Boat.*"

I started laughing. It triggered a cascade of laughter in Moose
and Riveaux, too.

Then it hit me.

Isn't your boat in the marina nearby? Riveaux asked Decker,
two days earlier, the morning I found Reese.

"There's a light on," I said, pointing to the window.

"Is that good or bad?" asked Prince.

"We need weapons. Sticks. Rocks. Anything that can cause
damage." Moose's focus was astounding. "Grab something.
Now."

I picked up a rusty metal folding chair from the dock.
Riveaux held up her cane. Prince pointed to BonTon. Moose
made a fist and cracked his knuckles.

"Let's go," I said.

8:02 P.M.

THE DOOR TO THE LOWER DECK was slightly ajar. I pushed it open, carrying my folding chair like a shield. The air was damp. I crept down the steps first, the crew behind me in a tight, single-file line. Sweat rained from my hairline down my neck.

The boat's interior was bigger than I had expected. A leather sofa ate up most of the living room. There was a large window and two can lights in the ceiling, but the kitchen area was tiny. Mini fridge, sliver of a stove, sink the size of a textbook. No table, two stools flush against the countertop. One chess set. Two framed pictures of Decker and Sue. Nine empty bottles of water. And one phone. I stopped and turned.

"Riveaux, look." I pointed at the phone.

She nodded furiously. "A burner?"

"Or Father Nathan's," said Moose.

"Don't think he had one, unless it's *his* burner."

I removed my gloves, turned on the phone, and checked the call log. Nothing. No photos. One app, a web browser.

"Check for email," Moose said.

"I don't know how." I handed him the phone.

"Ugh," he growled.

"What?" I asked.

Moose showed me an email thread. I recognized it instantly. Messages between Jasmine Norwood and the Redemption Detective Agency. "Decker set up the fake Jasmine Norwood account. To reel us in."

"Dang, Goldsmobile. She emailed the PI firm and set us up to find the body. But why?"

"Couldn't she have set up a free email address from, like, anywhere?" Prince asked. "Why get a new phone?"

"To control the location and IP address," said Moose.

Were Ruby Decker and her wife, Sue, behind the whole thing, the whole time? When life gives you a shove, retaliate with a roundhouse kick? What was justice in a broken world anyway?

Suddenly, BonTon barked and popped up on her hind legs.

"She hears something or someone," Prince said.

"Father Nathan," Riveaux said. "He's here. The dog smells Father Nathan."

"Or Decker," Moose said, dropping his voice. He mouthed the word *ambush*. "She could be here."

"Prince, let the dog do her thing," Riveaux said. Prince unclipped BonTon's leash and whispered into her ear. She set off into the living room, nose twitching.

"I'll check the bathroom," said Riveaux, strikingly calm, like she had been preparing for this moment her whole life, reading books about it, deploying the techniques. She pointed at me and instructed, "You take the bedroom. Prince, find a signal and call 911. Decker is either here or she'll be here any second. Brosmobile, you stand guard."

"Roger," said Moose, his blue eyes alert, loving the adrenaline.

That morning he was beating some guy in church to a bloody pulp, ripping him apart. Now we were tracking a killer together. The family that scraps together entraps together.

Hopefully.

I heard Prince on the upper deck, cursing at his phone.

"There's no fucking service out here! We're still in the city!"

The bedroom's wood paneling practically blinded me. The same background in the Polaroids. The carpet was thin and gritty as a striker strip on a matchbook. The space held a full bed dressed in linens. No pillows. No bedside tables or lamps. Two planks of wood. Razor wire. Oven light.

BonTon bounded into the bedroom, sniffing in circles.

"Father Nathan," I whispered. "Are you here?"

I didn't hear anything, but saw Decker's built-in closet. Big enough for a body.

That's where I found him.

Father Nathan.

Bound with zip ties, gagged and alive. Feral with fear. A storm cycle of a man.

"Thank you, God. Thank you," I exclaimed. *Hail Mary, fuck yeah. This is epically fucked, but thank you for leading us to Father Nathan. Thank you for keeping him alive.*

His eyes and mouth were covered in duct tape that had been soaked with tears and drool. I peeled the tape off his lips first then pulled out the wet towel gag. He gasped. Then I freed his eyes. He blinked away crust and grit. The tape had pulled off some eyelashes.

"Father." I didn't know what to say, so I held him, prayed, thanked Mary and God. "Who did this to you?"

"Water." Nathan's voice was so quiet it sounded like it was from the past.

"We're in the bedroom! Moose! We need you," I shouted. "Get water!"

Father Nathan looked twenty years older. That's what fear does. It rips you out of yourself. Terror is a thief. He was frail, exposed. He smelled like raw meat, old urine, and fresh sweat.

"He's okay?" Moose knelt, bit his knuckle so hard I imagined he hit bone.

"Father Nathan, can you hear me? He needs fluids right now."

Moose poured a trickle of water into Nathan's mouth.

Riveaux strode in with her cane and a box cutter. "Goldsmobile, damn!" she yelped when she saw us. With the blade, I cut his wrist and ankle zip ties. Nathan could barely lift his arms or keep his head upright, his spine like jelly.

"Goose, stand guard," Moose said. "Decker could be back any minute. And we need an ambulance."

Riveaux tried 911 again and cursed. "No service even though I can see the hospital from here."

BonTon had gone berserk, circling, licking Father Nathan's bare feet. A very *different* kind of anointing of the sick.

The boat was silent, like it had been swallowed.

8:31 P.M.

I JOGGED TO THE LIVING ROOM, to the big window, where I saw Prince. His shock of damp white garments.

He had made his way to the pier. He was waving his phone and darting around. Lifting his arms then dropping them. A crazed dance. Looked like he couldn't get enough bars to make a phone call. Emergency calls shouldn't depend on cell towers. But New Orleans had been battered by too many storms, couldn't fix what had been demolished.

I knocked on the window to get Prince's attention. From side to side I moved, knocking, but he didn't hear.

Then my foot made contact with something. Kicked it. In the weird light I couldn't tell what. It smelled disgusting. I knelt down and saw that it was a Styrofoam cup. Once filled and now emptied of brown soupy liquid, snot-thick, spreading across the carpet. The discovery stopped me cold.

Oh, fuck.

Grogan's chew.

I ran into the bedroom where Moose was tending to Nathan.
I grabbed Riveaux's wrist, hard.

"Ouch. Easy."

"This is Decker's boat, right?" I asked.

"Been here dozens of times for her holiday parties. Black
women working with white men . . . me and Decker, we got
along but—"

"It's Grogan, not Decker. He's using her boat. Grogan killed
Father Reese. He took Nathan hostage and sent me the Polaroids.
Isn't that right, Father Nathan?"

Nathan nodded.

What plan was Grogan working, killing Reese and keeping
Nathan alive? With no ransom.

For a minute I sat there, letting it sink in.

Father Nathan's eyes and ears adjusted. Moose took his
pulse. Riveaux tried to call 911 to no avail. We needed to drive
Nathan to the hospital, but her truck was back at the marina.
Moose would have to carry him.

The detective's long shadow was the first thing I saw out the
window.

Grogan lumbered toward the boat. A cistern of a guy with a
mean look on his mean face.

And Prince was still on the pier trying to get service.

"Prince cannot die," I said with my hands together. "I baptized that fucker an hour ago."

Nathan slumped against the bed. Riveaux, Moose, and I
huddled in the living room and watched through the window.

*Dear Lord, Hail Mary, Prince is a little shit, but please protect
him. It's not his time to die.*

I watched Prince's demeanor change. He must have known someone was coming, attuned to the fear on the boat. He slithered and hid behind a barrel. The momentary win of seeing Prince take cover was quickly overridden as the boat rocked gently with the weight of someone entering. Water gurgled under the hull. Grogan had stepped onto *Lez Boat*.

GROGAN BURST INSIDE, gun in his right hand and the folding chair I brought on board in his left. Riveaux and Moose jumped him at the same time and the gun went flying. I kicked it hard, so hard I expected every toe to break, and the gun slid with the determined grace of a hockey puck, vanishing under the huge sofa.

It was a short-lived victory since Grogan grabbed the chair and started swinging at anyone who came near him. A tangle of spit and limbs. Not all chippy and dancerly like fights in the movies, but awkward and blunt. And terribly, terribly messy. BonTon dashed back and forth, trying to wear him out. Grogan tried to kick her but she was too smart and fast. She clamped down on his leg, locked, and shook, ripping a very nice chunk out of his calf. Blood hit the floor. Enough blood to fill a Eucharist chalice. *Good girl.*

Riveaux cursed and banged Grogan in the torso with her cane. Grogan smacked Moose in the face with the chair. I feared for his teeth. There was room for only one golden grill in the Walsh family. I pushed myself off the wall and waded into the fists and metal. I didn't know what I was doing, but I did it anyway. Throwing punches, primal screams. Rusty metal scraped my skin. Grogan's fists were like steel maces. I bit Grogan's bicep, and he launched his arm back to shake me off.

At the right moment I ducked, avoiding the swinging metal chair. I grabbed the chess case and hit Grogan in the cheek. I made contact and put my whole body into the hit, but Grogan smiled and touched his face, like I blew a kiss.

It was his turn. He landed a punch on me, the side of my head, and knocked me out cold. As I fell, my soul peeled itself from my body. I didn't know who I was or what I was. Not my name or age or location. The only thing in that in-between moment was Nina.

Nina's face. Nina's smell, like a cedar forest on fire. Nina's voice.

My little mermaid, trapped in a net. I'll save you.

When I came to, I saw Moose behind the sofa, and Grogan swinging that fucking folding chair I wished I never brought on board.

"You're going down." Riveaux cackled as she used her cane like a scythe. She whacked Grogan in the crotch, and he yelped. The hit threw him off-balance. Moose took advantage of the moment and exploded an uppercut on Grogan's chin. It was so precise the detective finally went down.

Together, Moose, Riveaux, and I surrounded Grogan and kicked him. I kicked and kicked and kicked his stomach until I felt the glory of his body go slack. He spit blood and snot. Then I kicked him again. Anyone who says fighting doesn't feel good hasn't tasted its ecstasy, hasn't needed revenge.

"Goose, enough." Moose stood in front of Grogan, who lay on the ground, sweating, with the folding chair lying next to him.

Grogan stretched his arms as if he were relaxed in savasana. "I always enjoy a good fight." He flashed a relaxed smile.

We stood there, bruised, bloodied, destroyed.

On the edge of annihilation still meant I was close enough to life, to God, to hold on.

Then, a gunshot. The water beneath *Lez Boat* trembled.

A bullet hole had punctured the wall, and the air was smoking with gun powder.

During the brawl, Prince must have seen the action through the window. Used his scrawny body to his advantage, snuck onto the boat, and reached under the sofa to retrieve Grogan's gun.

And he fired it.

"Hey," I said, sounding like an actor in an after-school special as I tried to sound casual. "Prince, everything's fine. Can you look at me for a second?"

Prince eyed me with an unmistakably cold expression.

"Son," said Moose, in his smoothest de-escalation voice. "We've got Grogan. Prince, you did great, but can you give me the weapon?"

"Fuck no!"

"Prince, I just washed away your sins," I reminded him, "and now you're holding a gun."

"I'm protecting us," he said.

"Put it down, please. Don't do anything stupid."

"No," said Prince, who held the gun with two hands and pointed it directly at Grogan's face.

9:23 P.M.

WITH PRINCE POINTING THE GUN at Grogan's sculpted face, the detective spoke.

"The little PIs pulled in a big fish." He spat. "Proudest moment of your sad lives, huh?"

"Why did you even hire us?" I asked.

"I know what you're like when shit hits close to home." Grogan stuck out his bottom lip. "Had to keep y'all busy and under my thumb. Collect whatever y'all found and burn it."

"You were working a cover-up for the Diocese, right?" Riveaux asked.

"I'm not saying shit." Grogan wiped the blood from his chin.

"Better start talking!" Prince waved the gun, and BonTon howled, her black snout in the air.

"A big man now, huh? What are you, like five feet tall?"

"Talk!"

"Yeah, I got payouts from Reese once a month to make sure it all stayed quiet, to keep him from being charged. Hush up allegations. 'Lose' evidence."

"When did this arrangement begin?" I asked.

"Long before my time. I was grandfathered in. The bishop was always moving clergy around, one church to another, shufflin' after complaints were made to the NOPD. God only knows if those stories were true."

Riveaux threw the empty chew cup at Grogan.

"Why was Reese the money man?" I asked. "Why didn't the Diocese cut your checks?"

"Reese was there the longest, so they let him hold his own purse strings, gave him the keys to the kingdom."

"Until he locked you out," I said.

"The thing is, I'm in a hole, so I need that money."

"For gambling?"

"Extracurricular activity. Cards have a way of snatching you by the throat and not letting go. My wife ditched me."

"And you're crashing here because you lost the house," Riveaux said.

"Can't hardly pay for chew, even though I put my life on the line eighty hours a week."

I noticed Prince's hand quiver, worried he was losing his grip. "What happened between you and Reese?"

"Reese got a bit too full of himself." Grogan let his head rest against the wall. "Said he was ending my payments and I couldn't do anything about it. Since I got rid of all the evidence, he was right."

"So you offed Reese," I said.

"I snapped," he admitted. "It happened real quick."

"Kidnapped Nathan to cover your tracks?"

"This guy knew everything." Grogan pointed to Nathan on the ground, a heap of sunken eyes and breathlessness. "He was building a case against Reese and wouldn't hand over the goods."

Riveaux lowered her voice. "What about cutting up Reese's face, the Polaroids?"

"Made it look like a revenge killing. Even lined up the perfect fall guy." Grogan stared directly at me and smiled. I grabbed a vase off the counter, pulled out the dead roses and threw the sour, cloudy water into Grogan's face. Rank water dripped down Grogan's cheeks as he oozed blood, laughing. "Would have been pretty easy, too, after I got your RENEW crew and brother downtown. Who wouldn't believe that group of brain-washed, vindictive sheep got radicalized by a troublemaking 'nun.' But the flood wrecked that plan."

"Let's backtrack. You set up the Norwood ruse so that we would find the body first, hired Redemption to make sure we never got too close to the truth, sent the Polaroids with my name on them."

"Like father, like son," Nathan whispered from behind me, surprising all of us. I whipped around to face him.

"Don't you dare bring up my father. He was a great man, served the city as the chief of police for decades and—"

"I meant, your biological father," Nathan said.

Grogan paused. Then his laughter detonated and filled the room. "What the hell are you talking about?"

"The chief of police and the Diocese worked together for forty years, sending away the abused instead of dealing with the rapist. They managed it all internally," Father Nathan said. He was so weak Moose had to help him keep his head up. "They had to find a way to deal with Sister Laurel's pregnancy inter-nally, too."

It started to click. "Father Reese wasn't just your conspirator and bankroller," I said.

"What the fuck are you saying?" Grogan asked.

Prince was still pointing the gun at the detective, who, despite the battering we gave him, could have jumped and swiped the heat from the kid's hands any second.

Father Nathan marshaled the energy to explain more. "I did an investigation of my own. After Sister Laurel confided in me about the abuse. Forty years ago, when the Sisters of the Sublime Blood reported what happened to Police Chief Albert Grogan, the Diocese sent her away. Grogan Senior and his wife took in her child and raised him as their own. That was how the whole deal started."

"Wait, now. Really, what are you saying?" Grogan asked again, his voice brittle.

"Reese was your biological father," Nathan said.

"No fucking way." Grogan's fists were clenched so hard his knuckles had turned white. "Y'all are insane. My father would never—"

"Nathan came to our church to spy on Reese," I said. "The hair I found in the jar was Reese's, which he dyed brown. You were going to order a DNA test, to confirm Grogan's paternity?"

Nathan nodded.

"I don't believe you. The *woke mob* over here." Grogan's expression changed. Cracks had formed in the wall. The realization was too much to bear. "You're saying my own father was paying me to eat the evidence of his crimes. That I killed my *father*. What is this, *Star Wars*?"

Everyone was silent. But something was still bothering me.

"Why didn't you kill Father Nathan? You could have," I said.

Father Nathan's face crinkled with concern.

"You would have had to eventually since he knew so much," Riveaux said.

"I'm not a goddamn killer." Grogan thrust his fist in the air, making Prince flinch. "I needed Nathan's evidence so I could go straight to the Diocese. Resume payments, no middle man."

Prince let the gun fall to his side during the conversation but raised it again abruptly, aiming at Grogan's heart.

"Please, Prince," Moose tried again, "give me the weapon."

"It's mine," Prince replied coolly.

"Go ahead," said Grogan, fulfilling the prophecy of violence. "Kill me. If you are telling the truth, then do me the favor and kill me now." Grogan tried to squeeze his eyes shut, but his face was too swollen for his eyelids to close all the way. He leapt up but Moose pushed him back down.

"Men don't know how to deal with disappointment." Riveaux sighed.

It was hitting Grogan, landing in the way horrific news always lands, with more pain than you ever thought was possible. So much pain it can stop your heart. Were any of us taught how to grieve?

Would I grieve forever?

"I wish every day could be Easter," my seven-year-old self said to my mother. She wore the same simple dress every Easter for ten years in a row. No jewelry. No need for it. No embellishment. Simplicity is complex. She looked elegant. My mom held my hands in hers.

"If Easter was every day, then it wouldn't be unique, would it?"

"No, but we'd have more Peeps."

My mom put her rosary in my palm and said, "You're my special girl."

Then I heard it.

A bang so loud the curvature of the Earth must have buckled.

The second gunshot of that Easter night.

10:01 P.M.

THIS TIME THE BULLET MADE CONTACT. Tore through Grogan's flesh, unleashing a wild howl.

A holy rush of adrenaline had given Father Nathan the sudden resolve to grab the gun from Prince Dempsey and shoot Grogan in the kneecap. Edge-of-death Nathan had hobbled out of his waking nightmare and pulled the trigger.

Moose clicked into medic mode, leaned over Grogan, then quickly backed away.

"Help me!" Grogan's high-pitched screams sliced through the air. For a moment, I forgot what he had done. The bullying, intimidation, lies. And all I saw was a bloody creature on the ground. "Please!"

"Help him," I urged Moose.

"No," Moose said. "I can't."

"This isn't an eye for an eye." I put my hand on Moose's shoulder, one of the many places he was hurt. "I need you to keep this asshole alive."

Grogan's blood poured out. He was trembling, thrashing, the gunshot echoing through him. I grabbed Riveaux's phone. Still no reception.

"I can't do this without you," I said, but Moose wouldn't look at me.

He walked in reverse until his back hit the wall.

"Please save this life that isn't worth saving. We need you."

Moose grabbed supplies from the kitchen—towels, a bowl of water, first aid kit from under the sink, tape, alcohol. He made a tourniquet and applied gauze around the wound as Grogan growled.

"Might have nerve damage," Moose assessed, "but he's stable."

"I had to stop him from running," Father Nathan said, coming down after the adrenaline spike. "Lord, forgive me. It was him or us. I know his strength, his temper, and I had to—"

"We'll back you up," I interrupted. "Let's get the story straight."

"Please," Father Nathan said, meeting my eyes.

One by one, we all agreed to lie, to sin. Was he aiming for the heart? Didn't matter.

Grogan was too wrecked to protest, or maybe he chose not to.

On the day a dead man came back to life, a priest, a PI perfumier, a gay veteran, a juvenile delinquent, a pit bull, and a nun walked onto a boat and shot a cop.

Some punk rock shit if you ask me.

"Nathan shot Grogan in the leg in *self-defense*," I said.

"Yep," Riveaux said. "A clear-cut case of self-defense."

"Self-defense," Moose recited.

"Prince, what happened?" I asked.

"Dude was defending himself!" Prince lapped up the chance to lie. Or join a group.

Even lone wolves could find warmth in a pack. I should know.

A revelation is not always a big production, like God's and Adam's fingertips almost meeting in a fresco. It's recognition. Seeing something small for the first time and knowing it could be *true*.

The moment the rain started again, Decker and Sister Laurel rolled up.

"SCANNER REPORTED GUNSHOTS at the marina," Decker explained. "Said I'd handle it. This lady was looking for Grogan, pushed her way into the car. I didn't have time to argue."

Sister Laurel whimpered at the grisly sight, Grogan's bloody body.

"What in the hell is going on?" Decker surveyed the scene, the hole in the wall. "Why are you all on my boat?"

Riveaux explained it all to Decker, who was eerily silent as she absorbed the details.

"GROGAN!" Pure fury launched Decker as she swung at her NOPD partner. She tried to kick him before Moose and Riveaux intervened.

Decker wept for Sue. Riveaux hugged her for the length of a blessing as she cried. Decker's face, her entire existence seemed seized by grief, by shame. For her role in the police force and an interrogation that went horribly wrong.

Sister Laurel crouched close to Grogan, and with the help of Moose and Decker, carried him to Decker's car. Sister Laurel whispered in his ear. Words I could not hear. A prayer? A memory from the day he was born? I'll never know. She cried over him, but he stayed stone-faced.

Father Nathan held my hands, and said, "This is a sign from God, Sister Holiday. Take your permanent vows, please."

"Can we change things?" I asked.

"From the inside," he said.

I remembered the key I found in Nathan's classroom, pulled it from my pocket. "What's this for?"

"That? The key to my childhood home." He held a smile for a moment, but it was too heavy to hold for too long.

"You are *famous* now," I said, giving him the key. "Living up to the nickname."

"Take permanent vows," Nathan implored with a deep faith I needed to feel.

As head priest, maybe Nathan could veto the Diocese. And one day, I'd become what, Mother Superior?

Jesus Christ.

"You were right." Riveaux looked at our rescued hostage, who was sitting in the front seat of Decker's cruiser. "Nathan's a good man."

"I think you're taking a shine to our young priest," I said. "I'm a PI, remember. I catch things."

"PI *apprentice.* You better not bomb the exam. I've got a stellar reputation now. And don't you dare happily-ever-after me." Riveaux dropped her voice. "He's a damn priest."

Moose carried BonTon's leash to Prince on the pier. They reenacted the fight—fake punch and a block, fake gun and a caricature of being hit, hand to hand as if they were dancing. BonTon joined in, up on her hind legs, black nose in the air. Not a half an hour after the scrum, and it was already a legend.

A moment is just a moment, then it passes to become a memory. But clues remain. Residue. Nina's voice in my ear. Rosemary's perfume in my hair. Maybe I believed in Jesus and the empty tomb—his rebirth—because I needed a second chance. And a third and a fourth. We're all punished, we're all punishers.

We deserve love, whatever love is.

Decker turned on her siren, with Nathan riding shotgun and bloody Grogan handcuffed in the back.

"Wait!" Sister Laurel yelled. She leaned into the back seat. "I'll visit you."

Grogan was her son. The flesh of her flesh, blood, DNA. This meant more to Laurel than the circumstances of his being. Did they like their sandwiches the same way, their coffee? Did they both look up at the same moon and think, *wow*? Would they forgive each other?

Why, we so often ask. Why? *Why, God, has this happened to me?* We cry and beat our chests and tear our hair. But the asking is the answer. The *why* means we care, we can still feel, we want to know. We're not numb or dead. Not yet.

There's no happy ending for Sister Laurel. But she had a new beginning. Seeds can sprout anywhere, even in water. Between cracks. Life grows back after a flood.

Little by little.

"Why didn't you try to find me?" Grogan replied, staring at his cuffed wrists and avoiding Sister Laurel's eyes. He shrank in his seat. "You never sent me a birthday card. Never came to my baseball games."

"Gotta go now," said Decker, giving the orders. "Take them both to the hospital."

"Reese told me if I tried to contact you, the Diocese would have me killed," Sister Laurel explained. "Those men are capable of extreme evil. I had to stay alive for you. For this moment."

Grogan sniffed the air through the window, rubbed his cheek with his torn knuckles. "I wish I had known. Things could have been different. Could have gone another way."

"You can start now." She put her hands on Grogan's blond head and smelled his hair, like a new parent inhaling their infant.

"But it's over," Grogan said. "I'm finished."

"There's still time to start again," Laurel said.

And time is as tricky as water, the shape of a raindrop. There is a beginning, a middle, and an end, but not in that order.

Decker sped to the hospital with Nathan focused in prayer. Grogan's forehead pressed against the back of the passenger seat.

If we were lucky, Grogan would be shipped off to the same jail he'd sent countless people to. It wouldn't deliver Sue back into her wife's arms. Ruby Decker was grieving, looking for her own redemption. But hope stirred.

Two wrongs make for a compelling Bible tale or noir ripper, but two wrongs never make it all right. Grogan in the slammer wouldn't undo Laurel's years of pain. But it was one stroke of justice. A trial that would expose the cover-up.

Would the bishop have to pay? Doubted it. But I knew I could trust my gut.

Was the rosary bead still inside me? Not sure and never checked. I chose to imagine it there, a perfect piece of faith.

Riveaux was onto something. To be a sleuth or nun, you have to learn how to feel for your own way through the dark. Trust you can stay afloat, keep the basket upright on the river.

And that's how it ended, with a beginning. My decision to take permanent vows. Before leaving the marina on Easter, a prayer like liquid fire inside me, I waded back into the ruinous river.

"Why the fuck you swimming?" Riveaux called out.

Back into the same and different river. The water that held the rain, Father Reese's curse, Prince's blessing. A day ending as life begins, floating in a body of water, drowning in light.

ACKNOWLEDGMENTS

Thank you to my agents, Laura Macdougall, Olivia Davies, and Jennifer Thomas, for your steadfast vision, insight, and tremendous energy. Thanks for rolling the dice with me and Sister Holiday.

Thank you, Gillian Flynn, my book angel and feminist mystery/warped thriller visionary. No words. Only wow. I am grateful to be published by you, and I hope to make you proud. Thank you for taking a chance on me, an oddball poet and mystery fan from Scranton. Can I say that I'm your biggest fan? Too late. I said it. Big thanks to Kendall Sullivan.

Thank you to my editor supreme, Sareena Kamath—you genius. I have never met anyone who sees both the big picture and the molecular details with such astounding clarity. Your deep belief in radical texts and genre joy, and your incredibly kind nature are some of the reasons I'm grateful to collaborate. I am a better writer and storyteller because of you—thank you.

Team Zando: Molly, Chloe, Sara H, Amelia, TJ, Nathalie, Anna, Sarah S, Sierra, Andrew, Khalil, Dennis, Jessica, Jed. Superstars, that's what you are. How did I get so lucky?

Mara Wilson, your voice is noir perfection. Thanks for your artistry.

Thank you to my parents, Francine Mackinder Douaihy and Thomas Douaihy, for nurturing my love of art. My twin sister, Christa, kept me grounded during some big storms. To my exceptional niece, Lina, I love you so much.

Thanks to Geri Tisdale-Brock for believing in this series and for naming the character of Sister Helga.

Support from the Monson Arts Residency and the F. Lammot Belin Arts Foundation helped me keep my creative writing practice experimental and immersive.

Thank you to Constance Adler, Miriam Belblidia, Pearl Bell, Marc Bardon, Rebecca Castro, Dr. Leora Cohen, Tonya C. Hegamin, Rebecca Ferris, Brent Korson, and Todd Wonders, for inspiring and supporting me. Eden Young, rest in power. Anthony Psaila, you are the wind beneath my glitter wings. Summer J. Hart, enjoy the moon. Bianca Grimshaw, you provided such generous guidance. Puya Abolfathi, I'd be lost without you. Thank you to Bri Hermanson, my partner, first reader, collaborator, joyful and divine spirit.

To the nuns, mystics, believers, misfits, storytellers, teachers, nurses, carers, activists: I celebrate you. To anyone who deeply *listens*, you are my heroes.

Acknowledging the harms perpetuated by the Catholic Church is an important part of this work. I stand in firm solidarity with those who seek healing and justice.

Dear reader: This book is for you. Art brings us together, whether we meet or not. What a miracle.

ABOUT THE AUTHOR

MARGOT DOUAIHY is a Lebanese American originally from Scranton, Pennsylvania, now living in Northampton, Massachusetts. She received her PhD in creative writing from the University of Lancaster in the United Kingdom. She is the author of *Scorched Grace* and the poetry collections *Bandit/Queen: The Runaway Story of Belle Starr, Scranton Lace,* and *Girls Like You.* She is a founding member of the Creative Writing Studies Organization and an active member of Sisters in Crime and the Radius of Arab American Writers. A recipient of *Boston Magazine*'s Best Author Award and Mass Cultural Council's Artist Fellowship, she was a finalist for a Lambda Literary Award, *Aesthetica Magazine*'s Creative Writing Award, and the Ernest Hemingway Foundation's Hemingway Shorts. Her writing has been featured in *Queer Life, Queer Love; Colorado Review; Diode Editions; The Florida Review; North American Review; PBS NewsHour; Pittsburgh Post-Gazette; Portland Review; Wisconsin Review;* and elsewhere. Margot is an assistant professor in Popular Fiction Writing & Literature with Emerson College in Boston. As a coeditor of the Elements in Crime Narratives series with Cambridge University Press, she strives to reshape crime writing scholarship, with a focus on the contemporary, the future, inclusivity, and decoloniality.